SOFT TARGET

SCOTT MATTHEWS

vinci
BOOKS

By Scott Matthews

The Adam Drake Series

The Assassin's List

Oath to Defend

Dark Trojan

Call It Treason

Special Counsel

Soft Target

Sacred Target

Tipping Point

Coverup

The Deterrent

The Skysage Affair

Black Dragon

False Target

Conspiracy to Spy

Vinci Books

vinci-books.com

Published by Vinci Books Ltd in 2025

1

Copyright © Scott Matthews 2017

The author has asserted their moral right to be identified as the author of this work in accordance with the Copyright, Designs and Patents Act 1988.
This work is a work of fiction. Names, characters, places and incidents are the product of the author's imagination or are used fictitiously. Any resemblance to actual persons, living or dead, places and incidents is entirely coincidental.
All rights reserved. No part of this publication may be copied, reproduced, distributed, stored in any retrieval system, or transmitted in any form or by any means, including photocopying, recording, or other electronic or mechanical methods, nor used as a source for any form of machine learning including AI datasets, without the prior written permission of the publisher.
The publisher and the author have made every effort to obtain permissions for any third party material used in this book and to comply with copyright law. Any queries in this respect should be brought to the attention of the publisher and any omissions will be corrected in future editions.
A CIP catalogue record for this book is available from the British Library.
Paperback ISBN: 9781036701239

Printed and bound in Great Britain by Clays Ltd, Elcograf S.p.A.

Chapter One

THE LOW ROAR of the rapids echoed off the rock walls of the canyon. It was time to run the most feared white water on Oregon's famous Rogue River. More flips and rafters overboard happened in the raging water ahead on the Blossom Bar rapids each year than any other place on the wild and scenic river.

"Wait for my call," Josh Tanner, the guide, told the two clients in the front of his thirteen foot white water raft. "I'll steer to the left side. Then, Drake, dig hard on my call to turn us to the right into the center eddy. Then both of you pull to get us around the big boulder on the right."

The woman on the left in the front of the raft swept her wet blonde hair out of her flashing blue eyes. "If this is the last big one, Josh, let's really get wet this time."

"You're already wet, Liz," Josh reminded his excited rafter. After three days on the Rogue, she was still yelling for more through each set of rapids. "If we hit the rock wall on your side, be sure to brace yourself for the impact. If you go swimming, remember what you're supposed to do."

"If she goes swimming," Drake said, "she buys dinner tonight at the lodge."

"And if I don't—" she laughed as she splashed him with a stroke of her oar "—you owe me another raft trip next year."

Tanner ignored their banter and focused on the narrow gap between the sheer rock wall ahead on the left and the huge boulders on the right. Before it had been blasted with dynamite years ago, to make a passage through the boulder garden, you had to portage around the treacherous waters. Blossom Bar got its name from the wild azaleas that bloomed there but Tanner knew they were the only pretty things about the rapids. Too many close calls made him uncomfortable with what lay ahead.

He knew his friend and the beautiful woman beside him could take care of themselves.

He played football with Adam Drake at the University of Oregon and number 45 had been an

NFL-quality middle linebacker. But he passed on the opportunity to play pro football because he'd promised his mother that he would go to law school. Drake's mother had been killed by a drunk driver in his last year at law school. After the 9/11 terrorist attack on 9/11, he'd enlisted in the army. Instead of beginning a law career, he honored the memory of his Green Beret dad and harnessed his grief and anger over the senseless death of his mother to become an elite Special Forces warrior. Drake knew how to take care of himself.

His lady friend and former FBI agent was another matter. From what he'd learned from

Drake, she had climbed the FBI ladder quickly and landed a top job in the Department of Homeland Security. But Tanner was suspicious of women who were so quickly successful in a boys' club like the FBI. Had she been successful because of her sex and good looks or was she as capable as she seemed to be? So far, he hadn't seen anything that answered the question.

Tanner steered the raft to the left, aiming straight at the towering rock wall ahead. The river narrowed to no more than fifteen feet between the wall and three jagged boulders then veered sharply to the right. The raft would accelerate through the channel then drop ten feet just before they hit a wall of white water. If they slipped too far to the left at that point, the raft would flip to the left and throw them all into the raging river. If they hit the huge boulder on the right, that impact could flip them as well.

"Dig hard, Drake," he yelled. "I'm too far left!"

Drake pulled deeply with his oar three times before the raft slammed into the rock wall. The impact threw Liz overboard as the raft careened off the wall.

Drake jumped across the raft to grab her, but the current pulled her down deep under the raft and out of sight.

"Drake," Tanner yelled, "dig hard or we'll join her!"

Drake threw himself back across the front of the raft and into position and started rowing as fast as he could. He searched frantically downstream for a flash of her orange life jacket.

As they scraped against the huge boulder on the right and bounced out into the center eddy of the river, Drake saw her life jacket pop to the surface. Liz was floating face down thirty yards ahead of them.

Drake tossed his oar onto the floor of the raft and jumped into the river. In the swift current, he swam furiously, raising his head every fourth stroke to make sure he didn't swim past her.

After a long, eternal minute, his right hand slapped down on the back of her life jacket. Reaching ahead, he lifted her head back with his right hand and pulled her tight against him with his left arm. Her eyes were closed and she wasn't breathing.

Drake twisted around to see where the raft was and saw Tanner pointing to the riverbank at the end of the eddy. A narrow strip of a gravel bar offered the only break in the steep walls of the canyon.

Drake turned around and side-stroked across the current, pulling Liz behind him; when he reached the shallow water next to the gravel bar, he crab-walked back until he could drag her upper body up onto the gravel bar. Kneeling beside her, he began CPR and waved to Tanner to join him.

As he dragged the raft as high onto the gravel bar as he could, he asked, "How is she?"

"Unconscious and not breathing," Drake panted. "There's a deep gash on the back of her head."

"Let me call for help and then I'll spell you," Tanner said and reached back into the raft beside him. He kept a Motorola waterproof two-way radio for emergencies in the raft and knew the other guides on the river did as well.

He checked his Seiko dive watch. The jet boat from Gold Beach ended his run at the bottom of Blossom Bar before turning around and, if it was on schedule, should be close.

"Dick," he said, holding the radio close to his mouth, "this is Josh Tanner. We're at the bottom of Blossom Bar with an unconscious rafter. Are you close?"

"Five minutes away," the jet boat captain answered. "What do you need?"

"The lifeguard first responder bag, if you still carry it, and a fast run to Gold Beach."

"You got it."

Drake was leaning down, checking to see if Liz was breathing. "She coughed up some water and is breathing but still unconscious," he said.

"My friend's jet boat is close, he'll run her down to the hospital. I'll call ahead and have an ambulance waiting," Tanner advised and sat down on the gravel bar next to Liz. He watched her for a moment and looked up at Drake. "I'm so sorry. I've never had a swimmer at Blossom Bar before. I thought I knew that stretch of river."

"You warned us, Josh. It's not your fault. I should have kept my eye on her until we got through there."

Drake took his life jacket off, put it under Liz's head and turned to watch for the jet boat racing toward them. It wasn't the end to the three-day adventure he'd planned. That was supposed to be two nights with Liz at the luxurious Tu Tu Tun Lodge down river; dinner prepared by its French-trained chef and a hot tub on the balcony of their room overlooking the river.

Chapter Two

THE PASSENGERS on the jet boat made space for them in the aft seating area. Drake sat with Liz's head in his lap, cushioning it from the pounding of the boat running at top speed down the river. She was now conscious but dazed and murmuring softly with her eyes closed. The gash on the back of her head was deep enough that it required a towel pressed against it to stop the bleeding.

Over the roar of the jet boat's hydro drive, Drake leaned down and softly reassured her that everything was going to be all right. "We're taking you to the hospital to get you checked out, Liz. You're going to be fine, but this is going a little too far just to get out of buying my dinner tonight."

A soft jab of her elbow in his ribs was followed by a whispered question. "Why am *I* buying?"

He leaned down and said, "Because you went swimming."

"Where?"

"Blossom Bar rapids."

"Where's that?"

"I'll explain later, just rest."

Drake had seen soldiers with mild traumatic brain injuries and knew Liz was probably suffering from a mild concussion. She'd been unconscious for close to ten minutes and that meant her injury might be more than just mild.

When they finally reached the jet boat's excursion dock, two EMTs and a stretcher were waiting. Liz was quickly lifted out of the jet boat and transferred to the ambulance. Drake climbed in with her to provide as much information as possible about what had happened.

At the ER, he was left standing, looking through the small windows in the swinging double-doors. The little wave of her hand as she rolled away sent a jolt of fear through him as he remembered two other women he'd lost; first his mother and then his wife. Mom had died in her car, T-boned by a drunk. Kay had died in his arms at home after a swift and deadly fight against cancer. When Kay died, he vowed he'd never let himself feel the pain of losing someone he loved again.

The sudden emotion forced him to admit something he'd been unwilling to admit; Liz was an important part of his life that he was not willing to lose.

Drake retreated to the ER waiting room and bought a cup of coffee from a vending machine. The coffee was too hot to drink and too bitter to enjoy. *Get used to it*, he thought, *you might be here awhile.*

He started to walk to the nurses' station when he saw Tanner coming down the hallway.

"How is she?" Tanner asked.

"No word yet. How'd you get here so fast?"

"I left the raft at Foster's Bar and hitched a ride here

with a guy at the landing. One of the guides said he'd tow my raft to my dock."

Over Tanner's shoulder, Drake saw a doctor come through the ER doors and speak to the nurse at the nurses' station. When the nurse nodded in their direction, the doctor walked over. "Mr. Drake?"

"Yes."

"Your friend should be fine. She has a concussion and a gaping wound on the back of her head that we're stitching up. Her CT scan doesn't show internal bleeding or fractures but we'll keep her overnight for observation," the doctor said.

"Where are you staying?"

"We have reservations at the Tu Tu Tun Lodge," Drake said.

"Tell the nurse and leave her your mobile number. You'll be called if there's any change. Give us half an hour and you can see her."

Drake and Tanner said thanks and they shook hands with the doctor.

While Drake was at the nurses' station leaving his information, Tanner saw a young man he recognized coming out of a side-door of the ER.

"Billie? Billie Walid?" Tanner called out as the young man headed toward the exit. His face was bruised and his head was bandaged.

The young man hesitated and then turned around. "Mr. Tanner. What are you doing here?"

"Waiting to see if a friend's okay. What happened to you?"

The young man looked down at his well-worn running shoes. "Nothing really, Mr. Tanner. I was driving home after working out at school and some men made me pull over.

They were shouting that I looked like a Middle Eastern refugee. They tried to convince me to leave town."

Tanner knew that his dad was the chef at the Tu Tu Tun Lodge. He had immigrated from Lebanon with his wife, who was also Lebanese. His son's coloring was a light olive shade, but he didn't look that different from any of the other teenagers in the area.

"Did you know the guys? Did you tell the police?"

"Everyone around here knows them, Mr. Tanner. Going to the police isn't going to help. Hope your friend's okay."

Before Tanner could ask another question, Billie Walid turned and jogged down the hallway. He appeared to be afraid of something and that surprised Tanner. The kid played football and was a solid two hundred pounds or so. He didn't look like someone who would walk away from a fight if one came his way.

Drake returned from the nursing station and asked, "Who was that?"

"The son of the chef who's cooking your dinner tonight."

"Looks like he took a beating. Is he okay?"

"He wouldn't say much. I'll ask his dad tonight when I drop you off at the lodge."

"Why don't you join me for dinner since they're keeping Liz overnight?" Drake asked. "We'll catch up on what you've been doing since college."

"That sounds good. Go see how Liz is feeling. I'm going to call a friend and see if I can find out what happened to Walid's son."

Drake checked in at the nurses' station and was escorted into the ER. Liz was on a bed in a curtained-off bay with a nurse checking the bandages on the back of her head. She smiled when she saw Drake.

"How are you feeling?" he asked. He walked to the side of her bed and took her hand.

"Sleepy. They gave me something while they stitched me up."

"They didn't want you restless when they shaved your head." Drake kept a straight face as her hand flew to the back of her head. "Just kidding. It's just the back of your head. You'll look great in a month or two."

She saw that he was trying hard not to smile. "Not funny, Adam!"

"Sorry, just glad you're okay."

"I don't remember much. What happened?"

"You went swimming at Blossom Bar. When you popped up, you were unconscious with a big gash on the back of your head. What's the first thing you do remember?"

"You telling me I'd do anything to get out of buying your dinner."

"I'm still holding you to that when you get out of here, just so you know." Drake leaned down and kissed her gently. "They want you to rest so Tanner's going to take me to the lodge. Is there anything I can get you before I leave?"

"Just make sure you come back for me."

"He leaned down and kissed her again. "Don't worry. We still have the drive up the coast

I promised you."

Chapter Three

DRAKE FOUND Tanner outside talking on his cell phone. The muscles in his friend's jaw flexed like a bodybuilder working his pecs.

"Call me if you hear anything, Sam." He slid the cell into the rear pocket of his jeans, shaking his head. "Son of a bitch!"

"What's up?" Drake asked.

Tanner turned and started walking to the street. "You up for a short walk? My truck's down at my docks."

"Sure."

"My friend's a deputy in the Sheriff's Office," Tanner said when Drake caught up with him. "He thinks he knows who beat up Billie Walid but he says not to expect much to be done about it. They also broke all of the windows in his dad's car that he was driving."

"Why won't the sheriff do something?"

"Because he doesn't want to kick a hornet's nest is my guess. We have a lot of white supremacists or Neo-Nazis or skinheads, whatever you want to call them, around here.

The sheriff knows who they are, but everyone's afraid to testify against them. The sheriff can't do much until someone does."

Drake knew all about white supremacists and their dream of creating a homeland in the

Northwest. He'd prosecuted members of the Volksfront during his time in the Multnomah County District Attorney's Office. Volksfront got started in 1994 by some skinhead Neo-Nazi gang members serving time in Oregon State Prison. In 2004, the founder of the group had boasted in the papers that they were going to build their headquarters in Southern Oregon. The man later resigned his leadership role in Volksfront, but others quickly took over and continued the movement. White supremacists were still active and committing violent crimes in the northwestern states of Oregon, Washington, Montana and Idaho.

They walked north four blocks and stopped at a new spirit house and brew pub. Drake had listened to Tanner talk about his guide business, his divorce and his love of the outdoors, all the way thinking about men who would beat a young man because of his father's place of birth. There had been plenty of racist violence in Portland when he'd been a prosecutor. But the recent flood of illegal immigrants coming across the border was a powerful primer for a racial explosion among members of the white supremacists across the country. Drake knew it because it was already happening in Europe.

"Want to taste a good local beer before we march on?" Tanner asked. "It's another mile or so to the docks."

"Why not."

Tanner held open the door and let Drake enter. It was after five o'clock and most of the tables were taken.

Drake pointed to an empty table near the door to the

kitchen. "Why don't you grab the table and I'll get the beer? What do you want?"

"Get me a Pistol River Pale."

Drake walked to the end of the bar and waited for the young bartender to notice him. As in most of the popular restaurants and brewpubs up and down the coast, the servers and bartenders were young. College grads living at home with their parents, waiting for the economy to improve so their expensive general study degrees could land them a better job.

The bartender finished pulling a pint for another customer and came over.

"What can I get you?" she asked.

"Two Pistol River Pale ales and an order of your grilled Cajun oysters," Drake said.

"You got it, mister."

Drake waited for her to bring the two pints he ordered and returned to their table.

"I ordered grilled Cajun oysters to go with our beer. Hope you don't mind. They're a favorite of mine."

"Good choice. I hear they're good here, but save some room for dinner at the lodge." They touched their glasses and tasted their beers.

Drake nodded and said, "This is good. You come here often?"

"Never been here before."

"Why did we come this time? You afraid I couldn't walk all the way to the docks?"

Tanner looked toward the kitchen. "I wanted to check something out."

"Care to tell me what?"

Tanner didn't answer as the swinging doors of the kitchen opened. Their server set a platter of the grilled

Cajun oysters down with napkins, forks and two small plates and left without saying a word.

Drake followed the man with his eyes until he disappeared behind the swinging doors. He was in his mid-twenties, medium build, white with a shaved head. Drake had recognized the tattoo on the back of the man's right hand. It was the Valknut or Odin's knot. Three interlocking triangles, the symbol of a Viking warrior. Odinism was the ancient religion dedicated to the gods of the Norse pantheon and now the new religion of choice for white supremacists.

"That was Todd Davis," Tanner said. "He's the son of the leading white supremacist in the area. His dad has a muffler shop on the other end of town."

"Did your friend tell you he worked here?"

"He thought he worked the dinner shift. He's got quite a juvie record but nothing they've been able to pin on him since high school."

Drake speared an oyster and dipped it in the garlic aioli sauce. "Does your friend think he was involved with the chef's son?" "He's at the top of the list."

"Try an oyster," Drake said, pointing with his fork. "Is his dad involved with this kind of stuff?"

"He might not have ordered it, but he'd know about it," Tanner said and tried an oyster.

"James Davis isn't the kind of man or father you cross or embarrass."

"Any chance the chef's son will change his mind?"

"I'll give it a try when I drop you off. He and his dad live in a small house on lodge property."

Drake and Tanner finished off the oysters and beers, paid the bill and left.

It took longer to walk the rest of the way to the docks

than it did to drive the eight miles up the North Bank Rogue River Road to the Tu Tu Tun Lodge and Resort.

When Tanner turned his new Ford F-150 off the road and into the lodge, they were surprised to see blue LED strobe lights flashing atop two SUVs parked next to the lodge.

"I've got a bad feeling about this," Tanner said.

So did Drake.

Chapter Four

TANNER STOPPED behind the white Ford Expedition of Curry County Sheriff John Barker. Sheriff Barker stood in front of a deputy flipping through the pages of a small spiral notebook.

Drake followed Tanner, who walked past the sheriff and deputy to an older man standing alone with his arms folded across his chest.

"What's going on, Bob?" Tanner asked.

The man shook his head and wiped a hand across his eyes. "Walid is dead. They found him late this afternoon stomped to death. He said he had to go to town to pick up some fresh produce because his regular supplier had car trouble or something."

"Does Sheriff Barker know who did it?"

"If he does, he isn't saying. His deputy's been here for a while interviewing me and the staff, and then the sheriff shows up wanting to talk to Walid's son."

Tanner glanced at Drake and said, "Sorry Bob, I forgot

to introduce my friend, Adam Drake. Adam, this is Bob Morgan. He owns the lodge and resort."

Drake shook hands with the man. "Does this have anything to do with the trouble his son had in town?"

Morgan raised his eyebrows, surprised. "What trouble?"

"We saw Billie at the hospital," Tanner said. "He'd been in a fight. He said some guys thought he should leave town because he looked like a refugee." "Sons of bitches," Morgan hissed through clenched teeth.

Sheriff Barker walked over. "Did I hear you mention Billie Walid?"

Tanner nodded. "He was at the hospital, coming out of the ER. He was bruised and bandaged, but you probably know that. Just like you probably know who killed his dad." The sheriff's eyes flashed a warning. "Watch your mouth, Tanner. No one says they witnessed anything when Walid was killed and there was nothing at the scene that points one way or the other. If you can find me a witness who knows something then I'll do my job. Until then, do your own damn job. See if you can keep your clients from winding up in the hospital."

Sheriff Barker marched off and motioned for his deputy to wrap things up. When he reached his SUV, he turned and hollered, "Morgan, when Billie Walid shows up, tell him I want to see him."

They watched the two SUVs in silence until they reached the North Bank River Road and left the lodge property.

"I need a drink," Morgan said. "You two care to join me?"

Drake and Tanner followed their host to the bar in the lodge. After they each had a drink of their choice, poured for them by a pretty bartender who was as somber as her boss, Morgan led them out of the bar to a deck and sitting area.

There were guests sitting around a pool down a slope below them drinking wine, but they were alone outside on the deck.

"Wine's on the house tonight," Morgan explained. "We're having dinner catered from town, but it'll be later than our guests are used to. It will take time to find a chef as good as Walid, but I have a friend who's flying down from Portland to help out in the interim."

Drake walked to a low stone wall and looked down to the river flowing by the resort. His romantic evening at the picturesque lodge was a bust. Liz was stuck in the hospital for the night and the resort's renowned chef wouldn't be cooking any of their meals. He wasn't naïve, but he wondered what warped brand of hatred motivated the murder of the chef and the attack on his son.

He joined Tanner and the lodge's owner at a table under a dark blue umbrella. A bed of flowering yellow roses lined the back of the flagstone deck.

Drake raised his tumbler of Pendleton Midnight whisky in salute to his host. "I forgot how good this is. Thanks for reminding me." "Glad you like it," Morgan said.

"You acted like you know who beat up the chef's son," Drake said.

"I have a good idea."

"Care to share that idea?"

Morgan set his drink down and looked away to follow the flight of an osprey as it flew up the river hunting a meal for its young. He seemed lost in thought for a long minute.

"I grew up around here," he began. "My father was a foreman at the mill and my mother was a teacher. We lived in town and I was never afraid to be out on my bike after dark. Even the drunks my father had to fire from time to time never scared me. There were fights at school when I got older but those were always over girls. I don't remember anyone ever being killed.

"I left here for college and lived in Portland for thirty years. I was a civil engineer and made a fair amount of money, enough to buy this lodge and come home twenty years ago. But it wasn't the small town I remembered. It wasn't that much bigger population-wise, but it was meaner in a way I didn't understand at first.

"There used to be some old Klansmen living around here because, as you may not have heard, the State of Oregon was originally meant to be a white man's utopia. Oregon's founding constitution prohibited black people from living in the state as a matter of law. Oregon opposed slavery itself back then, but people didn't want to live anywhere near people who weren't white.

"I didn't see racism when I was growing up because there weren't many blacks around. Today America is thirteen percent black, but just two percent of Oregon's population is black. If there were incidents of overt racism when I was young, you didn't hear about them.

"But when I moved back here in the early 1990s, prison gangs like the Volksfront were starting to flourish. Members would get out of prison and find their way to southern Oregon to live close to their like-minded friends. Like James Davis and his son Todd. James Davis brags that he's a descendant of Jefferson Davis, but I doubt it. He has an auto repair shop on the south end of town and is said to be the leader of the white supremacists in Oregon. He's a mean SOB and so is his son. I'll bet the ranch he was involved in killing Walid and roughing up his son. If he wasn't, he knows who was."

"I took James Davis and his wife rafting a couple of years ago," Tanner added. "He was a foul-mouthed bigot, even with his wife in the raft. If Walid being Lebanese is what got him killed then I agree James Davis was involved somehow."

Drake looked at Tanner over the top of his tumbler as he finished his whisky. "Why now? Walid was the chef here for the last eight years, according to the resort's website. If Davis wanted to run the Walids off, why wait until now?"

"It's the refugees," Morgan said. "The government relocated thirty Syrian refugees over in Roseburg last month. There were protests at the VA hospital and Davis was front and center with a sign saying, 'Take care of our vets first!' Davis promised he'd make sure it didn't happen here."

Chapter Five

JAMES DAVIS ROCKED BACK in a wood banker's chair behind his desk when his son entered his office. At six foot four and two hundred fifty pounds, his mass was at the upper limit of what the old chair could support.

"Sit," he said gruffly. "What the hell happened?"

"It's taken care of, Dad," Todd Davis said. "The old man followed me on my hog to work this afternoon. Said he'd talked to his son and knew I was the one who beat him up. He was going to the police. When I pulled his kid out of his old truck, I left prints all over the door and roof. So I called Boss and Pete and they found Walid at the farmers' market."

"So you think it's 'taken care of'?"

Todd Davis smiled. "The old man won't be going to the police."

James Davis sprang forward in his chair. "I know. Boss called. I told them to head up north to the farm to get the gathering at the park set up. You're gonna do the same, 'cuz it's not *taken care of*, son! The sheriff will be headed straight here asking questions and I don't need that right now. So don't tell me it's *taken care of*! Take the van and drive to Portland tonight. A parts order from China is arriving on Monday so you'll have a reason to be out of town. Stay at the farm with the parts and don't talk to anyone."

Young Davis glared at his dad. "I did the right thing," he said defensively.

"Like hell you did. Now get out of my sight."

He watched his son stomp out of his office and leave through the side door of the shop. The two bay doors in the shop were down and his employees had left. He was alone for a change and needed time to think.

The culmination of two years of planning was happening in ten days. All of the movement's important groups had agreed to gather and pledge themselves to his plan; a plan to make the Pacific Northwest a White Homeland for believers who wanted to preserve America. The country was a cesspool of multiculturalism, a tower of Babel with no official language and no borders, run by a government that ignored the will of the people and did whatever it wanted in the name of enlightenment and liberal compassion. It had to stop.

His plan wasn't new. Reverend Richard Butler, the former head of Aryan Nations, had developed a similar four-phased plan in the mid-1980s for building a homeland in the Northwest for White Americans.

After resettling desirable elements of the existing racially conscious White community in the Northwest, Butler's plan called for the formation of a fighting revolutionary party, the insertion of the party into politics and the seizure of power in the power vacuum created by the inevitable collapse of the United States.

But Reverend Butler's plan had been too utopian, a

paper fantasy. It called for building up a revolutionary movement throughout the country to engage in guerrilla warfare. Acts of insurrection were supposed to goad the government into acts of repression and retaliation until people demanded the creation of a new republic in the Northwest.

His plan was simpler. People were afraid. People didn't trust their government to protect them from a jihadist army that wanted to kill them. Thousands of refugees had infiltrated the country. Some were jihadists or were radicalized over the internet and they were all Muslims. When the violent acts of these Muslims became intolerable and the government was unable to prevent terrorist attacks, people would flock to strong new leaders. His plan called for an outbreak of violence that could be blamed on the refugees they already feared. Then the political power Reverend Butler dreamed about would be theirs as alternative strong leaders the people would follow. It was already happening in Europe. Why not make it happen here?

So he sought out the leaders of the various far-right movements in Europe for guidance and support. He learned that they all seemed to have received financial support of one sort or another from a shadowy South American organization that called itself the Alliance.

When he'd tried to connect with the organization, he was ultimately directed to meet with the president of a bank in Seattle. After several lengthy interviews and, he assumed, a thorough background check, he was offered a line of credit for his business that could be used for anything he wanted, including a coded reference to political activities to the far right of normal.

There was only one condition required in exchange for the line of credit; he had to agree to perform certain favors for the Alliance if asked, from time to time. Over the last eighteen months, he hadn't been asked to do anything by his sponsors, as he now thought of them.

But the previous week, he'd been summoned to the bank in Seattle and given an envelope containing a room reservation at a luxury resort in Washington on the Columbia River. The envelope also contained a short note directing him to be in his room alone on a certain date and time, and be prepared to meet with the head of the Alliance.

That meeting was to take place the middle of the following week, one week before the gathering north of Vancouver, Washington. There was a lot to do between now and the gathering and he didn't need to be distracted by the stupid actions of his son.

Davis took a prepaid cell phone out of a box of cheap devices he kept in the bottom drawer of his desk and called his second in command.

"Walter, the sheriff is looking for a couple of witnesses who saw Walid meet his maker. Find a couple of our guys who could have seen something. Have them describe some vagrant hitchhiking up the coast highway they saw get into it with Walid behind the farmers' market.

Tell them to keep it vague, just enough information to get the spotlight off us. Call me when it's done."

Chapter Six

DRAKE WAITED for Liz in the hospital's small waiting area Sunday morning. He brought her red Tumi carry-on, as requested, and had been told to wait until she changed from her ultra-attractive hospital gown into something more suitable and did something with her hair.

He knew that could take a while. The deep gash in the back of her head had needed stitches and Liz would not want them to show. She wasn't pretentious about her looks, but Drake anticipated that she would hide the scars of her misadventure as carefully as she could. Allowing herself to be thrown out of the raft was not something she would want to be reminded of every time someone asked how she'd been hurt.

When she walked out of her room and headed down the hall toward him pulling her carryon, he was pleased to see a broad smile on her face. As gorgeous as ever and wearing a pair of jeans and a pink polo shirt, she looked as perky as he'd ever seen her.

She stopped in front of him and curtsied. "Shall we be on our way, kind sir?"

Drake pivoted and slipped his arm through hers. "And where would my lady like to go?"

"I'm starved. Somewhere we can get a good breakfast and a Bloody Mary."

"Can you endure a short drive up the coast? I know a great place in Bandon that offers a terrific Sunday brunch. I can get us there in an hour."

"I can wait an hour, but why can't we go to the lodge where we're staying?"

"Let's wait until we're in the car and I'll explain."

Drake led the way to his gray Porsche Cayman GTS in the parking lot. He stowed her carry-on in the trunk and opened the passenger-side door for her. When he joined her and they were belted in, he started the 340 hp flat-six engine and let it warm up.

"The lodge is in a bit of turmoil right now, so I canceled the rest of our reservation. The chef was killed yesterday and a new chef won't arrive for a day of two. I think we'll enjoy the rest of our vacation more if we head up the coast. If we decide to stop for the night, we'll find another place."

Liz turned to face him. "You're troubled about something. Is it about the chef who was killed?"

Drake engaged first gear and drove out of the parking lot onto Fourth Street. The Oregon Coast Highway was a block and a half away to the west.

"It's more than that, I guess. The chef's son was leaving the ER just after you checked in. He'd been beaten and Josh thinks some of the local white supremacists did it. The kid goes to high school here, but he's Lebanese. His dad was stomped to death and the sheriff here doesn't seem too anxious to find out who did it."

They waited for a string of RVs to go by at the stop light and then turned north onto the highway.

"If is this a hate crime, something the DOJ could be involved with, I could ask your father-in-law to make a request. He is the senior U.S. senator from Oregon."

"I don't know enough about it, Liz, to ask him to do that. Maybe if Josh learns more about it, we could consider that down the road."

Stuck behind the caravan of three luxury Marathon RVs driving up the coast highway, Drake didn't notice the swarm of bikers racing up behind them until they were fifty yards behind his Porsche.

The rumble of a dozen or more motorcycles made Liz turn her head to look.

"If you don't flirt with them," Drake said, "they'll race on by."

"Generally, bikers aren't my type," she teased, "but you never know until you take a look."

"Make it a quick one then because they're right on our tail."

Drake checked his rearview mirror and saw a dozen or more bikers riding two abreast. The first row of rumbling Harleys were just ten yards off his rear bumper, revving their engines to signal their impatience.

It wasn't like there was anything he could do about the slow speed of the RVs ahead of him, but the lead biker on the left pulled up beside his driver's side door anyway. With a wave of his hand, he motioned for Drake to pull out and pass the RVs.

"Looks like he wants to see how fast the Cayman will go," Drake said and nodded at the biker. "That's one bit of fun I think we'll pass on, however."

Liz swiveled her head to the right as the other biker in

the first row pulled up alongside her window. "That may not be an option. This one's trying to force you to pull out and pass."

Drake watched as the biker alongside his window drifted left across the centerline. Simultaneously he heard the biker alongside Liz's window pound twice on the roof of the Cayman.

"All right, enough of this." He signaled his intention to pass the RVs and put his left wheel on the centerline. The coast was clear ahead in the other lane for the length of a football field.

A Porsche Cayman GTS is capable of speeding from 0 to 60 mph in 4.3 seconds, but Drake didn't need that long to slingshot around the three RVs and speed away.

"Sorry about this, Liz," he said as he saw that the bikers were following his lead singlefile around the RVs and chasing after him.

"Not your fault, Adam. What now?"

"I'm not sure. Let's see what they have in mind."

Drake continued to accelerate until the speedometer read 150 mph. The road ahead was clear as far as he could see, but he knew he would catch up to slower traffic eventually. Port Orford, the most westerly city in the continental U.S., was twenty-seven miles away. They would never get there before the bikers caught up to them.

He drove on at twice the posted speed limit until the bikers were out of sight around the curves behind them.

"Maybe they've had their fun," Liz said with a tight smile as she snugged her seatbelt a little tighter.

A quick look in his rearview mirror answered that question as the first of the bikers came into view. Looking ahead, Drake saw another RV a quarter of a mile up the road before it disappeared around a corner. He was going to have to think of something soon.

"Don't suppose you have your old Homeland Security special agent badge with you?" he asked. Liz had served as the director of DHS's executive assistant after she left the FBI.

"No such luck. Not sure it would scare these guys off anyway."

"Maybe I'll just have to—" The beep-tone alert from the radar/laser detector he had installed in the Cayman signaled that a highway patrol car was headed his way.

Drake smiled and started slowing down.

Liz quickly turned to check on their pursuers. "What are you doing?"

"Making sure we're not speeding."

"So they can catch up to us?"

"Exactly, relax and enjoy the scenery. This should be fun."

The pack of speeding bikers closed on the gray Porsche like wolves moving in for the kill. The leader and his sidekick pulled abreast and then swerved directly in front while the rest boxed the car from the rear in rows three abreast. The cacophony of revving big V-twin engines drowned out the beeping alert of the radar/laser detector.

The lead biker continued to slow down and then extended his right hand, signaling for them to pull off the highway.

"Not quite yet," Drake said, shaking his head.

Looking ahead, he saw the headlights of a dark blue Oregon State patrol car come around a curve in the other lane. As it approached, Drake began flicking his lights off and on and honking his horn.

The pack maintained its tight formation around the

Porsche as the patrol car sped past and then slowed to turn around.

When the LED lightbar on the patrol car lit up and the siren started, the pack of bikers roared off.

"Lucky us," Liz said.

"Yeah, lucky us," Drake said to himself. He'd recognized the interlocking triangles on the back of the lead biker's right hand and the Volksfront logo on the back of his black leather biker's vest. It was the second time he'd seen signs of the West Coast Neo-Nazi group in or near Gold Beach. A whisper in his brain told him it wouldn't be the last.

Chapter Seven

THE DRIVE on north to Bandon and brunch was uneventful, except for the conversation.

Liz had been quiet for a while after the biker gang sped off. "I've decided to accept Mike's offer to join Puget Sound Security."

On the flight home from Nicaragua the previous week on the Puget Sound Security's Gulfstream, Mike Casey, the CEO and president of PSS, had asked Liz to become the vice president of the company in charge of governmental relations. It had become clear to Casey, after being involved in an international crisis in Nicaragua, that he needed someone in the company with close ties to his own government and the intelligence services of other countries. Liz's resume with the FBI, DHS and the Senate Intelligence Committee made her the perfect choice for what he had in mind.

"Have you told Mike?"

"I wanted to talk with you about it first."

"If that's what you want, I'm okay with it. You know that."

"I was hoping for a little more enthusiasm than that."

Drake knew what she was asking for, but it was more complicated than that. With her living on the West Coast and his work for PSS as special counsel, they would be seeing a lot more of each other. And that meant, sooner or later, he would have to decide how far he wanted the relationship to go. He'd slowly allowed himself to consider a future with someone else after Kay's death and he had to admit that his attraction to Liz was more than just fondness and friendship.

But was it the same kind of burning passion he'd felt for Kay? She'd taken his breath away the first he'd seen her at a post-marathon event at his athletic club. She was beautiful and bold, asking him to dance and challenging his views on the appropriate punishment for convicted criminals.

He was then the lead prosecutor in the Multnomah County District Attorney's Office. She was a do-gooder socialite celebrity trying to save the world, the daughter of the state's senior U.S. senator. They were opposites in most ways and that had somehow flamed their love into something white hot.

Liz was different. She lived in his world. She had a law degree and experience as a crack FBI agent. She'd served as the executive assistant to the director of DHS and then joined his father-in-law's senate staff as his intelligence specialist.

She was also beautiful, and his initial attraction to her had been immediate. It was, however, muted by a sense of guilt for admiring another woman so soon after losing Kay.

It was possible that he loved Liz but differently than he loved Kay.

Drake decided to keep it light.

"I guess I was thinking about how I will miss those crab cakes you made for me."

Liz punched him on the shoulder and laughed. "There might be more crab cakes for you in Seattle if you treat me right."

It was Drake's turn to laugh. They'd enjoyed Maryland crab cakes their first night of intimacy and mention of the meal had become their veiled reference to the pleasure they'd enjoyed.

He smiled and took her hand. "The crab cakes will always be a bonus."

Liz turned so she could read his eyes and held his right hand in both of hers. "Have you decided to keep practicing law in Portland while you work for PSS as special counsel?"

Drake left his hand in hers for as long as he could before returning it to the steering wheel for the sharp corner ahead. Using the paddle shifter to downshift, he hit the apex of the corner and drifted slightly toward the centerline.

"I'm still wrestling with that. Keeping my own office gives me flexibility. It allows me to take on cases that interest me and still do the stuff with PSS that I enjoy."

"You mean stuff that lets you live dangerously from time to time?"

Drake grinned. "I can do that whenever I get behind the wheel of this car. No, it's more than that. I joined the army the day after I passed the bar exam because we were at war. We still are. Troubleshooting for the government and your old boss allowed me to contribute a little to the effort. Working for PSS will occasionally give me the same opportunity. Besides, Mike's my best friend. I owe him for saving my behind more than once."

He decided not to tell her the rest of it, even though she

might understand. He hated the enemy! 9/11 had left a deep, aching scar on the soul of America but it had triggered in his mind an anger he had to fight to control, even today. The evil brutality of the Islamic terrorists he'd witnessed firsthand in Iraq and Afghanistan only added to his resolve to avenge the innocents he'd seen jumping to their deaths from the burning twin towers.

"When will I see you, if you keep your office in Oregon?"

Drake relaxed the tension he felt in his shoulders. "You'll probably see me more often than you'd like. I'll be in Seattle every week. How long will it take you to wrap things up in

D.C.?"

Liz shrugged. "If Senator Hazelton asks me to stay until the end of the session, I will. Otherwise, I'll move to Seattle as soon as he can find my replacement."

They were both quiet, looking at the road ahead as they approached a sign welcoming them to the city of Bandon. Life was going to be different for them in ways they were each imagining expectantly. Like the lazy Sunday brunch at Alloro's Wine Bar and Restaurant that Drake had been promoting since they left Gold Beach.

Chapter Eight

RYAN WALKER SAT IN A DEEP, red leather armchair in his suite at Skamania Lodge on the Columbia River reviewing a file. He'd been ordered to kill the man he was reading about; a man who had interfered in his business and that of his clients one time too many.

For the last twenty years, he'd served as the director of the Alliance, the powerful organization his grandfather had started after World War II. Working closely with the Nazi Martin Bormann, Rainer Walkur had smuggled gold out of Germany to build a new empire before the end of the war.

When his grandfather was assassinated years later in Brazil by Jewish assassins, his father, Rolf Walkur, inherited the leadership of the Alliance. He changed his name to Walker and set out to build a vast financial empire with the gold of the organization. From a ranch in Argentina, his father brought together drug lords, a couple of criminal syndicates and the leading terrorist organizations in the world and offered to launder their profits through the banks the Alliance owned. With the fees that he charged and the profits from other legitimate businesses he purchased, the holdings of the Alliance soon exceeded five hundred billion dollars.

When his father died, he had taken over and expanded the services of the Alliance once again. He offered to coordinate the various illegal activities of his clients to achieve a more robust financial return. With the Master of Science degree in financial economics from Columbia University he'd earned, the task had been easy due to the immense wealth his clients earned from the commonality of their illegal drug enterprises.

But the last several operations he'd coordinated for his two most dangerous clients had been abject failures, largely at the hands of the attorney Drake. As a result, his clients had ordered him to remedy the situation by killing a barrister who lived across the Columbia River in Portland, Oregon.

Walker dropped the file he was reading on the coffee table and walked to the window of his suite. The broad waters of the river outside flowed west down the Columbia Gorge and provided a majestic backdrop for the one hundred and seventy-five wooded acres of the resort and its splendid golf course. It was a shame he wouldn't have time for a round or two while he was there. The events of the next week, however, would provide all the pleasure he needed.

He pulled up the sleeve of his pale gray cashmere sweater and checked the time on his gold Patek Philippe watch. His man was five minutes late.

Walker used his phone to text his bodyguard Eric in the lobby. "Has he arrived?"

"Walking in now, alone."

"Follow him up and then join Josef in the second bedroom in case I need you."

He hadn't met James Davis, but there was no need to take any chances. When Davis learned about the quid pro quo for the money he was receiving, there was no telling how the man would react.

Walker sat down in the leather armchair and waited.

As arranged, Eric knocked three times on the door of the Hood River Suite.

"Come in."

His bodyguard entered and held the door open for their guest.

Walker stood and assessed the man. Davis was a bull of a man with a thick neck and barrel chest. He wore a three-quarter length black leather jacket over an unbuttoned white shirt and black jeans. His hair was cropped close, almost shaven, and his nose appeared to have been broken several times.

Davis stood across the coffee table and extended his hand.

Walker motioned for him to sit. "Tell me about your plans for the additional money you're seeking."

"I explained all of that to your bank president in Seattle."

"Humor me, Mr. Davis. Another five million dollars is a lot of money."

Davis leaned forward, resting his arms on his knees and steepling his sausage-like fingers. "People are fed up with a government that sends them refugees they don't want in their towns, paid for by their tax dollars, then expects us to welcome them with open arms. If we don't, we're accused of discriminating because of their religion and investigated for hate crimes every time one of them stubs a toe or gets in a fight when they harass our women.

"The money is to help elect local officials in the Northwest who think like us and will push back against Washington and the president. When we have control of enough of the local governments in Oregon, Washington, Idaho and Montana, there will be a safe place for our race to live."

"And by 'our race', you mean white people?"

"I mean the white working class in America. I mean people who are against homosexuality, multi-culturalism, mass immigration that displaces white workers, and Zionism. People who are tired of paying for people who won't work and aren't forced to be drug tested before they get government benefits. Parents who are tired of having their kids come home from school telling them they're learning about the Koran and Islam. This isn't America and it has to stop."

Walker nodded in agreement. "All right, the money will be used to support candidates in the Northwest. Have you identified these candidates and are you one of them?"

"We know enough of them and, no, I'm not one of them. With my record, I need to stay in the background."

"How much of the five million do you intend to keep for yourself and your organization, Mr. Davis?"

James Davis sat back in his leather armchair and smiled. "As much as the groups you sponsor in Europe and the Golden Dawn in Greece keep for themselves, Mr. Walker. The activities we organize are often expensive."

"If you've spoken to these groups, you know that sometimes I ask that certain favors be carried out in exchange for the money they receive. Are you willing to do the same thing for me?"

James Davis stood and again extended his hand to his host. "Anything you need done,
Mr. Walker."
After a short discussion, Walker gave Davis the file on the attorney. The two men shook hands before parting.

Chapter Nine

WHEN DAVIS LEFT, Walker's two bodyguards joined him in the suite's conference/dining area and took seats on opposite sides of the long table.

Walker sat at the head of the table and opened another file. "Did you put the devices on his truck?"

"The GPS tracker and the listening device were installed," Eric confirmed.

"I want to know where he is at all times. He said he would take care of the attorney for me. I need to make sure he doesn't interfere with our other business."

Josef, his communications man, flipped over a 2-in-1 ThinkPad and opened a file. "When do you want me to give him the rest of the information we have on the attorney?"

"When you've confirmed that Drake has returned to Portland and is alone. The woman with him on this rafting trip is too well connected. If she's involved when Drake is killed, it will guarantee an investigation by the FBI. If she's not, local law enforcement will handle the investigation. We have people inside law enforcement in

Portland who are loyal to us and will keep an eye on things."

Eric checked his own ThinkPad. "The surveillance cameras on Drake's office and reserved parking space show that he's not back yet. I called and asked for an appointment with him and his secretary said he wouldn't be back until today or tomorrow." "I want it done before we leave next week. Make sure it happens."

Josef opened another file on his ThinkPad and studied it for a half a minute. "How soon do you want to meet with our jihadist from Seattle? He's stayed in his room as we told him to, but he's on his second scotch, judging from the little empty bottles from his mini bar."

Walker slapped his folder down on the table. "Damn Arabs; another rich Saudi on a student visa living the good life and still wanting a shortcut to paradise and his promised virgins! You would think he'd be satisfied with the young women at his university."

Eric laughed. "Maybe he can't find any virgins there."

Josef joined in. "Or they prefer young boys like their prophet."

"Enough! Ali is the cell leader and we have to work with him. So he *will* be respected. No more jokes. Give him ten minutes and then bring him here. Make sure no one sees him enter this suite. We can't be linked to him in any way."

The bodyguards stood as one and left Walker at the conference table with a second file. The plan in this file detailed an audacious attack on the mass transit system in Seattle. The plan itself mimicked in many ways the 1995 nerve gas attack on the Tokyo subway.

That attack had involved five two-man teams riding on separate subway trains who released lethal sarin gas into the air. Each man carried a small plastic bag filled with liquid sarin. At an appointed time, the bags were dropped onto the floor and punctured with the steel tips of their umbrellas. When the liquid sarin evaporated, the vapor rose into the air, blinding commuters and leaving them gasping for air. Twelve people died and fifty-five hundred had been treated in hospitals.

A later study by a U.S. Senate subcommittee estimated that if the sarin gas had been disseminated more effectively, tens of thousands might have been killed.

Now, thanks to the stupid Assad regime in Syria, stockpiles of the nerve gas were in the hands of terrorists eager to use the deadly nerve agent. Small, concealable canisters had been developed that were capable of releasing clouds of tiny droplets fine enough to be inhaled by unsuspecting commuters on mass transit systems all over the world.

Walker had been asked to coordinate the funding of the operation and deliver the sarin gas to one Ali Mohammad. He was a University of Washington foreign student who'd been chosen to lead the deadly attack on the United States. Walker's own direct involvement in the plan was meant to guarantee he would carry through on his order to eliminate the attorney.

He was furious that he had let himself be coerced into such a reckless plan. Smuggling nerve gas into the U.S. and then allowing himself to be put in direct contact with the foolish young Arab was madness. This had to be the last time. He had to find a way to break free of the Brotherhood and cut his ties to the crazy Islamists who wanted to rule the world.

There was plenty of money to be made serving the needs of his other clients without taking the risk he was being forced to take in America.

Walker secured the second file in his brown leather briefcase and splashed two fingers of a rather good eighteen-year-old Macallan Scotch in a tumbler at the wet bar. If the young jihadist tried to make a show of his devout beliefs and willingness to die for Allah, a subtle reminder of his sinful taste for Scotch might keep him in his place.

Three knocks on the door announced the arrival of Ali Mohammad, a graduate student in biochemical engineering at the University of Washington. He was close to six feet tall with short, black hair, wire frame glasses and beady eyes that reminded Walker of a hunting falcon. He was dressed casually but expensively; a tan cashmere sportscoat over an unbuttoned white shirt, jeans and gray hand-stitched Italian driver moccasins.

Walker conspicuously finished his Scotch and set the tumbler on the bar before moving to greet his guest.

Mohammad walked past Walker to the wet bar and poured some Scotch in a tumbler like

Walker's. "Next time we meet it will be in Seattle. I don't have time for your games."

"If you want my help, you'll make time."

Mohammad sat down in one of the leather armchairs, crossing his legs. "You have been paid to make a delivery, nothing more. I understand the need to be discreet about the transfer of the canisters, but I have classes to attend, exams to prepare for. It's as important that I maintain my image as a serious student as it is for you to remain in the shadows as the leader of the Alliance. I know who you are, Ryan Walker, but I'm not sure you know who I am."

Walker sat in the other armchair facing Mohammad. "You are the son of a Saudi prince and a trained operative of Al Qaeda in the Arabian Peninsula, or AQAP. You received your training in the mountains of Yemen before coming to the U.S. on a student visa. You lead a cell of martyrs who plan to kill as many Americans as possible with sarin gas stolen in Syria from Assad. Did I leave out anything?"

"Why would I want your help? Your track record sucks."

Walker managed to smile at the reminder of his failures. "Because my bank financed the installation of the new chemical detection system for the Link Light Rail system you want to attack. I have the complete schematics for that detection system. That's why I was chosen to assist you."

Chapter Ten

AFTER ENJOYING a relaxed brunch at the Alloro Wine Bar and Restaurant in Bandon, Drake drove north on the Oregon Coast Highway to their destination for the night. Past forty-seven miles of shifting white sand dunes in the Oregon Dunes National Recreational Area, past the most photographed lighthouse on the West Coast at Heceta Head (with its haunted Light Keeper's house) and the world's smallest fishing harbor at Depoe Bay.

Liz was dazzled by the natural beauty of it all. "What a treat! It's so beautiful."

"You've only seen the south and central coast. We'll finish up with a drive to Astoria at the mouth of the Columbia River tomorrow before we head back to Portland. Then you will have seen it all."

They drove past the town of Newport until Drake slowed and turned into the Salishan Spa and Golf Resort. When he stopped in front of the lobby, he got out and walked around to open Liz's door.

He offered his hand to help her out of the low-slung

Cayman. "While I register, why don't you check out the menu for the dining room? If you don't see anything you like, there's a restaurant nearby that's pretty good."

While she was gone, he picked up the keys to their room overlooking the Siletz Bay and ordered a bottle of champagne. He was tempted to arrange a visit to the spa for her before dinner then thought better of it. The rafting and coast trip was meant to be a short vacation with time to relax together. Why was he trying to rush her off to get a facial or a manicure?

Liz returned and slipped her arm through his. "Great wine cellar and the menu is wonderful. But after five hours on the road from Bandon, do we have time for me to take a shower and freshen up before we eat?"

"Take all the time you need. We're here to relax."

Drake drove them to their deluxe room and retrieved the Cayman's two custom fitted luggage bags from the bonnet. Liz rushed ahead to check out the room. When he set the bags down and closed the door behind him, she was standing out on the deck. In the distance, an osprey was flying over the bay looking for its dinner.

He joined her on the deck and wrapped his arms around her from behind. "In Seattle, they call the osprey a sea hawk. Thought you should know that if you're moving there."

Liz leaned her head back on his chest and watched the hunter search the waters. "My dad was a real estate developer in San Diego but also a conservationist. For decades, there were no known osprey nests in all of Southern California. Fishermen killed them because they competed with them for fish. After World War Two the pesticide DDT killed a lot of them. Dad's group built nesting platforms for them and they slowly made a comeback. I've always admired the patience they have hunting to feed the babies back in their nests."

"And here I thought you were a city girl who didn't know an osprey from a sea gull."

She twirled around in his arms and pushed out of his grasp. "There are a lot of things about

me you don't know, Mister. Now get out of my way, I'm going to take a shower before I let you buy me a very expensive dinner."

Drake watched with admiration as she marched to the luggage bags and carried them both into the bedroom with ease. Her toned arms and shoulders handled the luggage as if they were filled with feathers. He also admired the way she filled out her designer jeans and her pink polo shirt.

He only had a moment to savor the sight of her before his phone buzzed in his pocket. He saw that it was his buddy Josh Tanner.

"Adam, do you have a moment? I don't want to tear you away from anything important, but I need a favor."

If he only knew, Drake thought. "What's up Josh?"

"I know you probably aren't in Portland yet, but when you get there could you check with chef Walid's sister and see if she's seen Billie? He hasn't been seen around here since his dad was killed. I'd like to know that he's okay."

"Sure, send me her phone number and address and I'll get in touch with her. Has the sheriff identified the guys who killed Billie's dad?"

"A couple witnesses came forward and said they saw some hitchhiker fighting with

Walid, but no one believes them. They're a couple of good old boys who ride their

Harleys with James Davis and his son."

"Is there any reason to think Billie's in any danger?"

"No, unless he decides to go after Davis and his guys on his own. Volksfront is hosting a white supremacist gathering up in Battle Ground, Washington this year. If Billie believes Davis had something to do with his dad's death, he might head up there." Someone was knocking at the door.

"I have to go, Josh. I'll call you when I've talked with Billie's aunt."

Drake opened the door and tipped the young man who handed him an ice bucket and a chilled bottle of Oregon's best sparkling wine, Argyle's Tirage Brut. It was time to introduce Liz to another of Oregon's great wines.

He found two champagne flutes in the rack above the wet bar and quietly opened the bottle of Argyle. When both flutes were filled and bubbling away, he set them on the glass coffee table in front of the gas fireplace and waited for Liz to make an entrance.

When she did, he was speechless.

"Would it be okay if we ordered dinner from room service?" she asked as she let her white spa robe slide down her naked body to the floor.

Chapter Eleven

THEY WERE both in their spa robes sitting on the balcony the next morning when Mike Casey, the CEO of Puget Sound Security, called from Seattle.

"Tried to reach you at your office and Margo said you were still driving up the coast with

Liz. Care to tell me what you've been up to?"

Drake recognized the barely concealed smirk in his friend's voice. "None of your business. A friend would have waited until I got back to Portland to call, so I'll assume this call is important in some way."

"That response tells me all I need to know about what you've been up to. And, yes, this call is about something important. I have a new matter that I need you to handle." Liz reached over and squeezed his knee. "I'm going inside," she whispered.

"My coffee's getting cold, Mike. What is it you want me to handle?"

"Sounds like Liz needs you inside, I'll explain it all when you get here. Why don't you bring her here and I can talk to you both? She hasn't told me if she's going to accept my offer."

"I'll mention it to her. Goodbye Mike."

Drake went inside shaking his head. "Mike wants me to drive you to Seattle. He wants to know if you are accepting his offer."

Liz refilled his coffee cup from the carafe they had ordered from room service with breakfast. "What else did you boys talk about?"

Drake stepped in front of her and put his arms around her neck. "I told him it was none of his business what you looked like wearing a spa robe."

"What about what I look like without a spa robe?"

"Hmm, not sure I remember. Care to show me again?"

AFTER SHOWERING AND CHECKING OUT, Drake drove Liz north to the old town of Astoria on the mouth of the Columbia River, keeping his promise to show her the Oregon coast. They arrived in Portland by noon and stopped at Drake's office before heading north on I-5 to Seattle.

Margo Benning, Drake's office manager/legal assistant/secretary and friend, was working on her computer when they came down the back stairs from the parking garage into the office. She stood and warmly hugged Liz while giving her boss a frosty look.

"When I didn't hear from you this morning, I canceled your eleven o'clock. He's a good client we don't want to lose if you want to pay my salary this month."

"Good morning, Margo. Liz insisted on stopping by to

say hello. We're on our way to Seattle. Mike has a new matter he wants me to handle."

"And you were going to tell me you won't be here this afternoon when?"

Liz came to Drake's defense. "It's my fault, Margo. Mike just called this morning and talked him into driving me to Seattle. He should have called you though."

"Oh, I'm used to it, honey. I've been covering his hindquarters for so long he's forgotten what it's like to be a real attorney."

Drake headed toward his desk in the loft above and said over his shoulder, "Margo, is Paul available? I have something I need him to do for me."

The Bennings lived in the condo directly above the office. Drake had purchased it along with the rare bookstore below when its owner decided to move to Palm Springs and play more golf. The bookstore and its upstairs living quarters were a part of the RiverPlace, a development of retail shops, restaurants and a marina on the Willamette River in downtown Portland. It was Drake's favorite place in the city. He'd renovated the bookstore into a classy and comfortable law office that was perfect for a single attorney and his highly-qualified and sometimes cranky secretary.

Liz followed Drake up the stairs to his loft office. "Margo called Paul. She said he'd be down in a minute. This is some office you have here."

"Thanks, I like it. Check out the view of the marina. I do some of my best thinking standing at that window looking at the river."

Drake put a new legal pad in his laptop case and was ready to go. "I'll just need a minute with Paul. You can stay here, if you like, or go down and visit with Margo."

The mischievous smile on her face told Drake he just

made a mistake. "Margo said there were things I needed to know about you. Take all the time you need with Paul."

Before she reached the bottom of the loft stairs, he heard Paul Benning enter the office and greet his wife. "Up here, Paul."

Benning was Drake's second best friend, next to his former Delta Force partner, Mike Casey. He was still on medical leave from the Multnomah County Sheriff's Office, where he was a senior detective, and was contemplating retiring. At fifty-six, he had a full pension earned and was in relatively good health after a prostate surgery. Drake was interested in seeing if he was interested in working out of the office as a private detective. The thing he was going to ask Benning to do would give him some indication.

Drake stood to shake his friend's hand and waved him to a seat in front of his desk. "Thanks for coming down. How are you feeling, ready to do some work for me?"

"If it's anything like our Nicaraguan adventure, Margo's made me promise to say no the next time you ask. What did you have in mind?"

"The son of a man who was killed in Gold Beach is missing. A friend of mine down there is worried about him. He's asked me if I could find out if the kid's okay. The boy's aunt lives around here."

Benning leaned forward and looked at the piece of paper Drake handed him. "She lives in

Oregon City?"

Drake nodded. "That's her address and phone number. If you're up to it, give her a call and see if she knows where Billie Walid is."

"Why's the boy missing?"

"We don't know for sure. He's Lebanese and was beaten up and told to leave town. Then his dad was murdered the same day. It's possible he's afraid the same thing would happen to him if he stayed around."

"What does his being Lebanese have to do with it?"

Drake shrugged his shoulders. "You remember the Volksfront? The gang's leader lives in Gold Beach. He's been protesting the government settling Syrian refugees over in Roseburg. Maybe his guys can't tell the difference between a U.S. citizen who's Lebanese and a Syrian refugee."

"Or they just don't like anyone who isn't white. I remember the Volksfront and their Neo-Nazi hoodlums. We've had our share of trouble with them."

"Well, you shouldn't run into any of them when you contact the aunt. Will you check into this for me? I'm happy to pay for your time and out-of-pockets."

Benning smiled and got up. "Gives me a reason to get out and see if I'm ready to get back to work. Glad to help out."

Downstairs they found Liz and Margo sitting on the sofa in the client waiting area, in deep conversation.

"If I were you, Adam, I'd get Liz out of here as soon as you can. My wife knows way too many of your secrets and it looks like she's sharing some of them right now."

Drake agreed. "Liz, we better get going if we want to beat the rush-hour traffic in Seattle. Sorry to have to interrupt your time with my ever-loyal secretary." The two women continued talking, ignoring the men.

Drake leaned closer to Benning. "Find out what she's telling Liz and dinner's on me."

"Why do you think my wife would tell me? Have you ever been able to get her to tell you anything she didn't want to? Relax and assume she's sharing the good stuff. If she isn't, you'll know it long before you get to Seattle."

Chapter Twelve

PAUL BENNING WAS RIGHT. They didn't make it across the I-5 Columbia River Bridge before Liz turned in her seat and punched his arm.

"I understand you thought I was the 'Ice Queen' when we first met. What other first impressions did I make?"

For the next three hours, Drake tried to explain his initial impressions and feelings for her. It required him to share a lot more of his life leading up to their first meeting than he wanted, including his courtship and marriage to Kay. Sharing his feelings about losing his wife to cancer brought back all the memories that had started to fade just a little.

He was glad when they finally arrived at the new corporate headquarters of Puget Sound Security on the eastern shore of Lake Washington. He'd had enough sharing for the day.

Drake watched Liz as she examined the modern, three-story office building. The two top floors had wrap-around windows providing a floor-to-ceiling view of Lake Washington. The ground floor's exterior walls were fortified concrete with an overlay of stamped black concrete in an interlocking stone pattern.

"It's not what I was expecting," she said. "Security firms don't look like this in D.C."

"Mike will give you the tour, but prepare yourself to be impressed. In addition to offices, conference rooms and training facilities, it has a firing range, armory and machine shop. PSS is the complete package."

Drake drove to the lift gate for underground parking and entered the security code that changed on a random basis. His reserved parking place was two down from the CEO's. He saw that his friend's space was occupied by a new two-tone gray Land Rover.

He opened her door and gave Liz a hand. "Let's go see what the boss has in store for us."

When they stepped out of the elevator on the third floor, Mike Casey was waiting for them.

"Hi Liz. Would you like to look around and then accept my offer or can we discuss your salary and perks and then go take a look around?"

Drake stepped forward and extended his hand. "Hello Mike, good to see you too."

Casey pulled his friend in, gave him a man hug and slapped him on the back. "Missed you too, but Liz is about to make me a happy man. Aren't you, Liz?"

"Why don't we talk later?" she suggested with a coy smile. "I would like to look around first."

"Sure thing. Let me go grab my assistant. I'll have him give you the grand tour while I brief Adam on his next project."

Casey left and Drake took the opportunity to say softly,

"See if you can learn as much about him from his secretary as you did interrogating mine."

"I don't think that's possible. Besides, you're his best friend and you'll tell me everything

I need to know."

Casey returned with his assistant and introduced him to Liz. "Ken will show you anything you want to see. When you're finished, he'll bring you to my office and we can talk."

When the two left for the grand tour, Casey turned to Drake with a big smile. "Did you really leave Liz alone with Margo?"

"How'd you know that?"

Casey pointed to the security camera above the elevator door. "It records audio as well. We listened to you on Ken's monitor. You'd be amazed how much you can learn about people as they finish their conversations stepping out of the elevator. Let's talk in your office."

Drake's office was next to Casey's, with black lettering on the glass panel beside the solid mahogany door announcing it as the office of Special Counsel. The light gray walls on two sides were bare. A black and white framed picture of the Twin Towers before the attack on 9/11 hung on the wall above a mahogany credenza. A red folder lay in the middle of his mahogany desk.

Casey slid into one of the two black leather chairs in front of Drake's desk.

"You need to personalize your office."

"I have a personalized office in Portland."

"Yes, but when clients visit and walk by this office, it would be nice if it looked like someone worked here."

Drake sat in his stiff, new, black leather executive chair and opened the file.

"What's my new project? I hope it doesn't take me out of the country like the last one."

"I thought Nicaragua was growing on you?"

"Yea, like a bad fungus. Margo will go through the roof if I'm gone again for any length of time."

Casey pointed out the window toward downtown Seattle. "We've been asked to assist Sound Transit in completing a security assessment for its Link Light Rail trains. They're installing a new chemical detection system and want to make sure they've covered all the bases."

"What can I add to your assessment? You have guys far more qualified than me to do an assessment."

"The company that won the bid and is installing the new system is Martin Research, your old client in Portland. Richard Martin asked for you when he learned that you were my special counsel. Review the contract, look at the new detection system and then see if Sound Transit is installing the system in all the right places. It shouldn't take you more than a week."

Drake flipped through the thick file. "All right, but I have to get back to Portland after I take Liz to the airport. Is there a deadline on this?"

"Department of Homeland Security is asking all the mass transit systems in the country to review their security measures. They're worried that the next wave of terrorist attacks will target mass transit. Sound Transit would like us to complete our assessment by the end of the month." "Is there anything to support the DHS concern about attacks on mass transit?"

Casey shook his head. "There's no new intelligence. They've been worried about the growing trend over the last decade of jihadists going after subway and commuter rail systems. They've killed over two hundred people that way.

But I think the real concern is about nerve gas stolen by ISIS in Syria and the number of Syrian refugees given sanctuary here and coming over the border down south."

Two light knocks on the door and Liz poked her head in.

"I'm ready to talk, Mike, if you are. Adam's promised to take me to dinner to celebrate my new position with Puget Sound Security before I catch the redeye home."

CEO Casey sprung out of his chair and clapped. "Excellent! Let's leave him to read his file and get a start on saving Seattle from the enemy while we go over your compensation package."

Drake watched them leave and knew his life was changing.

Chapter Thirteen

JAMES DAVIS SAT on the end of his double bed in a room at the city center Econo Lodge. He was waiting for a call from his spotter.

Adam Drake had returned from Seattle that morning and had been in his office most of the day. At noon, he walked down the esplanade at RiverPlace to the Harborside restaurant for lunch and then returned to his office for the rest of the day.

It was now a quarter to six in the evening and Drake was about to walk down that same esplanade to a fancy wine bar nearby to meet a new client. Davis knew this because he was the fictitious new client that Drake was supposed to meet.

Posing as a wealthy out-of-town investor wanting to invest in a new Oregon winery, it had been easy to schedule a meeting with Drake. The file he'd received on Drake detailed his ownership of an old vineyard where he lived and his interest in wine. By insisting on a first meeting at the nearby wine bar, ostensibly to see if Drake really knew anything about Oregon wine, he had presented a challenge he hoped the man would not be able to resist.

It had worked and the target was about to walk right into the trap awaiting him. Four of his men were sitting in a white Ford Transit Connect borrowed from the Oregon Premier Wine Company for the night. It was parked in a turnaround half a block from the wine bar. When Drake approached, his men would grab him and take him to a gang member's tire shop where they would finish the job their sponsor assigned to them.

Davis jumped when his cell phone buzzed and laughed. He'd been waiting for the damn call and it still startled him, spilling beer from his growler down the front of his shirt.

"Drake just walked by. He's walking south down the esplanade."

"Is he alone?"

"He's alone. He's wearing a blue blazer and tan pants."

"Follow him. I'll tell the others."

Davis ended the call and alerted his lead man that Drake was heading his way.

"Get ready and remember he's former Delta. Don't pussyfoot around. Use the Taser and get him in the—"

"Relax, Davis. He won't know what hit him."

DRAKE WAS off to meet an intriguing new client.

It wasn't the first time a prospective new client had asked to meet outside his office. Business clients liked to show off their facilities to a new attorney they wanted to hire as a way of demonstrating what they did and how important they were. That didn't bother him. Attorneys did the same thing with their high-rent, impressive offices.

What intrigued him about this prospective new client was that he knew the nearby wine bar was a favorite of his and that he would be tested on his knowledge of Oregon wine before he was hired. He was looking forward to meeting this out-of-town investor.

He looked down at the marina on his left as he walked and saw that boaters were taking advantage of the warm night, preparing for a late cruise on the river. With sunset in late June around nine o'clock, they had plenty of time to enjoy their time on the water.

Out of the corner of his eye, he noticed the man on the bench he'd just passed stand and walk his way. There was something about the way he studied Drake's face that triggered a silent alarm. He knew it was a remnant of his training as a soldier, and a reflex that he'd learned to trust doing house-to-house searches in Iraq. The wary look of an enemy staring down from a rooftop was often the only warning you had of imminent danger.

Drake let his right hand swing back and brush against his Kimber Master Carry Ultra handgun under his jacket and then felt foolish. It was broad daylight on a busy esplanade in downtown Portland, Oregon, not a sidewalk in Chicago. He shook his head to turn off the triggered alarm and continued walking past the marina.

As he neared the Harborside at the Marina, he turned his head enough to look behind him. The man was fifteen yards back, looking in the window of a shop. Drake walked on to the corner and turned right, toward the wine bar half a block away.

He checked his watch and saw that he was right on time for his six o'clock meeting. It was time to relax and interview a new client. This client might think he was the one doing the interviewing, but he would soon learn that Drake chose the clients he worked for very carefully. Life was too short to spend it solving legal problems for a client he couldn't stand to be around.

The squeal of tires from a vehicle coming from the turnaround at the end of the street caused him to stop to see what was happening. The turnaround was too small for a car to speed around it.

A white delivery van accelerated out of the turnaround and sped toward him. As it got closer, he recognized the purple cluster of grapes logo of the Oregon Premier Wine Company, the biggest distributor of wine in the state.

Drake stepped back from the curb as the van slid to a stop. *They must be late for a delivery*, he thought, *with the front door of the wine bar ten feet away*.

The passenger door and sliding side door flew open and two men jumped out. They wore black ski masks and leather biker vests. The taller one exiting from the shotgun seat held a Taser and motioned for Drake to get in the van.

"Get in and I won't have to use this."

The second man moved to block a retreat on the sidewalk.

Another man, bigger than the other two, came around from behind the van and stood next to the second man. Drake was alone, facing three men who weren't there to deliver wine.

He raised his hands in surrender. "I don't really have time for this…"

Drake moved his hands in front of his face in a fighting stance and launched a high kick with his right foot that landed on the jaw of first man. The Taser dropped out of the man's hand as he flew back into the open passenger door of the van.

Pivoting on his left foot, Drake bent his knees to slip

under a blow aimed at his head from the second man and shot a body blow into the man's ribs. The man groaned and dropped to his knees.

The third man squared off with Drake and raised a police baton in his right hand. He flicked his wrist to expand it to its full length and smiled.

Drake returned the man's smile as he reached back to draw his Kimber from its concealed holster. "Ever hear the saying, 'Don't bring a baton to a gunfight'?"

The man started to lower the baton when a loud voice shouted, "What's going on out here?" from the door of the wine bar.

Drake turned his head slightly over his right shoulder to tell the person to call the police when a terrible pain exploded on the left side of his head. His eyes fluttered and a black cloud hid the sun.

Chapter Fourteen

A THROBBING PAIN behind his left ear was the first sensation when he regained consciousness. It seemed to be keeping time with a beating bass drum somewhere. As the drum beats began to fade a little, he heard a soft tapping sound near his head.

He opened his eyes and turned his head to the left. A nurse was tapping an IV bag on its stand beside his bed.

"Keep your head still and it won't hurt as much."

"Now you tell me," Drake said and cautiously turned back to look up at the ceiling. "Where am I?"

"OHSU Emergency Care. An ambulance brought you here."

"How long ago?"

She patted his arm. "I'll see if I can find your doctor. He'll answer your questions."

He closed his eyes when the nurse pulled the curtain closed around his bed and left. Other than the pain at the back of his head and a major headache, the rest of his body seemed to be okay.

The curtain was pulled back and a man wearing blue surgical scrubs moved to his bedside.

"Mr. Drake, I'm Doctor Sands. How are you feeling?"

"Pain in the back of my head and a whopping headache. How long have I been here?" "Not long. We kept you sedated while we ran some tests. Can you tell me what happened?"

Drake ran a hand down his face and tried to remember. "I left my office to meet a new client and woke up here. That's all I remember."

The doctor nodded. "I'm sure you'll remember in time. A witness says you were hit in the head with a police baton. You were in some sort of altercation with three men in front of a wine bar. Does that help?"

"No, it doesn't. Sorry."

"Well, let me tell you what we know. Your CAT scan shows that you have a fracture of your occipital bone, a linear fracture from the blow of a blunt object like a police baton. You don't have a concussion, but that doesn't surprise me. Not all skull fractures result in concussions, but we'll keep you overnight just to make sure. The police want to take your statement, of course, but you'll be released tomorrow unless something else turns up. Is there someone you'd like us to call?"

"Yes, thank you."

"Give the nurse the number and she'll make the call for you. Get some rest, Mr. Drake. You'll feel better in the morning."

Drake waited for the nurse to return and gave her Paul Benning's number.

He remembered more than he told the doctor. He had left his office to meet someone and now doubted that the person was really a potential client. The timing of the van's arrival and the attempted snatch in front of the wine bar was too perfect. It wasn't a random act of violence. The person or persons responsible targeted him for some reason he didn't understand.

But he *would* figure it out. He remembered seeing something that identified his attackers as clearly as his nurse's ID badge. The man holding the Taser was left-handed. When he motioned for him to get in the van, there was a tattoo of three interlocking triangles on the back of his left hand. It was Odin's symbol of a Norse Viking Warrior and the chosen tattoo of Volksfront, the white supremacy biker gang, like the gang of swarming bikers that chased him on the coast highway near Gold Beach the previous weekend.

He closed his eyes for what seemed a short minute. When he opened them, Paul and Margo Benning were standing at the foot of his bed. Margo had a stern but concerned look on her face.

"What happened?"

"I'm okay, if that's what you're asking."

"I know you're okay, we talked to the doctor. What happened?"

Drake looked at Paul Benning and grimaced. "I guess I'm not getting a sympathy card from my secretary. Have you talked to the police?"

Margo came around to the side of his bed and clamped a hand on his forearm. "You're right; I'm sorry you have a skull fracture and a bad headache. The doctor says you'll live. Now, what happened after you left the office?"

"Three men tried to pull me into a van. I disabled two of them and then made a mistake. I allowed myself to be distracted for a second and got whacked by the third man. Then I woke up here. That's all I know, Margo."

"Did this happen before you met with the new client Margo mentioned?" Benning asked.

Drake nodded. "It happened before I entered the wine bar. I never met the client. I'm not sure he was a real client."

Margo pulled on his arm. "Wait a minute. I talked with the man for twenty minutes. He was very specific about why he wanted you to represent him, gave me a lot of information. He also knew a lot about you and was very complimentary. He didn't say anything that made me suspicious. Why do you think he wasn't a potential client?"

Drake elevated the head of the bed and took her hand in both of his. "This isn't your fault, Margo. Someone went to a lot of trouble to set this up. They knew all the right things to say to get me to one of my favorite places. I think the man you talked with wasn't legit because the men who attacked me knew where I was going. They waited for me."

Paul Benning started drumming his fingers on the bed next to Drake's foot. "But why go to all this trouble? If someone wanted to hurt you, there are easier ways than trying to abduct you in broad daylight."

"I don't know why, Paul, but I might know who. One of the men had a tattoo I recognized. Check with your friends at the Sheriff's Office and find out what they know about Volksfront gang members living here in Portland. It can't be a coincidence that the gang is suspected of killing the father of the boy I asked you to find and was also the biker gang that hassled us on the coast two days ago."

Margo poked him in the chest. "I know what you're thinking and I don't want you or Paul going after some biker gang. Let the police handle this, please."

"I will, but I have to know who put me in the hospital.

When I know, I will gladly let law enforcement do the rest. I just want to get them pointed in the right direction."

He knew when she squinted her eyes that this wasn't the last of the conversation. She knew him well enough to know that he wouldn't rest until he got another shot at his would-be captors. Just as he knew she wouldn't stop trying to talk him out of it.

Chapter Fifteen

JAMES DAVIS KNOCKED SOFTLY on the door of the fifth-floor suite in the Portland Downtown Embassy Suites. The stately, old hotel was too fancy for his taste and he was glad he wore a coat and tie for the meeting.

He stood facing the door when people walked by, keeping his eyes fixed straight ahead. He didn't think anyone would recognize him, but why take a chance? Some cop he'd run into might be having a night out with a mistress or favorite hooker.

The door opened and he walked in without a word from his host. He saw that the suite had a living room and beyond that a separate bedroom. A bottle of Jack Daniels and a bucket of ice sat on a glass coffee table in front of a gray sofa.

"There's a glass over there if you want a drink," Michael Flynn said.

Davis didn't react when Flynn remained seated in the armchair at the end of the coffee table. The man was a master manipulator and slick politician. If the slight was meant to establish the man as his equal, it wasn't going to work.

Flynn was a politician he had chosen to lead the political wing of the movement. He was running for congress in Washington's fifth congressional district and was increasingly popular in his hometown of Spokane. His public positions on most matters were mainstream conservative, but privately he was as far right as David Duke. He wanted to drug test all welfare recipients and sterilize welfare women after their second child. He hated affirmative action and wanted to eliminate all minority set-asides. His latest rant that caught the attention of the movement was about the settlement of refugees in communities where they were not wanted. That was what had led to their first meeting.

Flynn needed money and lots of it. Davis had promised to get it for him, if he pledged to support and work for the establishment of a white homeland in the Northwest. It would take time, Flynn was told, but building a solid political base in Congress and the state legislatures was necessary for their success. Flynn could lead the way and be assured of the money he needed for his campaigns. And Flynn had eagerly agreed.

But Davis could see that something had changed. Flynn wasn't deferential and no longer had the look of a supplicant with an outstretched hand. He looked angry.

Davis took his time getting a glass from the wet bar. He poured whiskey over two cubes of ice before he sat down in the armchair facing Flynn across the coffee table.

"Something bothering you, Flynn?"

"Your boys screwed the pooch, Davis. Now he knows he's a target. If you can't get the job done, maybe we need someone who can."

Flynn refilled his glass and sat back in his chair.

Davis savored the moment as well as the whiskey. Flynn was trying his best to look tough, to be the leader. It was time to break him down.

"There is no *we*, Flynn. I speak for the movement. I picked you to be the public face of the movement. Without the funds I provide you, there would be no *you*. If you don't change your tune, there might not be a *you* when I leave this room."

Flynn stood up and tried to make his five feet eleven inches look as intimidating as possible. "Don't threaten me, Davis. I know who Ryan Walker is and I know he likes to spread his money around funding little groups like yours. But I'm running for Congress of the United States. He's never had a far-right politician like me in America, someone who has a shot at doing what he's been able to do in Europe. He's got people marching in the streets, rioting against the flood of refugees and wanting to take down governments. He needs me more than he needs you to make that happen."

In a way, Davis admired Flynn's delusion and the courage it gave him. He could give a good speech, and maybe even get others to believe he was the man he claimed to be. But inside Flynn was a little man.

He stood to face Flynn and drew his .44 caliber Charter Arms pistol from its Italian leather holster on his right hip. Releasing the cylinder with a flick of his thumb, he took one cartridge out and held it up.

"Sit down, Flynn. Do you know what this is? It's a .44 caliber cartridge with 246 grains of lead in its round nose. That's 16 more grains of lead than a typical .45 cartridge you used in the Army. It tears an awful hole in a man. Believe me. Have you ever fired a revolver like this?" Flynn's eyes looked away and then down. He nodded no.

Davis walked around the coffee table and handed Flynn the gun, butt first. "Here, why don't you hold it while we finish our conversation?"

Flynn took the revolver as Davis turned his back and returned to his chair. When he sat down, he saw that Flynn had laid the revolver down on the coffee table.

"I called this meeting to make sure that you were ready to speak at our gathering this weekend. You are ready, aren't you?"

"Yes."

"Good. We have sixty-three groups coming from all over the country. I don't want them to be disappointed, so send me a copy of your prepared remarks. When you're finished speaking, we have a party planned for the boys. I want you to be available at the party to meet anyone who wants to meet with you, is that understood? Good. When we wrap it up for the weekend, I'll have the first installment of your money."

"I thought I was getting the full ten million."

"You were, until you insulted me tonight."

Davis got up and picked up his revolver from the coffee table. "You have any questions?" Flynn's silence gave his answer.

"Good. See you on Saturday."

Davis took the stairs down to the lobby and leaned against a pillar where he could see the stairs and the elevator. He flipped open his burner phone and called the leader of the Portland cell.

"I need a soldier over here to keep an eye on someone. Even if he leaves town, I want eyes on him 24/7. Give me a report every four hours."

Chapter Sixteen

PAUL BENNING'S Ford F-150 pickup was idling at the curb when Drake walked out of the hospital on Wednesday morning. Clouds filtered the sun, the kind that would burn off by noon, unlike the anger Drake was struggling to control.

"How's the head?" Benning asked.

"Sore and throbbing. You have time for breakfast? I need some coffee."

"Sure, where to?"

Drake checked his watch. "They're still serving breakfast at Three Degrees in the

RiverPlace Hotel, let's go there. It's close to the office in case Margo needs me."

Benning drove slowly through the complex of buildings that made up the Oregon Health Sciences University complex. OHSU sat on top of Marquam Hill and it towered above the city. Some of the best views of Portland could be seen from the hospital, but Drake wasn't interested in sightseeing as they drove down SW Sam Jackson Park Road.

"A detective stopped by to question me this morning," Benning said. "From his line of questioning, he made it sound like this was your fault. He said maybe you were the aggressor, a tough guy with a gun. That maybe the man who hit you was just defending himself."

"He asked if I thought that might be the case. He said he'd seen your file and knew about your military training. He wanted to know if you saw yourself as some kind of vigilante." Drake shook his head. "Terrific, that's just what I need people thinking."

Traffic was light and, twenty minutes later, Drake and Benning arrived at the Three Degrees Restaurant in the RiverPlace Hotel and were seated at a table with a view of the river.

Drake quickly ordered coffee and scanned the menu. Steak N Eggs with a side of whole wheat toast and marmalade looked good. "I'm ordering steak and eggs. What looks good to you?"

"Steak and eggs. I'll join you."

The waiter brought a carafe of coffee and a small pitcher of cream and left.

Drake added a splash of cream to his cup and stirred it with a spoon. "Did you get a hold of your friend?"

Benning was a senior detective on medical leave from the Multnomah County Sheriff's Office. His "friend" was a detective assigned to the department's gang task force that monitored the activities of gangs, including prison gangs and skinhead groups.

"I did. Ron has a file on Portland members of Volksfront and said he'd bring me a copy. He'll get the last-known locations for as many of them as he can. What are you planning on doing with the information?"

Drake grinned. "Don't you think you're better off not knowing the answer to that? Margo won't be satisfied until she pries it out of you, if she thinks you know something."

Benning raised his cup in agreement. "Then don't tell me everything."

"Let's say the file on these guys allows me to identify one big guy who's left-handed and has a tattoo of three interlocking triangles on that hand. Let's say the file also has his last-known address. What would a good detective do with that information?"

Their orders of steak and eggs arrived with a flourish and gave Benning time to consider his answer. "Let me answer your question with a question. If a good detective knew what he would do with the information, would a smart attorney consider letting the detective do what needed to be done?"

Drake watched a thirty-two foot Bayliner motor yacht move out of the RiverPlace marina and head north toward the Columbia River. He knew what his friend was asking. He also knew the problem it would cause them if his wife found out.

"Do you really want to take this on? You're still on medical leave from the Sheriff's Office. You know how Margo feels about me going after "some biker gang", as she put it. She'd raise holy hell if she knew I asked you to do it for me."

Benning cut off another piece of hanger steak and stared at it before putting it in his mouth. When he finished the bite, he looked at Drake for a long moment. "Adam, I'm thinking about leaving the Sheriff's Office. Dealing with my prostate cancer and realizing how much time my job takes me away from Margo got me thinking.

"I'd like to set my own hours and choose the things I work on, like you do. I think I'd like to open my own office and work as a private detective. I know some attorneys who might send me some cases. You might even have some work I could do, like finding the guys who tried to snatch you off the street."

"Will Margo back you on this?"

"I don't see why not. It's the same thing I've been doing for the last thirty years. With early retirement and Margo's income, we'll have enough to live on even if I flop as a private detective."

Drake recognized the cautious excitement in his friend's voice. He probably sounded the same way when he decided to leave the District Attorney's Office and hang out his own shingle.

Still, it was a big undertaking to start a new business and go out on your own.

"Tell you what, Paul. If you can get Margo to go along with this, let's give it a try. You can work out of my office and I'll be your first client. You find the guys who attacked me and the chef's son. See if this is what you really want to do and we'll go from there."

Benning reached across the table to shake Drake's hand and seal the deal. "I'll get started right away, but I'll tell Margo when the time is right."

Good luck with that, Drake thought. For both their sakes, he hoped there was a right time.

Chapter Seventeen

JAMES DAVIS SAT ON A FOUR-LEGGED, wooden stool leaning back against the workbench in Clint Buddy's tire shop. A black tire iron dangled from his right hand, tapping the heel of his steeltoed work boot.

Three of his men stood in front of him. Only one of them looked him in the eye.

"So far, I haven't heard one thing that explains why you failed to grab him," Davis said. "Clint's the only one who got a lick in."

"We had him if that guy hadn't come out of the wine bar."

"Mooney, when you joined us you were supposed to be a real bad ass. One wine-sipping suit steps out and you guys run? You don't deserve to ride with the big boys if you can't deal with one civilian."

The man in the middle, the biggest of the three, continued to meet the gaze of the Volksfront commander. "Maybe you should have let us clip him right there. We didn't need to take him to the old warehouse to kill him."

Davis jumped off the stool and poked Tom Brasco in the chest with the tire iron, knocking him back. "You sure you want to second-guess my orders, son? There's only room for one man giving orders around here."

"I'm just saying the man has skills and he's packing. It's not going to be easy to get the jump on him. Shooting him would be a lot easier."

Davis kept the tire iron touching Brasco's chest until the big man lowered his eyes. "The reason I wanted him taken to the warehouse is because I need to ask him some questions before you kill him. He's been causing problems for a man who wants to know why. I agreed to find out why for the man. So, we'll try again."

Back on his stool, Davis flipped the tire iron end over end for a minute as he thought about a plan B. "Let's give it a couple days to cool off. I've got some things to do for the gathering, then we'll take care of the attorney. Finish what you need to do here before the gathering and we'll meet."

Davis left the tire shop and drove back to the Econo Lodge to check out. Before he got there, his cell phone vibrated in the nylon holster on his belt.

"Mr. Walker wants to meet with you before he leaves for Seattle tomorrow. Be here by five tonight, same place as before."

The call ended and Davis shouted profanities at his phone. He didn't have time to drive to a damn fancy spa and he didn't want to explain why the attorney was still alive. He knew that was the real reason for the summons.

Walker had made it clear that the five million dollars was contingent upon the successful termination of the attorney. Why this one attorney was so important to the banker was a mystery.

But the answer to that just might provide a little leverage to guarantee the five million he needed.

He arrived at his motel on SW 4th Avenue and parked in front of his first-floor room. Staying in his truck, he called a source in Gold Beach.

"Deputy Rawlings."

"Toby, this is James Davis. Got a minute?"

"Sure, Mr. Davis."

"Toby, you've been to a couple of our meetings. You know how we help each other out from time to time, right?"

"Yes, I do, Mr. Davis. I know you put in a good word for me with Sheriff Barker."

"I was glad I could help, Toby. Here's the thing. I need to find out things about somebody and I don't have a way to do that. It's possible the National Crime Information Center might have something that would help me. Do you have access to the NCIC?" "We use the NCIC here, but I don't get to use it myself."

"Is there a way you could use it if you wanted to, Toby?"

"Mr. Davis, Sheriff Barker would fire me if he found out I used the NCIC."

"Don't worry about the sheriff. I'll speak with him if there's a problem. I need your help, Toby. Can you help me out here?"

Davis could feel the kid squirming at his desk where he filed misdemeanor complaints and handled nuisance calls for the department.

Toby all but whispered his answer. "Mr. Davis, I'll do what I can. What's the man's name?"

"His name is Ryan Walker. He owns a bank in Seattle and might be from another country, he's got a slight accent of some sort. That's all I know."

"It might take me day or two to get on the NCIC when nobody's around, will that be okay?"

"That'll be fine, Toby. I'll call you tomorrow and see how you're doing. And Toby, if you'd like to come to the gathering this weekend with your dad, you're welcome to."

"Thanks, Mr. Davis, I'd like that."

After grabbing his duffel bag from his room and checking out of the motel, Davis drove to his favorite steakhouse and strip club, the A-Crop. He had time for a steak and a beer before heading up the Columbia to meet with Walker.

JOSEF, Walker's communications expert, played the recording of Davis's call for Walker.

"Davis is more resourceful than I anticipated," Walker said. "When he arrives, relieve him of any weapons. Find a way to put a bug on him. I want to know what he's planning. After he takes care of Drake for me, he's a liability we can eliminate. Until then, make sure he doesn't interfere with our other work."

"If he becomes a problem before he kills the attorney, do you want Eric to take care of him?"

Walker considered the question. "If he's going to expose us or interfere with our young Saudi's plans in Seattle, kill him. I'll find another way to get rid of Mr. Drake."

Chapter Eighteen

PAUL BENNING WAS PARKED across the street from the Acropolis Steakhouse, one of Portland's oldest gentleman's club and strip joints. He'd followed James Davis from a tire shop owned by a known and active member of Volksfront.

His friend in the gang taskforce at the Sheriff's Office had provided a file on known Portland members of the gang. It was complete with criminal records and photos. The photos were mug shots for the most part, although some of them were surveillance photos taken at a distance.

He figured the tire shop was as good a place as any to start hunting down the men who attacked Drake and he was right. He parked half a block away from the tire shop, and within thirty minutes, three members of the gang had shown up. Two were locals who lived in Portland and one was from out of town. The out-of-towner was from Gold Beach and was believed to be the current leader of Volksfront.

Benning decided it was time to report in to his new client.

"Drake, you busy?"

"I have time to talk. What's up?"

"If I'd known being a detective was this easy, I would have left the department a long time ago. I located the leader of Volksfront." "How'd you manage that so quickly?"

"My friend Ron Rivera gave me a copy of a file the task force keeps on known Volksfront members. I started with one of them who's supposed to be actively involved in gang activities and got lucky."

"Give me your location, I'll be there in fifteen minutes."

Benning told him he was across the street from the Acropolis Steakhouse and turned on the radio to listen to some classic rock. He had time to think before Drake arrived about a possible link between James Davis and the men who put his friend in the emergency room.

It could be that the Volksfront leader had something to do with the murder of the chef in Gold Beach when Drake and Liz were there. And it was possible Drake had seen or learned something about the murder that led to his attempted abduction. Maybe it had something to do with the chef's son that Drake had asked him to find or maybe Davis just wanted to find out if Drake knew where the kid was because the kid might have seen or heard something. But those possibilities were pretty tenuous. Whatever the reason was for going after Drake, he knew Drake was determined to find it out one way or another.

Which was going to put him between a rock and hard spot if sleuthing for his wife's boss put either of them in danger. When the time was right to tell her what he was doing, he would have to find a way to minimize the danger or his career as a private detective was going to be a very short one.

Deep in thought, he didn't hear Drake arrive until there

was a knock on the passengerside window of his Ford F-150.

Drake climbed into the leather bucket seat beside him. "You looked like you were in a galaxy far, far away. You sure he's still in there?"

"He's still in there. His truck is in the parking lot."

Benning reached back and grabbed the file from the floor behind his seat. "Here's the file Rivera gave me. Anyone look familiar?"

Drake flipped through the pages, stopping on the mug shot and surveillance photo of Tom Brasco. "From a distance, it's hard to tell how tall this guy is, but he's big enough. How big is Davis?"

"He's big but heavy. He doesn't sound like the guy you described with the Taser."

"How long has Davis been in there?"

"Forty-three minutes, long enough for a steak or a show. The food's pretty good here."

Drake turned to look at Benning with a big smile. "And what about the strip shows? They pretty good too?"

Benning kept his eyes looking straight ahead and said as seriously as he could, "It was work. Like I said, the food's good. Don't remember much about the pretty waitresses or the nimble pole dancers. But the food was good."

Drake chuckled. "Good to know the food's good."

"What do you want to do when Davis comes out?"

"Let's see what he's up to. He's been to the tire shop. Maybe he'll go back there and meet with his boys. If not, we'll see where he's going. I'd like to know why he's here in Portland."

"Have you heard anything more about the murder of the chef in Gold Beach?"

Drake shook his head. "I need to call Josh and—"

Benning pointed across the street. "That's Davis." They watched Davis walk toward the parking lot.

"He's a big old boy, isn't he? But you're right; he's too heavy to be the guy I'm looking for."

The headlights of a black Ram Big Horn 2500 truck blinked at the back of the lot.

"The truck suits him, big and mean looking," Drake said as he opened the door to get out.

"You follow him at first and then we'll switch off. Call me when you want to rotate."

Drake walked back to his gray Porsche Cayman and got in. They both started their engines and waited for Davis to pull out of the Acropolis parking lot.

The rumble of a big V8 engine moved toward and then away from them as the black truck turned onto McLoughlin Blvd. and headed north. Benning waited until it was half a block ahead and then followed. Drake was two car lengths behind him.

Davis continued driving north on McLoughlin Blvd. Ten minutes later, when he turned west onto SE Belmont St. and took the exit onto I-5 North, Benning hit the Sync button on the center console and called Drake.

"Do you want to keep following him if he stays on I-5 and crosses the Columbia into Washington?"

"Let's stay with him a little longer and see where he's going."

Three minutes later, they knew. Davis exited again and headed east on the Banfield Expressway. He was staying in Oregon.

Chapter Nineteen

FOR DRAKE, it was déjà vu all over again. Two years before, he'd followed a terrorist on the
Banfield and up I-84 to Hood River. That pursuit ultimately ended at the lakeside home of United States Senator Hazelton, his father-in-law. In a firefight with terrorists, four of whom died that night, the life of the Secretary of Homeland Security and both his in-laws were saved.

The night also saved his life. Grieving over the death of his wife of only three years and drinking to excess, he had been neglecting his law practice and practically everything else as well. But because of that night, he was later approached by the Secretary of Homeland Security and asked to be a troubleshooter for the DHS from time to time. The assignments and adventures that followed had given him a new purpose and reinvigorated his life.

This time, however, he wasn't after a terrorist. He was following a man he suspected of being involved with the men who beat him and put him in the hospital. James Davis was a felon who led a gang of Neo-Nazi white supremacists that marched to the drum of hatred and fascist intolerance.

In many ways, he guessed Davis and his followers weren't that much different than terrorists. Both groups wanted to return to a former time, a time when their race was unchallenged in the world, and they were willing to use violence to achieve their goals.

Drake looked ahead and saw that Davis was staying on the Banfield Expressway and heading east up the Columbia River.

Benning called again. "What now? He could be visiting family in eastern Oregon for all we know."

"My gut tells me he's up to something. Trade places. Let's give him another hour and then we'll turn back."

Benning slowed a little and Drake took his place. Davis was two cars ahead and maintaining a steady seventy miles an hour. They passed the exit for Portland International Airport and continued on I-84 toward Troutdale and points east.

The caravan of three drove along the Columbia River, past the picturesque Multnomah Falls then Rooster rock and the Bonneville Dam. When they reached the Cascades Locks, Davis slowed and took exit 14 for the Bridge of the Gods.

Hanging back while Davis stopped to pay the bridge tool, they saw him turn right and head east on Hwy. 14.

Before they followed him across the bridge, Drake called Benning. "Let's trade places again. The city of Stevenson's a mile up the road and his biker friends might have told him what
I drive."

They followed Davis's black Ram Big Horn as it entered

the city limits of Stevenson and immediately turned left on Rock Creek Drive.

Benning pulled to the curb and called Drake. "I know where he's going. "We had a sheriffs' conference at Skamania Resort and Spa a couple years ago. The road to the Skamania lodge is just a spitting distance up Rock Creek Drive."

"You sure?"

"Stay here and I'll go see if his truck is at the lodge. If it isn't, you can follow him on Rock Creek and I'll catch up."

Drake waited five minutes before Benning confirmed that Davis was at Skamania Resort and Spa.

"He parked and walked right in. No luggage or golf clubs. He's here to see someone."

"See where he's going and I'll join you."

Drake parked the Cayman in the rear parking lot and jogged down the path to the lodge. On the way, he spotted Benning's white Ford F-150 parked two rows behind the black truck in the lower parking lot.

Benning was waiting for him standing beside a ten-foot chainsaw carving of a bear just beyond the registration desk.

"I just caught a glimpse of him getting in the elevator when I walked in."

Drake looked around for a place where they could watch the lobby and not look out of place. He pointed to a sitting area in front of a tall flagstone fireplace just off the main lobby. A stack of neatly folded newspapers occupied one end of a coffee table; four leather armchairs and two elegant rocking chairs surrounded it.

"I think I'll catch up on the news."

Benning nodded toward the gift shop. "I'll watch from in there."

Drake walked to the sitting area, picked up a copy of the *Wall Street Journal* and sat down.

Benning headed the other way and entered the gift shop to browse the lodge mementoes and apparel on display. He fingered the soft wool scarves and examined the sweatshirts with lodge logos. Then he moved on to the reading material display and selected a copy of *Outdoor Life* to read while he waited for Davis to return to the lobby.

Neither man would remember much of what they read during the next twenty-three minutes as they feigned interest in the reading matter in their hands. They did pay attention, however, to two men when they walked out of the elevator.

One man was young and muscular and carried two leather suitcases.

The other man was older and wore oval, wire rim glasses. He carried a leather suitcase in one hand and a silver aluminum laptop case in the other. The strap around his neck for the laptop case pulled diagonally across his chest and stretched the fabric of his windbreaker tightly over a cross-draw holster under his left shoulder.

Drake called Benning. "Someone's bodyguards, from the look of them. Wonder who they work for."

"Classy place like this, could be anyone. We'll know when he or she joins them. How much longer do you want to wait for Davis?"

"We've come this far, we'll give it another ten minutes. If he doesn't come out, you go use your charm and your badge, if you still have it, and ask the woman at the front desk if she knows who Davis is meeting."

Chapter Twenty

WALKER ADMIRED the view out the window of his suite on the fourth-floor executive level of the Skamania lodge one last time. The Columbia River Gorge was a magnificent canyon that stretched for eighty miles. It had more waterfalls along those eighty miles than any river in North America and he intended to see them all on his helicopter flight back to Portland.

James Davis, his acolyte fascist gang leader, sat quietly behind him in a chair. He wasn't worried about turning his back on the man. Not after the tongue-lashing he'd just given him for failing to kill the attorney. The man was begging for another chance.

Walker turned around and folded his arms across his chest. "You're a smart man, Davis, but you have foolishly underestimated Adam Drake. The dossier I gave you detailed his military training and activities as a Delta operator. If I allow you a second opportunity to kill him, what would you do differently this time?"

"Do I still have to question him first?"

"I need to know what Drake and the government know about my organization, so, yes, I want him interrogated."

"We'll have to grab him where we won't be interrupted again. He parks his Porsche in the parking garage behind his office, we could grab him there."

"Then take him where?"

"One of my men owns a tire shop. We've used it before."

Walker considered the plan for a moment and then said, "Perhaps there's an easier way. Drake only has one employee, his secretary. Get Drake in his office. Use the threat of killing the secretary to get Drake to talk. Then kill them both."

A grin spread across James Davis's face. "We could do that."

"If you do it in the next couple of days, I'll have the money for you in time for your gathering this weekend."

"Consider it done, Mr. Walker."

"Excellent, then that concludes my business here. Walk out with me. I have a flight to catch and you need to get back to Portland. Call me when it's finished."

WHEN THE ELEVATOR DOOR OPENED, Drake saw James Davis walk out with another man and instinctively raised the paper to hide his face. Then he smiled. Davis would have to turn completely around to see him in the sitting area.

His phone vibrated in his pocket.

"Nice move, rookie. I can tell you haven't done a lot of surveillance work."

"Thanks. Think the guy with him is the one with the bodyguards?"

"If he is, they'll be outside waiting for him. I'll go see."

Benning walked out of the gift shop and followed Davis and his friend.

Drake folded and laid his paper down and started across the lobby. Before he reached the door, Benning stepped back inside.

"The bodyguards and Davis's friend are waiting for a ride to a heliport. Davis is walking to his truck. What do you want me to do?"

"You stick with Davis. If he returns to Portland, see where he goes then meet me at the office. I know where the heliport is. I'll see if I can find out who Davis met with." Benning jogged to his truck while Drake strolled leisurely to his Cayman.

He wasn't in a rush because the heliport was nearby, if you could call it a heliport. It was just an open area about a half mile away across the railroad tracks that ran south of the city of Stevenson. A helicopter could land there but that was all it could do.

From the upper parking lot, he saw Davis's black Ram Big Horn back out of its parking space and drive toward the exit. Benning's white F-150 was rolling before Davis left the lower parking lot.

Drake slipped on his Ray Bans and rested his hands on the top of the steering wheel. The resort's white transport van was pulling away from the front of the lodge below. It would drive past him in the upper parking lot on its way to the heliport.

What business did a redneck like James Davis have with a man with two bodyguards? He didn't know a lot about the man's business, but for him to drive this far for such a short meeting meant it had to be important.

He started the engine and drove out of the upper lot. When he reached the end of Skamania Lodge Way and turned left onto Rock Creek Drive, he saw Benning's F-150 pulling on to Hwy. 14 to follow James Davis.

Drake reached the heliport before the lodge transport and found a black Bell 429 helicopter waiting for its passengers with its rotor blades slowly spinning. It was a charter from Pacific Edge Aviation, operating out of Portland International Airport, according to the gold lettering on its side.

He scanned the open area and decided that parking there wasn't an option. Davis's friend might not pay any attention to someone so obviously watching his departure, but his bodyguards surely would. He made a U-turn and drove back across the railroad tracks to a wide spot in the entrance road. From there he had a clear view of the Bell 429 in his rearview mirror.

The resort's white van turned off the highway onto the entrance road and headed his way. Drake kept his eyes lowered as if he was studying a road map until the van passed him. As it rolled to a stop beside the helicopter, he hit the release for the bonnet and got out. Lifting the bonnet, he stood to one side so he could click a few shots of the men getting out of the van with his cell phone.

The driver got out first and opened the rear doors for the bodyguards to lift out the luggage. Three leather suitcases and silver aluminum laptop case.

Then the bodyguards stood to one side as their boss got out. He had gray hair, almost white, wore a black blazer and gray slacks. The man looked to be fit and in his sixties judging from the way he moved as he stepped out and jogged to the helicopter.

Drake closed the bonnet and stood beside the Cayman. He watched over the roof as the bodyguards loaded the luggage and followed their boss into the helicopter. Whoever this man was, he needed to know how he was involved with James Davis.

The Bell lifted off and Drake watched it climb and then veer off toward the river. He had no idea where it was going but he knew someone who could find out.

Chapter Twenty-One

THE DRIVE along the Columbia River back into Portland took an extra thirty minutes with the early go-home traffic.

Drake parked in his reserved space and took the back stairs down to his office. His secretary was at her desk talking on the phone and writing on a legal pad. She waved him over and wrote something then turned the legal pad around. It said Paul was on his way and would be there in ten minutes.

He gave her a thumbs up and took the stairs to his loft office and sanctuary. A half-wall on one side let him look down to the client waiting area and reception counter. He could see Margo's desk and secretarial work area behind the counter but not the break room and storage room adjacent to her desk. A small, unisex office restroom was located under the stairs down from the parking garage.

Drake leased the condo above his office to Margo and Paul Benning. He loved the arrangement and so did they.

A stack of files occupied the center of his desk with documents attached, each waiting for his signature. They would have to wait until he called the one person he knew who could find out the destination of the Bell 429 helicopter and who had chartered it.

He called Mike Casey at Puget Sound Security.

"Hi Mike, am I interrupting anything?"

"You are, but my pedicurist can keep working while we talk."

"I don't know whether to laugh or call your wife."

"Laugh but don't call Megan. I was kidding about the pedicure. What's up?"

"Can you track the flight of a helicopter?"

"The FAA can."

"Do you know someone there?"

"I might, why?"

"The guy I'm interested in is an acquaintance of someone we're looking into. I'll tell you all about it when I get to Seattle."

"Give me the tail numbers. What kind of helicopter is it?"

"A Bell 429 owned by a charter service out of PDX." Drake repeated the Bell's tail numbers.

"I'll see what I can do. How soon do you need this?"

"I know you're busy with your pedicures and stuff. Sometime this week will be fine."

"I'm not going to hear the end of this, am I?"

"Probably not. See you soon."

The thought of Mike Casey, Delta sniper and Night Stalker pilot, sitting in his office getting a pedicure was a picture that was going to take up space in his mind for a long time. Even if Casey was just joking.

Drake headed downstairs to get a cup of coffee just as Paul Benning was coming down the back stairs from the parking garage.

"Say hello to your wife and come upstairs when you're finished."

He didn't know if Benning would take the opportunity to tell Margo where he'd been all afternoon, but if he did he didn't want to rush him. Telling her he was venturing out as a private detective for the office, instead of returning to the Sheriff's Office, was going to require a delicate touch.

Back in the loft, he started signing the letters in the stack on his desk and waited for his friend to arrive. He only finished two files before Benning showed up with a worried look on his face.

"Looks like I'm not going to be able to put off telling her about your offer. She wants to know where I was all afternoon and she wants to know it now. I told her I'd tell her tonight."

Drake leaned back in his chair holding his coffee cup in both hands. "Paul, whatever you decide is fine with me. I would like to work with you here, but walking away from your position as a senior detective in the Sheriff's Office is a big deal. It's something both of you have to be comfortable with."

Benning nodded his agreement and changed the subject. "I followed Davis to the

Downtown Econo Lodge where he has a room. He was still there when I left to come here."

"Is he alone?"

"As far as I could tell, he's alone."

"The man I want to have a word with is the guy I recognized from his mug shot and surveillance photo."

"Tom Brasco."

"Does the task force file have an address or tell us where he works?"

"No, but I'll get back with Ron Rivera and see if he can find out. What are you planning on doing if we find him?"

"I'm not sure. Let's find him first. Have you made any progress on the other matter, finding the chef's son?"

"His aunt hasn't seen him and I don't have any other leads. He lived with his dad at the resort and the aunt says he doesn't have any relatives here in the northwest. He doesn't sound like a kid who would just take off with no means of support."

"Unless he's afraid that what happened to his dad will happen to him if he stays in Gold Beach. He was a good athlete. Check with the school and see if he had any close friends who might know where he is. Let's keep trying to find him a little longer."

Drake's phone rang. It was Mike Casey. "Paul, you might want to hear this. I'll put it on the speaker."

"Mike, Paul Benning's here with me and I have the speaker on. What did you find out?"

"Buddy, the man who chartered the helicopter, is Mr. Big as far as I can tell. He chartered back to PDX on the Bell 429 and then got on his private jet to fly to Seattle. He's staying on a mega yacht on Lake Washington, according to the charter company."

"Do we know who he is?"

"The manager of the charter service wouldn't tell me."

"See if you can find out who owns the jet or the yacht. Maybe that will tell us who he is." "Care to tell me why you want to know?"

Drake knew that Casey didn't know about the three men who tried to abduct him. He'd made Margo and Paul promise they wouldn't tell anyone unless they checked with him first.

He shook his head to signal Benning not to say

anything. "Mike, at this point I'm just curious. He met with someone who caused me a problem. I need to know how they know each other, that's all."

Casey knew him well enough to know that wasn't the full story, but his prolonged silence indicated that he wasn't going to push it.

"All right, amigo, I'll see what I can do."

Benning started to get up when Drake said, "I didn't want Liz to know about my trip to the ER just yet. Mike would have told her if he knew about it."

"I figured it was something like that. How do you think Mr. Big fits into all of this?"

"I don't have a clue, but James Davis is getting more interesting by the minute."

Chapter Twenty-Two

DRAKE FINISHED off the paperwork on his desk and was ready to leave the office when Margo buzzed him.

"There's a man at the front door who wants to see you. It's after hours, do you want me to tell him to make an appointment?"

"Let me have a look."

The high definition digital security camera system the previous owner had installed provided a view from the security cameras at both the front and rear doors over the internet.

Drake clicked the icon on his desk monitor for the security system. The man had turned away from the door, but something about him seemed familiar.

"Margo, I need to see his face. Tell him I'm on a conference call. If he wants to wait, you'll ask if I have time to see him as soon as the call ends."

From the loft, Drake heard Margo key the intercom and ask the man if he wanted to wait. He watched the man turn toward the front door and say he would wait. It was the man who hit him with the baton outside the wine bar!

"Margo, see if he's alone."

"Just a second."

The zoom lens on the security camera pulled back. Two men stood to the left of the door with their backs to the wall.

Drake pushed his chair back and ran down the loft stairs to Margo's desk. "It's the three goons from outside the wine bar. Tell Paul to get down here with his shotgun. Get your revolver out and cover him at the front door. When I call you, open the door for Paul and let them see the wrong end of his shotgun. I'll go down and get behind them."

He took the back stairs three at a time and slammed the push bar on the rear door to the parking garage. Five parking spaces to the right from where he parked the Cayman was an access door. Stairs from there led down to the boardwalk.

If they were bold enough to come for him at his office, they'd better be brave enough to die. This was going to end then and there, one way or another!

At the bottom of the stairs, Drake stopped and took out his cell phone. "Is Paul there?"

"He's ready."

"Are they still at the door?"

"One at the door, two on either side of it."

"Go cover Paul at the door. When you get there, count down from three so I can hear you then pull the door open. I'll get behind them and we'll invite them in for a little chat."

Drake held his phone to his ear with his left hand and drew his Kimber .45 with his right hand.

"Three, two, one."

He shoved the phone in his pants' pocket and hit the push bar with his hip. Twenty feet away to his right, three men stood frozen. Before the men had a chance to do something stupid, Drake ran to cover them from behind.

"Let's all go inside where we can talk. We don't want anyone out here to get hurt."

Tom Brasco was closest to Drake at the door. He raised his hands and said with a smile, "You've got this all wrong, counselor. We're here to apologize for the other night. You weren't the man we wanted."

"Then you can apologize inside. We're drawing a crowd out here."

A couple with a baby in a stroller and two women walking arm-in-arm watched them from a safe distance. One of the women held a phone to her ear.

Benning stepped aside and motioned them in with the barrel of his Remington 870. Drake followed the men inside and closed the door behind him. Margo moved to her husband's side with her Taurus Judge revolver loaded with five .410 shotgun shells. She switched her aim from one man to another, as if she couldn't decide which man to put down first.

"This is my secretary and her husband, gentlemen. He's a detective with the Sheriff's

Department but she's the one I'd be worried about. She's seems to be a little twitchy with that .410 revolver. Stand real still with your hands raised while I remove your weapons."

The men stood three abreast facing the Bennings. Brasco, the apparent spokesman for the trio, said over his shoulder to Drake, "You're making a mistake, Drake. We're trying to settle this friendly like, make amends for hurting you."

Drake finished searching the three men and walked around them holding three of their handguns, two wicked looking tactical folding knives and a police baton.

"What's the old saying, 'Beware of friends bearing gifts'? You gentlemen didn't come here to make amends, but I'll give you that chance by telling me who sent you. I'd rather see him in jail than you three, because that's where you're going if you don't tell me before my secretary walks to her desk and calls the police."

"You got nothing on us," the shorter of the three blurted out. "It's your word against ours."

Drake laid the guns and knives down on the waiting area coffee table and walked back with the baton. "Really? I think I recognize this baton."

He flicked his wrist to extend the baton and poked it in the chest of the short man. "And I remember the last time I saw you with it outside the wine bar. Besides, you're going to be arrested for the weapons you were carrying in addition to attempted murder and aggravated assault. See I know you are felons in possession of weapons you're not supposed to have. Anyone have anything to say before we call the police?"

Drake's question was answered with stony silence and menacing glares. "All right then, they're all yours, Detective Benning."

"Get down on your knees and lace your fingers behind your heads. The deputies will be here shortly. We'll let them do the honors."

Margo went to call the Sheriff's Department while Drake stood beside Benning. The men got on their knees without saying a word, staring at the floor in front of them.

"Do you think James Davis is going to be pleased with these three?" Drake asked Benning.

Brasco raised his head and said, "What makes you think Davis had anything to do with this?"

"Because you belong to Volksfront and he's your leader. I recognized your tattoo outside the wine bar and when you tried to run me off the road on your Harley in Gold Beach. He sent you and I'm going after him next."

"Go ahead, but he's not the one who wants you dead."

"Shut up, Brasco," the man next to him hissed. "You'll get us all killed."

Drake thought of the man and the bodyguards Davis met with at the resort on the Columbia. "You mean the man from Seattle?"

The three men kept their heads down. No one answered.

They didn't need to.

Someone else wanted him dead and Drake thought he knew who it might be.

Chapter Twenty-Three

WHEN THEY FINISHED SORTING things out with the deputies from the Multnomah County Sheriff's Office, it was seven o'clock in the evening.

The Bennings were upstairs in the privacy of their condo where Paul was trying to explain to Margo what he'd been doing that afternoon.

Drake was at his desk in the loft trying to decide whether to drive to Seattle that night or wait until the next day. He needed to get started on the security assessment review for Seattle's Link Light Rail installation, but he also needed to investigate "Mr. Big" on his yacht. He had no way of knowing how long the man would remain in Seattle.

Mike Casey might know something by now about the man's travel plans.

Drake reached his friend at his home. He heard kids splashing in the pool in the background.

"Sounds like a party."

"We're having a sleepover. Want to join us?"

"Tempting, but it sounds like you have it under control. Did you find out anything more about Mr. Big?"

"Yes and no. Are you coming to Seattle this week?"

"I'm thinking about driving up tomorrow. Any idea how long he'll be in Seattle?"

"His moorage is rented for the month, but there's no way to know if he'll stay that long."

"Then I better come up tonight."

"There's a file on your desk. It seems your man is a bit of a mystery. We're not even sure what his real name is. Have a look and you'll see we may need to get some help on this one." "Thanks Mike. I'll stay at the Woodmark if that's okay."

"That's what it's there for. See you tomorrow."

PSS had an account at the luxury hotel on Lake Washington for visiting clients and out-of-state employees. Drake always felt guilty for using the perk when he stayed over in Seattle.

He called Margo to let her know he was leaving for Seattle. By the tone of her voice, she wasn't thrilled to have learned that her husband was working as a private detective. Or maybe it was the thought of them working out of the same office. Whatever it was, Drake knew they would work it out.

On his way out, he took two bottles of water and a handful of energy bars from the refrigerator in the break room and climbed the back stairs to the parking garage. If he made good time on the freeway to Seattle, he might get there in time for a late dinner and a glass of wine before turning in.

Drake gave his Cayman a quick once-over, to make sure Davis or his boys hadn't left a surprise for him, and settled in for the two-and-a-half-hour drive north. The canvas duffel bag with a change of clothes that he kept in the car with his travel shave kit was all he needed for a quick day or so out of the office.

———

JAMES DAVIS FINISHED the bottle of Jack Daniels and paced back and forth at the foot of the bed in his motel room. The men had orders to call him as soon as they had Drake and his secretary in his office. He should have heard from them an hour ago.

Damn it! How could they have screwed up again? Either Drake got the better of them again and they were dead or something had happened and they couldn't call. Neither possibility pleased him. How hard could it be to kill one man?

It was time to find a safe place to sort this out and he knew just the place.

He stuck the empty bottle of Jack in the open carryon on the bed and made one last walkaround to make sure he didn't forget anything. He left the room key on top of the TV and closed the door behind him.

His Ram Big Horn was right outside the room and a second after he tossed the carryon to the floor behind his seat, the Hemi roared to life and he was on his way.

At the first red stop light, he took his cell phone out and scrolled through his contacts. The man he wanted worked the swing shift in the police department and had time to check on his men before he left work.

"Tex, do you know who this is?" he asked when the man answered. Tex was in the Oregon National Guard and was injured when the Guard had been deployed to Iraq. His brother was a cop and got him the job in records when he returned. His brother was also a standing member in the Portland chapter of Volksfront.

"Yes," Tex said guardedly.

"You don't have to say anything, just listen. Three of my men are missing. Tom Brasco, Clint Buddy and Mooney. You met all of them at your brother's. I need to know if they've been arrested. Can you check and see?"

"Yes."

"Call me back at this number."

Davis turned his neck left and right to relax his tense muscles and kill the headache he felt developing. When the light changed, he drove on following the directions on his navigation system to the Acropolis Steak House and Strip Joint. A good distraction and a couple of drinks would help pass the time while he waited for news about his men.

He was on his second Jack Daniels, sitting alone in the Acropolis, when Tex called back. "They were arrested early this evening and charged with attempted murder and assault. They're being processed now."

Davis ended the call and signaled for another drink and a menu.

Chapter Twenty-Four

THURSDAY MORNING GREETED Drake brightly with a blue sky and a soft, warm breeze coming off Lake Washington. After finishing his bodyweight exercise routine and warm up stretches in his room, he pulled on a pair of black running shorts, a gray tee shirt and his Nike Pegasus running shoes. A five-mile run along the bike path bordering the lake before breakfast would help cool his simmering anger over the two attempts on his life in the last week.

Some force was warring against him that he didn't understand. His time in southern Oregon on the rafting trip with Liz hadn't involved the Volksfront or James Davis in any way that would explain their attacks on him. Outrunning the bikers with their gang tattoos on the Oregon coast highway might be something they weren't used to, but it wasn't something you killed someone over, even if you were a badass white supremacist skinhead knuckle dragger. At the three-mile mark on his run, no explanation he could come up with seemed likely, so he ignored a nagging headache and increased his pace on the way back to the Woodmark.

He was drying off from a shower when a polite knocking on the door signaled that room service was there with his breakfast of coffee, grapefruit, scrambled eggs and toast with marmalade. Slipping on the hotel's spa robe, he tipped the waiter and took the tray of food out to his room's lakefront balcony along with the complimentary copy of the *Seattle Times*.

The headline below the fold reported that elected officials and community leaders in the state were calling on citizens to reject fear and panic following weeks of harmful and discriminatory rhetoric aimed at the refugee resettlement program.

Drake set the tray on a small table between the two balcony chairs and poured a cup of coffee before starting on the grapefruit. The newspaper reported that Syrian refugees were not being welcomed with open arms as the officials had hoped. Rural communities and small towns were rebelling against the plans of urban elites to send them refugees they did not want and said they could not afford.

It was easy to see why a man like James Davis would seize on the anger and fear of people to build up the ranks of his movement. The attacks in Paris and Belgium and the threats issued from the Islamic State scared people. Fear was easy to direct against refugees who looked like the terrorists and shared the same religion.

Thinking of the problem the government had created and sitting in a spa robe at a luxury hotel made him think of Liz. He hadn't spoken to her since she flew back to D.C. Drake walked back into his room, picked up his cell phone and called her.

"Hi Liz. It's Adam. How are you?"

"An hour ago, I was fine. Then I got a phone call from a friend and now I'm not so fine.

Why didn't you call me after you got out of the E.R.?" Margo?

"I didn't want to worry you. A little bump on the head, nothing as bad as your concussion."

"Adam Drake, a skull fracture is not a little bump on the head. I need to know that you're okay. Please don't let me hear that you've been hurt from someone else ever again."

"All right, I promise. How did the senator react when you told him you're leaving?"

"He's trying to talk me into working out of his Portland office instead. I think he feels the only reason I'm leaving is to be closer to you."

"Anything I can do?"

"You could come see me."

"Maybe I can come as soon as I finish this matter Mike wants me to handle."

"I'd like that."

"Me too. I'll have an idea when that might be in a day or so."

"Okay. Call me."

"I will."

Drake returned to the balcony to finish his breakfast and found his scrambled eggs were cold. He didn't care; it had been worth it to hear her voice.

Reviewing the contract with the Link Light Rail for the installation of the new chemical detection system would take a day. Then he would think like a terrorist and go check to see if the placement of the monitors would get the job done. With any luck, he could be finished by the following Monday—assuming he stopped lounging around in a spa robe and got busy.

Drake finished his coffee and took his blazer and slacks out of the closet to dress for a day at PSS headquarters.

Before he left, he checked his laptop again for the location of the Nautical Landing marina on Lake Union where Mr. Big moored his mega yacht. As much as he wanted to see where Mr. Big was staying, it looked like he would have to fight the morning traffic to get there and he didn't have that much time that morning. Maybe he could talk Mike Casey into going with him later in the day.

If Mr. Big was the man giving James Davis his marching orders, he wanted to get eyes on the enemy. James Davis might just be a gun for hire, but he couldn't understand why a man with a two-hundred-foot mega yacht would select him to do his dirty work. The man had to know, or at least suspect, that Davis was on every watch list of every law enforcement agency in the country.

And he still couldn't understand why Mr. Big might want him dead, if, in fact, it was Mr. Big. There were other possibilities; enemies he fought against in Delta, men he prosecuted and put in prison. It was even possible there were even a few local radicalized Muslims who might still want revenge for the three wannabe-assassins he killed on his farm a year or so ago.

But seeing Davis at the Skamania Resort at the same time Mr. Big was there certainly raised the possibility that they knew each other and might be working together. If that was true, he needed to know a lot more about the man calling the shots.

Chapter Twenty-Five

THE DRIVE north to the PSS headquarters on Carillon Point took Drake five minutes. He parked his company car in his reserved space and took the stairs to his office. There were two files on his desk, one labeled Link Light Rail and the other Confidential.

He hung his blazer on the back of the door, slipped the Kimber Ultra Carry ll and holster off his belt and put them in the center drawer of the desk. It was time to find out how much they had learned about Mr. Big.

The confidential file was thin. Research hadn't turned up very much.

Mr. Big's name was Walter Guzman of Buenos Aires, Argentina, according to his passport. His mega yacht, Astrid III, was owned by a financial conglomerate based in Hong Kong, but his name wasn't listed anywhere as an officer or member of the board of directors. The yacht was built in a German shipyard for a Saudi prince, but it was unclear when the ownership of the yacht changed hands. The yacht could accommodate twelve overnight guests in luxury and carried a full-time crew of fifteen.

The PSS research section couldn't find any public record of Guzman living in Argentina or having a business or family there. The only mention of Walter Guzman was in a business journal that mentioned him as the representative of the Hong Kong financial conglomerate who negotiated the purchase of Buenos Aires' largest bank.

There were no known photos of the banker and the origin and source of Guzman's wealth was unknown. An investigative business journalist, however, had reported on his blog that unconfirmed rumors traced it back to Nazi gold smuggled out of Germany.

The mention of Nazi gold tripped an alarm in Drake's mind.

A *banker* by the name of Ryan Walker in Nicaragua the previous month was the moneyman for a Russian/Hezbollah terrorist plot to launch an EMT attack on America. The DEA believed he was the head of an organization known as the *Alliance* that operated out of

Paraguay as a go-between for the cartels and various terrorist groups. Paraguay after World War Two was a safe-haven for fleeing Nazi war criminals

The year before, a *banker* in London had funneled illegal foreign campaign money from the Muslim Brotherhood to America to assist a White House advisor in persuading the president to start a shooting war with Syria.

Then, in San Francisco, a *banke*r orchestrated a plot to hit the U.S. energy grid from a fortified bunker staffed by neo-Nazi members of the Golden Dawn party in Greece, one of the strongest far-right skinhead organizations in Europe.

In each case, the *banker* escaped capture and was still a

free man, despite U.S. and Interpol warrants outstanding for his arrest.

Was it possible that Walter Guzman was Ryan Walker and the head of the criminal neoNazi organization known as the *Alliance*?

Drake walked down the hall to Mike Casey's office with the file and knocked twice on the open door. Casey was on the phone and pointed to a chair in front of his desk.

"I'll have my assistant fax our proposal this morning. Call me if you have any questions." Casey ended the call and saw the file in Drake's hand. "Not very helpful, is it?"

Drake laid the file on the desk and sat down. "Did you notice the unconfirmed rumor that traced Guzman's wealth to Nazi gold smuggled out of Germany?"

"I did, but rumors like that have been attributed to a lot of wealthy families in Argentina and South America."

"Remember the bank president in San Francisco with the bunker in the basement of his mansion? The banker in London and the foreign campaign contributions from the Muslim Brotherhood? The banker in Nicaragua the DEA thinks is the head of the Alliance operating out of Paraguay? What if Guzman is the banker we keep running into?"

"What makes you think Guzman might be the banker in Nicaragua? Just because he's from South America and travels around in a hundred-million dollar yacht? That's pretty thin." "You're right, it is. But here are a couple things about Guzman you don't know."

Drake told Casey about the two attacks on him by members of the Volksfront prison gang and following James Davis to the Skamania resort where Guzman was staying.

"One of the goons who tried to take me in my office said that Davis isn't the one who wanted me dead. What if the banker on the yacht is the head of the Alliance, traveling with a false passport in the name of Walter Guzman?"

Casey sat back in his chair and considered Drake's supposition. "Why would the head of the *Alliance*, a criminal organization with connections to the drug cartels and terrorist groups, use someone like Davis to come after you?"

Drake shrugged his shoulders. "I don't know. It doesn't make a lot of sense. It's just a feeling I have that Guzman is Walker. He's had far-right neo-Nazi guys from the Golden Alliance in San Francisco working for him. Maybe he's using another far-right Neo-Nazi prison gang this time as well. I can't prove it, but I can't overlook the possibility either."

"What do you intend to do about it?"

"I'm not sure, why?"

"Because I know you and how you act on your hunches and because we have a deadline on the Link Light Rail matter. Is this feeling of yours going to keep you from meeting our deadline?"

"I'll meet the deadline, don't worry, but I could use your help with my hunch to make sure that I do. Come with me sometime today and let's take a look at Guzman's yacht. We're pretty good at picking out the bad guys."

Casey just shook his head. They had served together in Delta Force. Drake had been the best partner Casey had ever worked with in Iraq, when they were part of Task Force Black and operated on the hunter/killer teams. It was true they had been good at spotting the bad guys, but he had a company to run and not enough time in the day to do everything that needed to be done. But it was also true that Drake's hunches were usually spot on.

"You spend the rest of the day working on the light rail

matter and I'll see if I can free up some time this afternoon."

Drake got up to leave. "On it. Call me when you're ready to go." Back in his office, he made one call before he got to work.

"Liz, I need a favor."

"Will it help you to come see me sooner?"

"We'll see, if you can get what I need."

"If you get what you need, do I get what I need?"

Drake had to laugh. "Let's see if you can deliver before I answer that."

"Oh, I can deliver all right. What is it you need?"

Drake told her about Walter Guzman and his hunch that Guzman and Walker were one and the same. "Can you find out what the FBI, DEA and Interpol have on Guzman and whether Guzman is an alias that Walker might be using? If Guzman is Walker, he's here for something big if he's willing to risk being arrested in the U.S. He'd be tried as a terrorist and given a oneway ticket to Gitmo or executed."

"It's almost noon here in D.C. and I have to attend a closed-door session of the Senate Intelligence Committee for the senator right after lunch. I'll make some calls as soon as I can. Will that be soon enough?"

"Of course it will."

"Book your flight, cowboy. You're going to be traveling real soon."

Chapter Twenty-Six

WALTER GUZMAN SAT in his private study in the owner's suite on the main deck of Astrid III, looking out the window at gawkers taking pictures of his yacht from small boats motoring slowly by. The privacy that the yacht provided was well worth the millions of dollars it cost to shield him from prying eyes.

Still, the tight confines of Lake Union and the moorage at Nautical Landing concerned him. He wanted to be close enough to keep an eye on the young Saudi and his cell as they got close to the target date, but he also needed the safety of the open sea. If he was implicated in the attack on the light rail system before his planned departure, the narrow canal and the Ballard locks the yacht had to pass through from Puget Sound to Lake Union could be blockaded and he'd be trapped.

Which was why a new Sikorsky S-434 was sitting on the helipad. It would fly him to his jet at the airport if he needed to escape that way. No plan was perfect when you involved amateurs, but his plan to assist the young jihadi was as close to perfect as possible.

Unfortunately, his other endeavor to expand the limited vision of the American white supremacy movement was faltering, thanks to the bumbling efforts of James Davis and the internecine rivalries of the various groups and gangs. They all wanted the money he was willing to provide them, but they were not willing to jettison their petty turf wars to become a cohesive unit.

His vision was for a new movement that combined the strength of the rising militias and the election of patriot politicians with the founding beliefs of the white Anglo supremacy movement. The anti-government sentiment, with its anger over an open border policy, and the resentment and fear aroused by the unwanted settlement of thousands of Muslim refugees was the fuel that could ignite a revolution in the country.

Nurture and grow that movement and unite it with the growing popularity of the far-right parties in Europe and you would see a world power rise from the ashes of the "isms" to restore order and decency and peace.

Thinking about restoring order in the world, he wondered if Davis had made good on his promise to dispose of the attorney who persisted in interfering in his plans.

Guzman called his bodyguard on the ship's intercom. "Eric, meet me on the main deck salon."

He walked aft from the owner's suite and met his bodyguard at the salon's bar.

Guzman reached around to the refrigerator under the bar and selected a Perrier.

"Would you like one?" he asked. "No thank you, sir."

Guzman sat in one of the three swiveling bar stools. His bodyguard remained standing.

"Has Davis called?"

"No sir."

"Has he finished with the attorney?"

"No sir. He tried but his men failed."

"How do you know that?"

"I listened to a call he made from his truck. Three of his men were arrested after they attempted to take the attorney as you suggested."

Guzman glared at his bodyguard. "Are you implying they failed because of my suggestion?"

"No sir."

"What then?"

"Davis and his men are clumsy and crude. You should send me to do the job."

"I can't do that, Eric. Davis and his men know I'm the one who wants Drake dead. If you kill him, one of them might expose us someday. If they do it, they'll keep their mouths shut."

"What will you do then? Davis has tried and failed twice."

"Let me think about it. Are we ready for our meeting with Ali Mohammad?"

"Josef will fly the Sikorsky to get him and bring him. With sunglasses and a hat, no one will recognize him when he walks the short distance from the helipad to the bridge. When you're finished, Josef will fly him back to the helipad on the apartment building his father bought for him. He lives in the penthouse. The helipad is on the roof above."

"Have you listened to the tapes of the meetings he's had with his cell from the bugs planted in his penthouse?"

Eric nodded yes and smiled. "He conducts them after

the parties he hosts. They send the girls home and the men stay behind. The parties are rowdy, but he does get down to business afterwards with his men."

"Do you think his men are ready?"

"They seem to be. Each of the two-man teams have ridden the Link trains that run between the university and Sea-Tac and timed the thirteen stops along the way. The trains run every ten or fifteen minutes, depending on the time of day, so they don't have to wait long at any of the stations.

"The sarin dispersal devices you gave them to practice with are foolproof. Once they're activated, the men have plenty of time to get off the train at the next stop without risking exposure. The only thing that can go wrong is if his men panic or lose their nerve."

"Ali will just have to make sure they don't. I have a call to make and then I'll think about what we'll do with Davis. Thank you, Eric. Why don't you go work out in the gym or take a swim before Josef leaves to collect Ali? It will relax you before we have to suffer the arrogance of the young Saudi."

Guzman retreated to his study. Davis was a problem that had to be dealt with. The gathering he was hosting in two days was important to the plans for a resurgent movement in America. But the Muslim Brotherhood's edict that the attorney had to be killed was more important; his future and safety depended on a friendly relationship with the terrorist group and its allies. The jihadists wouldn't allow another failure to go unpunished. They had been quite clear about that.

There had to be a way to use Davis and his men to get the job done. If he couldn't find a way, he'd have to do it himself if he wanted to survive the fallout of failure.

Chapter Twenty-Seven

DRAKE FINISHED his review of the Link Light Rail contract with Martin Research and walked down the hall to Casey's office. The PSS CEO was eating a foot-long burrito at his desk.

Casey smiled, pointed to his mouth and finished chewing.

"Are you trying to set an example for your employees by eating lunch in your office?"

"It's a breakfast burrito, so technically it's a late breakfast or an early lunch. I had an early meeting and all they had were pastries and coffee. I wasn't going to make it until lunch."

Drake leaned against the doorframe and motioned for his friend to keep eating. "I reviewed the light rail contract with Martin Research. There are a few changes I would have suggested to Richard Martin, but overall it's okay. I need a little more information about how the new carbon nanotubes detection devices work, but I should be able to complete the security assessment in a couple of days."

Casey finished off the burrito and chucked the wrapper into the waste paper basket under his desk. "You have plans for lunch?" "You still hungry?"

"No, but I'm sure I will be. I thought we might drive over to Lake Union and look at Guzman's yacht. There's a seafood restaurant nearby you might enjoy."

"Do you have time right now? Martin isn't available until this afternoon. There's not much I can accomplish until I talk with him."

Casey checked his watch and swiveled around in his chair to pick up a stack of files on his back bar. "Sure, grab your coat. I'll drop these off and meet you at my car in five minutes."

It took them twenty-five minutes to drive from PSS headquarters and across the floating bridge over Lake Washington to Nautical Landing on Lake Union. Guzman's Astrid III was moored along the second dock south of the office and showroom.

The two smaller yachts on either side the first dock were half the size of Astrid III.

"That's some boat," Casey said as he pulled the Range Rover into a parking space near the office. "Want to get a closer look?"

Drake took his Ray Bans out and slipped them on. "If Guzman is the man who wants me dead, I guess I should introduce myself. Let's go."

They crossed the parking lot and stopped at the end of the pier to gaze up at the yacht. Two crewmen were looking down at them from either side of what looked like an infinity pool at the stern. Two crewmen were stationed on the upper captain's deck and another two were standing down the pier beside an open gull-wing loading hatch near the bow.

"Looks like they're not going to invite you on board to meet Mr. Guzman," Casey said. "I see that. Sounds like the engines are running. Maybe they're getting ready to leave." Drake led the way down the pier to the two crewmen guarding the open hatch.

"Do you guys give tours of the Astrid, you know like they do on the Queen Mary?" he asked.

There was no response from the two men.

Drake tried again. "Are you leaving? I stopped by to say hello to Mr. Guzman." A tightening of their jaws and squinting eyes didn't answer his question.

"Maybe they don't speak English," Casey said.

"I think they do. They're just not very friendly.

He took his cell phone out, turned it on and tapped the camera icon. "Mind if I get a picture of you two before we leave? We might never see each other again."

As he started to raise his left hand, the nearest crewman stepped forward and grabbed his forearm. "No pictures, mate. Get off this pier before we throw you off."

Drake reached across with his right hand and jammed his thumb against the man's radial nerve just above his wrist. His hand flew open but Drake maintained the pressure on the nerve.

"That wasn't nice, mate. All I wanted was to say hello to Mr. Guzman. Now you'll have to say hello for me. Tell him Adam Drake would like to meet him. Will you do that for me?" Drake increased the pressure until the man nodded twice and jerked his arm away.

The second crewman put a hand on his mate's shoulder and pulled him back toward the open hatch. Once inside, the two men turned and glared out at Drake and Casey as the gull wing hatch closed.

"There are two more on the deck above watching us," Casey said as they started back up the pier.

"Add the four we saw at the stern walking in plus the two at Skamania Lodge and

Guzman has to have at least ten bodyguards. Seems like a lot for your average billionaire."

"I don't think there's anything average about Guzman. I'll have research dig deeper when we get back."

At the end of the pier, Drake turned and began taking photos with his cell phone. When he lowered it, he saw that the yacht was inching away from its moorage. He also heard the whine of the helicopter's turbine on the helipad starting up.

"Hope he's not leaving just because we stopped by," he said.

"We'll know soon enough if it turns toward the ship canal and the Ballard Locks."

The Astrid III glided to a stop a hundred yards off shore and the helicopter lifted off and swung to the northeast and the university district.

"What's this guy up to, I wonder. Do you carry binoculars in the Range Rover?"

"In the console. Be back in a minute."

Drake watched the yacht while Casey jogged to his SUV. When he returned, he handed the binoculars to Drake.

The bow of the Astrid III was pointed northeast at a forty-five-degree angle toward the western shore of Lake Union. With the compact Leupold binoculars, Drake had a clear view of the port-side of the yacht and a third of the helipad.

"Guzman's going to a lot of trouble to get that bird in

the air. Do you think he's just being nice so he doesn't disturb people in the other yachts around here?"

Casey tapped Drake on the shoulder. "Let me have a look. The noise would be a little louder if they took off from here, but the turbulence won't bother the other yachts. They're designed to withstand gale force winds at sea."

They took turns watching the yacht with the binoculars. Ten minutes after the helicopter lifted off they heard it returning.

Casey focused the binoculars on the helicopter. "Sikorsky S-434. Nice, light turbine helicopter. Let's see if I can get a look at its passengers."

Drake watched the helicopter slow its approach and then gently set down on the yacht's helipad.

"Get your phone out and take a picture," Casey said. "The door's opening and a man's getting out. We might be able to blow up the image enough to ID him. Looks Middle Eastern, in his twenties, wearing sunglasses."

The zoom on Drake's iPhone wasn't strong enough for him to see much detail. He started the video mode just as the man turned back to the helicopter to receive a briefcase the pilot was handing out to him. There was a flash of reflected sunlight from his sunglasses as he turned back and then he was out of sight as he crossed the helipad.

Casey lowered his binoculars. "I think I've seen Guzman's guest somewhere before. Let's get back and enlarge that digital image you took. Maybe we'll get lucky and discover who our man is associating with."

Chapter Twenty-Eight

ALI MOHAMMAD STORMED across the helipad and was escorted down to the sky lounge at the rear of the main salon. He handed his briefcase to Guzman's bodyguard and sat in one of the white armchairs in an alcove by a window.

"Where's your boss?" he asked.

"He'll be with you in a minute. Would you like something to drink?"

"I prefer to smoke, now that cannabis is legal. Do you mind?"

"Mr. Guzman doesn't allow smoking inside."

"Fine. How long is this going to take?"

"I'm sure that will depend on how long it takes you to brief him on your preparations," the bodyguard said and left the sky lounge with the briefcase.

Guzman watched a CCTV display in his study as the Saudi bounced his leg up and down while he waited. His bodyguard knocked once and then opened the door.

"He brought the last installment in his briefcase."

"Make sure the bearer bonds are all there and put them

in the safe. Let him wait another ten minutes and then take him to the media room."

Guzman had watched a video of the Saudi's last party in his penthouse several times and had seen enough to be worried. The men chosen to carry out the attack on the light rail system were too fond of their marijuana, as was their leader. They were all smart young men, but with no real experience and no mission discipline. If they were following him out of a misguided sense of adventure and chance to party, they would likely fail.

The sponsors were as concerned as he was and wanted to know if he thought the plan would succeed. If he did, he was to provide the sarin gas to the cell. If he didn't, he was ordered to kill the cell members and fly the young Saudi home to answer to his father. With the U.S. Congress wanting to investigate the full extent of Saudi participation in the planning or funding of 9/11, no one was willing to risk the young prince's involvement in a failed attack.

His role was, in part, to make sure the sponsors could plausibly deny their involvement. That's why they paid him so handsomely; he was a middleman willing to take the blame for a price.

Guzman left his study and took the stairs down to the media room on the deck below. Ali Mohammad was now standing in front of the touch-screen panel that displayed the movie choices for the month.

"Have a seat, Ali. I have something I want to show you."

Guzman nodded to his bodyguard at his side, who inserted a disc in the DVD player at the bottom of the control panel for the drop-down projector and wall screen.

The seven-foot wide HDTV screen came alive with the video recording of Ali's last party at his penthouse.

The young Saudi watched for a full ten seconds before he shot up and faced Guzman. "When did you have that installed?"

"Your father installed the cameras before he gave you the keys to the penthouse."

"Why are you showing me this?"

"Sit down, Ali, and watch a little longer. Then you tell me why I'm showing it to you."

Ali refused to sit but turned and did as he'd been told with his arms folded tightly across his chest.

He watched as the nubile young coeds were escorted out of his penthouse and a tray of traditional hashish pipes was passed around between the men who remained. He left the room and returned with a bowl of brown hashish that he ceremoniously presented to each man.

Ali turned with fire in his eyes. "This is none of your business!"

"It is very much my business. Now try again. Why do you think I'm showing this to you?"

"Because you think this is all just a big party and that we're not serious about killing Americans. But you don't know anything about us. I'm the only one from Saudi Arabia. The others are from Iraq, Afghanistan, Yemen and Egypt. They've all lost family and friends and they are willing to die to pay these bastards back.

"The hash is a way to relieve their fears and give them courage to go forward. It's been used like this for generations. Much like you Nazis used methamphetamine in World War II. If you're afraid we won't get the job done and want out, return the money and I'll find someone else to help me."

Guzman let the young man simmer for ten seconds and then began to clap softly. "Bravo Ali. Perhaps you are the leader your men need after all. Let's go outside by the pool and you can smoke your pot while you tell me how you're getting your men ready."

The bodyguard led the way to the infinity pool at the stern and two lounge chairs in the shade. Guzman told him to have the chef prepare a plate of tapas and bring him a cigar so that he could enjoy a smoke with his young friend.

He wasn't ready to hand over the nerve gas devices quite yet. He still needed to learn just how deep Ali's well of hatred for the West was, whether he was willing to die for his cause along with his men. If the attack on the light rail system appeared to be doomed to failure, he had no intention of flying the young man all the way back to his doting father in Saudi Arabia. He would make sure *all* members of the cell were dead and report that they had died as martyrs.

His only interest in aiding the jihadi was to fan the fire of resentment and fear of foreign refugees to aid his own cause, not win the world for Islam.

Chapter Twenty-Nine

AFTER LUNCH at the seafood restaurant on Lake Union, Casey returned to PSS to work with a tech in the IT section to enlarge the image on his iPhone. Drake went to his office and called Richard Martin at Martin Research to learn more about carbon nanotubes and the role they played in the chemical detection system.

"Richard, thank you for taking my call," Drake began. "I'm in Seattle going over your project for Link Light Rail. Can you give me a quick rundown on how your new chemical detection system works?"

"How technical do you want me to be?"

"Just technical enough for me to understand how a chemical weapon is detected on one of the light rail trains."

"Four detection devices will be installed in each light rail car. Each device has two electrodes with a microscopic amount of carbon nanotubes located between them. When there are no toxic or explosive substances in the environment, electricity will flow between the electrodes and the nanotubes at a consistent and known level. If molecules of a toxic or explosive substance are present in the air in sufficient quantities, the nanotubes will be affected. The current will either increase or decrease, depending on the substance in question."

"So the devices will only detect substances present in the air. What about substances that aren't in an aerosol or vapor form?"

"You mean in a liquid form? There are other detection methods for detecting toxic chemicals in water, but we aren't testing the water on these light rail cars."

"I guess I'm thinking about the sarin gas attack on the Tokyo subways in 1995. The sarin was transported in liquid form. It was only when the liquid was released and became a vapor that it was deadly."

"Well, it was deadly in the liquid form too, but only if you ingested it, but I see what you mean. If sarin is brought into a light rail train car in a sealed liquid container, it will not be detected by our nanotube devices until it's in the enclosed environment as a vapor."

"What about in an environment that's not enclosed, say at one of the stations between the university and Sea-Tac?"

"If the quantity was sufficient in the open environment, it might be detected. Sarin dissipates very rapidly. To carry on with your hypothetical scenario, if the person carrying the liquid sarin was involved in making it, they might have traces of it on their clothing or in their hair. In sufficient quantity, the sarin could be detected in the open environment in vapor form, but not from the liquid form they were carrying."

"All right, I think I understand. Do you have something that will show me where and how many of these devices will be installed? I'll take a ride on the Link Light Rail system and finish my assessment in a day of so."

"Thanks Adam. Call me when you're back in town and I'll take you to lunch."

Drake sat back and thought about what he'd learned. Suicide belts and other explosive devices would be detected by Martin's devices entering the light rail train cars. Toxic chemicals like sarin would also be detected, but only if they were in an aerosol or vapor form. It wasn't clear if either would be detected before they entered the closed environment of the train car and, if they were, what the reaction would be.

He needed to know more about how Link Light Rail was going to install the new chemical detection system because, at the moment, there didn't seem to be any reason why a nerve gas attack like the 1995 sarin attack in Tokyo wouldn't be successful.

Casey tapped on his door. "Guess who Guzman's visitor was?"

"Surprise me."

"His name is Ali Mohammad. He's a rich Saudi attending the university and living in a penthouse in a high-rise condo complex his daddy bought just before he got here. I thought I recognized him. We installed a bunch of security systems in the building after he started throwing some rowdy parties in the penthouse. Rightly or wrongly, the Middle Eastern types coming and going scared some of the residents pretty badly."

"What's their connection? Rich yacht owner from Argentina and rich Saudi here on a student visa? Maybe Guzman knows Mohammad's father?"

"Maybe."

"What, you think there's something else going on?"

"Rich Saudis don't usually hang out with other uneducated Arabs. A year ago, the police broke up a party in the penthouse and arrested two young men who were drunk and disorderly. The first resident, who wanted us to install a security system for them, got the police report and brought it to us to explain why they wanted a security system. The two men who were arrested were Afghanis and didn't speak English."

"Ali Mohammad has to be here on a student visa. If the two Afghanis couldn't speak English, they probably weren't students. Were they deported?"

"Come on, you know the answer to that. Seattle's a sanctuary city, just like Portland."

"If they weren't deported, do we know what they're doing? Guests of the government on welfare or working somewhere?" "There's no way to know."

Drake spread his arms wide and said, "Unless…"

"Unless what?"

"Unless someone sends a surveillance team to follow Ali Mohammad and his friends and find out what they're up to; say someone with an interest in helping a friend find out who's trying to kill him."

"That would have to be a pretty special friend to foot the bill for something like that."

"It would indeed. A brother-in-arms with a highly sophisticated international security firm at his disposal, for example."

Casey smiled and turned to leave. "If a guy had a friend like that, he would probably do just about anything he was asked to return the favor, I suppose."

It was Drake's turn to smile. "I suppose, if a guy had a friend like that."

Chapter Thirty

HE SPENT the rest of the afternoon reading two long online research articles on carbon nanotubes and everything he could find about the Sound Transit Light Rail system in Seattle. The science behind the evolving use of carbon nanotubes was interesting, but the new mass transit system in Seattle and the surrounding area was dazzling.

Drake looked forward to riding the Link Light Rail line from the futuristic underground station at Husky Stadium to SeaTac Airport and back as soon as possible. He had to see the light rail cars and the fifteen stations along the route through the eyes of an imagined terrorist to anticipate a future planned attack.

The reason the new chemical and explosive detection system was being installed was the increasing possibility of attacks on U.S. ground transportation. Counterterrorism analysts warned, after the foiled plot to blow up a Toronto passenger train in 2013, that terrorists were shifting their focus from attacking airlines to attacking mass transit.

Since 9/11, terrorists had plotted more than seven

hundred attacks on surface transportation internationally, including a Madrid train in 2004 and the London subway in 2005. There had been more than fifty foiled attacks in the U.S during the same period, most notably:

*2003, there was an Al Qaeda plot to release cyanide gas in a New York City subway.

*2006, the FBI stopped a gas attack on a commuter rail tunnel connecting New York and New Jersey.

*2009, seven terrorists were within days of a coordinated suicide bombing in the New York City subway system.

With more than 140,000 miles of train routes in the U.S. and more than 500 major urban transit operators, the public used ground transportation 32,000,000 times a day and that presented a smorgasbord of terrorist opportunities.

Drake's job was to spot as many terrorist opportunities as possible for Sound Transit's Link Light Rail line where the Martin Research chemical detection system was being installed and tested.

He closed the files on his desk and got ready to leave. He secured the files in the locked drawer on the back bar behind his desk and remembered to get his .45 Kimber from its hiding place before slipping on his blue blazer.

Casey met him in the hallway outside his office. "Tonight's Megan's book club and I'm picking up a pizza for the kids. Want to join us for dinner?"

"Have to take a rain check, but thanks. Tell the kids I'll come see them soon."

"What do you have going on tonight? Liz is still in D.C., isn't she?"

"She is, and I promised to go see her as soon as I finish your assessment for Sound Transit. I'm going to take a ride on the Link Light Rail tonight from the University Station and can wrap things up tomorrow. I need to get home for a few days before I leave for D.C. next week."

"All right, see you tomorrow," Casey said and walked away before turning to say, "Pick up a prepaid ORCA card at the front desk for the light rail before you leave. We have them for our employees to use."

The evening traffic and the unfamiliar route from Kirkland to Husky Stadium took Drake an hour to drive the relatively short distance to the U Link station and find a place to park. He took the escalator down under the artist-designed blue panels to the platform and got in line to ride the next light rail train headed south.

His wait was a short one. During peak hours, a train was supposed to arrive every six minutes and it did. He took a seat in the first of two cars and sat back to study his surrounding for the forty-six-minute ride to the SeaTac station.

All the seats were occupied and two thirds of the passengers were standing. Most of them were commuting home from work or school, judging from the scattering of briefcases and backpacks they carried. There were teenage kids and gray-haired seniors in the car, and every age in between. The ethnic mix was predominantly white with a healthy dose of Asian and Hispanic passengers. There were only two passengers who appeared to be Middle Eastern.

With the success ISIS had recruiting young Americans of all races to join the jihad, he reminded himself that ethnicity was no longer a helpful way to profile a terrorist. Male or female, the only characteristic that seemed to be a consistent identifier was the age of the terrorist—late teens to middle twenties. And with the way the tactics of the jihadist were evolving so rapidly, even that couldn't be counted on to remain a factor for long.

The ride south past thirteen Link stations to the end of the line at SeaTac Airport thinned out the passengers but didn't change his impression of the light rail system. It was efficient and fast. The stations were clean and well-lit with no obvious security presence. The stations with the largest number of human targets were the underground stations closest to downtown Seattle where people crowded to wait for their trains to arrive.

There wasn't much to see at the covered above-ground station at SeaTac, so Drake got on the next northbound train up the line to University Station. The car wasn't half full, but he decided to stand for the rest of the ride and calculate the potential damage an attack on the light rail system might cause. Each light rail train had two cars. Each car had a maximum capacity of two hundred passengers; seventy-four seated and one hundred twenty-six standing. If five trains were attacked simultaneously, as they had been in Tokyo in 1995 by five two-man teams, two thousand passengers were potential casualties if you assumed one hundred percent lethality of the attack.

No attack would achieve a one hundred percent kill rate, but even if you assumed a fifty percent casualty rate one thousand innocent passengers could die in a single successful, coordinated terrorist attack. Small wonder the terrorists were shifting their focus to ground transportation. One well-planned and successful attack could kill more people than were killed at any time since 9/11.

With that sobering thought, Drake spent the next forty-five minutes on the ride north trying to think like a terrorist planning an attack on Sound Transit's Link Light Rail.

Chapter Thirty-One

GUZMAN STARED at the image frozen on the screen of the wall-mounted CCTV display in his study. His two bodyguards stood quietly behind him.

"Who is the man with him?"

"We ran the plates on the Range Rover they left in," Eric said. "The vehicle is registered to Puget Sound Security. The taller of the two fits the description of the company's CEO, Michael Casey."

"What's their relationship?"

"I don't know."

"Well, Eric, why don't you earn your pay and find out?" Guzman said coldly. "When the man I've tried to kill twice shows up and says he wants to say hello, I expect you to find out how he found me and what he's doing here. Is that too much to ask of you?"

"No sir."

"Josef, hack the system of this Puget Sound Security and find out what we're up against. I need to leave for the gathering James Davis put together for me the day after tomorrow. We need to make sure Drake doesn't interfere in that or our work with Ali Mohammad."

"Yes sir."

"Sir, are we going to wait for Davis to take care of Drake?" Eric asked.

Guzman turned away from staring at the face of the man he'd come to both loathe and grudgingly admire and sat down at his desk. "I think Mr. Davis will have outlived his usefulness after the gathering on Saturday. Bring him back with us and we'll drop him off somewhere at sea when we leave next week."

"What about Drake?" Eric pressed.

"Find where he's staying and more about his friend's company, I'll think of a way to get rid of Drake and maybe his friend as well. Now go, I have a call I need to make."

Guzman waited for his two bodyguards to leave. When the door to his study closed behind them, he walked to the wet bar in his owner's suite and filled half a tumbler with Yamazaki Single Malt Whisky, his new favorite.

Revulsion was too lame a description of his feelings for the man he was about to call.

While the man was the best interrogator he knew, the man was also a sadist and a butcher. Guzman didn't mind that the men he interrogated suffered great pain and ultimately died, but the excessive blood and hacked off body parts was unnecessary.

He used the man when he absolutely had to, but he didn't trust the psychopathic cartel enforcer. The man had a reputation for killing anyone who belittled him or voiced criticism of his ways. There would be no trace of disgust in his voice when he asked the *Confessor* to take care of a current problem for him.

Before he returned to his study, he finished off his

whisky and took a small, black book out of the suite's safe. The man was reachable only by phone and only at an international number given only to a select few. A voice analyzer would then compare his voice with his voice exemplar before the call would proceed.

Guzman placed the call. "I may need your help. Are you available?" He waited for his voice to be analyzed.

"How soon?"

"In a day or so."

"That would require rearranging my schedule. My price would have to double."

"That is acceptable."

"I'll call you when I arrive."

Guzman returned to the wet bar and refilled his tumbler. His men would have to find Drake and find him fast. The *Confessor* was not a man you wanted hanging around for any longer than necessary.

In the meantime, he had to consider what it meant that Drake had found him. The only possible way was for him to have found a connection between James Davis and himself. Otherwise, the attorney would have no way of knowing he was in Seattle or that the Astrid III was his yacht. But even if Drake knew where he was, could he know who he really was? Could he know that he was the leader of the Alliance and that they had crossed paths before? They never met because he always stayed in the background, orchestrating but never directly participating in the endeavors of his cartel and terrorist clients.

Guzman crossed the suite and stood at the window, looking at the lit-up skyline of downtown Seattle. It was possible, of course, that Drake or someone on his behalf, like the CIA or the FBI, learned something from one of his many clients that had brought the man to Seattle. But it was more likely that one of the men James Davis sent after Drake had talked when he was captured.

It really didn't matter what Drake knew that brought him to Seattle. The *Confessor* would find out soon enough what it was. What would matter was if Drake had somehow learned about Ali Mohammad.

Guzman went to his study and summoned Eric, his bodyguard.

"Drake and his friend were here before Ali arrived. Check the security CCTV footage and see if they were still here when we moved away from the pier out into Lake Union. See if they could have seen Ali."

"Even if they caught a glimpse of him when he got out of the helicopter, they couldn't know why he was here."

Guzman sighed. "Drake shouldn't have known that I was here either. Do what I told you. If Drake finds out who Ali is, we need to make sure he doesn't do anything about it."

Chapter Thirty-Two

DRAKE ATE breakfast at the Woodmark's Beach Café and was at his desk by seven o'clock Friday morning. A dream the night before had featured terrorists wearing gas masks boarding a U Link Light Rail train.

Even with a state-of-the-art chemical detection system on the light rail line, nothing would stop someone from getting on with a chemical weapon that wouldn't be detected until it was deployed. He wasn't sure what he was going to say in the PSS security assessment he needed to finish.

On his way to get a cup of coffee in the break room, he saw Marco Morales walk into the conference room up ahead. Drake followed him in to say hello.

"Marco, where have you been hiding? Thought I'd run into you before now."

"I used some vacation time to spend time with a friend. This is my first day back."

"That friend wouldn't happen to be a pretty vice president named Stephanie at Trans World Marine, would it?"

The wide grin on the young man's face said it all.

"What are you working on these days?" Drake asked.

A voice from the hallway said, "I thought Marco would be the right person to run a surveillance operation I had in mind."

Mike Casey walked in with a PSS dark blue coffee mug in one hand and a file in the other. "You need some coffee before we get started?" he asked Morales. "Drake will be happy to get it for you."

"Cream and heavy on the sugar, Mr. Drake. Thanks."

"No problem, Marco. Be right back."

When he returned with two PSS coffee mugs in hand, he saw that Casey had opened the file and slid the enlarged photo across the conference table to Morales.

Casey said, "We need to know what this man is up to. He's here on a student visa at the university and hanging out with some dubious individuals. Put together a surveillance team and find out what he's up to."

"He looks Middle Eastern. What do we know about him?"

"He's a rich Saudi that likes to party in a penthouse his daddy's paying for. The information on the penthouse and some work we did in the building is here in the file. He likes to entertain in the penthouse with the dubious individuals I mentioned. You'll want to identify as many of them as you can. Find out where they live and how they support themselves. A couple of them don't speak English, so they're probably not working."

"How many men can I have and how soon do you need this?"

Casey looked at Drake and smiled. "The wealthy client we're doing this for has unlimited resources and said whatever it takes to get the job done. He'd like a report as soon as possible." Morales accepted the file from Casey and left.

Casey picked up his mug of coffee and sat back in his chair. "How'd the ride on Sound Transit go last night?"

"Fast and uneventful. That's quite a light rail they're building. But I don't think the chemical detection system from Martin Research is going to keep terrorists from killing a lot of people if they want to."

"Why? I thought the detectors were more sensitive than the older system and reacted a lot faster."

"They are, but that's not the problem. The nanotubes will detect explosives and toxic chemicals like sarin gas, for example, in the environment. But in the case of sarin in its liquid form, it can't be detected until it's a vapor. You could carry sarin in a liquid form into the train cars and the sensors wouldn't detect it until it was released as a vapor. That's what happened in Tokyo. They brought the liquid sarin in plastic bags and then broke the bags on the floor by poking them with the tips of their umbrellas."

"What about out on the platforms where passengers are waiting to board the trains? Wouldn't the sensors detect sarin gas there in time?"

"Only when it's released as a vapor. The underground platforms are bigger and the concentration wouldn't be as great as in a closed train car. And the above-ground platforms are covered but an open environment. The closed train cars with two hundred potential passengers on each is a more likely target."

Casey shook his head. "Sound Transit's not going to like our assessment if the Martin Research system isn't going to protect them like they want it to."

"They have to know it's not going to protect their

passengers from every possible kind of WMD. The only thing they can do is what the TSA is doing at the airports, and even that doesn't prevent everything from getting through."

"That would never work for mass transit. The Sound Transit trains run every six minutes during peak hours. You'd never get everyone searched in time to keep the trains running as quickly as they have to. That's why people use mass transit."

"I know. But that's the reality of life today. Not every risk can be eliminated."

Casey got up to leave. "Have you talked with Liz about this? Maybe she knows something we don't about how efficiently Homeland Security shares intelligence with mass transit operators that would minimize the risk somewhat. You could include that in the assessment to keep from scaring Sound Transit so badly."

"Assuming Homeland Security does efficiently develop and share intelligence," Drake said as he got up to leave and follow Casey out of the conference room. "But I'm happy to call

Liz and ask."

He looked at his watch on the way to his office and saw that it was ten minutes before eight o'clock. Plenty of time to catch her before she left the senator's office for lunch. He was anxious to know if she'd found out anything about Guzman.

The more he thought about the man and his meeting with the young Saudi on his yacht the more certain he was about his suspicions. A dark cloud had blotted out the sun for a moment as he watched the helicopter land on the yacht's helipad. He remembered wondering at the time if it was an omen of some kind.

Chapter Thirty-Three

THE RECEPTIONIST in Senator Hazelton's office remembered him from his last visit and promised that Liz would call him the moment she returned from a Senate Intelligence briefing.

It was twelve thirty in D.C. when she called.

"Hi handsome. How are you?"

"I'm fine. How's the concussion?"

"Right, yours or mine?"

"Yours."

"I'm fine. Just promise me you won't keep things from me."

"Okay, I promise. Are you busy?"

"If you call sitting through a two-hour briefing being busy, I am. Still trying to decide whether to sell my condo or lease it to someone."

"You won't have any trouble selling it, if that's what you decide to do."

"To be honest, I think it's the thought of leaving Washington that's holding me back. I've lived here since I joined the FBI and always called it my home."

"Are you having second thoughts about going to work for Mike and moving to Seattle?"

"You know why I'm moving to Seattle. It's not about working for Mike."

Drake knew he had to ask the next question. "Maybe you're having second thoughts because you're afraid you'll see too much of me and lose the freedom you've had since college."

"I'm having second thoughts about moving all the way to the West Coast and still not seeing enough of you."

He let out a sigh of relief. "You might change your mind when you find out you can't get rid of me."

His implied promise seemed to settle the matter for the moment.

"How are you doing with the security assessment for the light rail system?"

Drake told her of his concerns about a possible terrorist attack like the one in Tokyo in 1995. "I know the terrorist plots we've stopped since 9/11 happened because of good intel or fortuitous citizen involvement. But how confident should a mass transit operator be that it will receive intel from the FBI or DHS in time to prevent an attack?"

He heard her heels clicking on the floor and the sound of her office door shutting.

"The problem isn't getting the intel to the operator in time, it's developing the intel in the first place. When terrorist groups like ISIS use social media to encourage specific attacks, the NSA and the FBI have a chance to focus the investigation and develop good intel. But if there's nothing in the wind, it's hard."

"Is there anything in the wind?"

Not that I've heard and I attend all the Senate Intelligence briefings. The one I just sat through was about an anti-refugee vigilante group from Europe that calls itself the Soldiers of Odin. It's recruiting Americans from far right white supremacy groups and extreme antigovernment patriot organizations to patrol the streets like they're doing in Finland."

"That sounds like the Volksfront goons in Gold Beach. Which reminds me, have you been able to find out anything more about Guzman, our banker with the mega yacht?"

"Not much, I'm afraid," Liz said. "As far as the FBI and DEA are concerned, he's just a banker and Guzman is not an alias used by Ryan Walker of the *Alliance*. The only thing Interpol has on him is that the Hong Kong banking conglomerate he's associated with owns banks in Europe that most of the far right political parties are using. With the rising popularity of parties like the Front National in France, the Austrian Freedom Party and the National Democratic Party in Germany, any movement that sounds even a little like the Nazis of old is under surveillance. That includes the Golden Dawn Party in Greece and the Soldiers of Odin in Finland."

"Liz, that's exactly what you'd expect Guzman, the banker, to be doing if the rumors are true that his wealth is due to Nazi gold smuggled to Argentina after World War Two. That's also the same rumor about Ryan Walker, the *Alliance* and smuggled Nazi gold. Guzman has to be Walker."

Drake heard her sigh, a sigh that sounded a lot like 'Here he goes again'.

She began softly. "Adam, you know I love you. And you know that I haven't been a hundred percent supportive of your hunches in the past. Each time I was wrong. I'm just frightened. I know you're probably right about Guzman, or whoever he is, and I don't know how to help you. Whatever you decide to do, please be careful. Promise me you'll let the FBI take down Walker and that you won't go after him yourself."

He was partially wrong about her sigh; she wasn't being dismissive. She just wanted him to be careful.

He promised. "If I find anything that proves that Guzman is Walker, I'll let your old agency take care of him. If Guzman is Guzman and nothing more than a neo-Nazi financier, I'll let the Jewish Anti-Defamation League take care of him."

His poor attempt to end the call on a light note produced a resigned harrumph from Liz.

"Just remember your promise."

Chapter Thirty-Four

DRAKE FINISHED the security assessment before noon and walked it down to Casey's office.

"Here's a draft of the report for Sound Transit. Give it a quick once-over and let me know if it needs anything," he said as he dropped the file on the desk. "I need to get back to Portland." Casey smiled and said, "Margo's orders?" Drake nodded.

"See you next week then. I'll let you know if Morales turns up anything on the Saudi who visited Guzman."

Drake turned to leave and then stopped. "About Guzman. The only thing Liz turned up was that Interpol says most of the far-right political parties in Europe use the banks owned by Guzman's banking group."

"That might explain why James Davis met Guzman at Skamania Lodge."

"Maybe, but I don't see Davis using some international banking conglomerate. He strikes me as someone who would be more comfortable at a local bank where his tough-guy reputation counts for something when he doesn't want to wait in line."

"If that's all it takes to get to skip to the head of the line, I need to work on my street creds. My bank still makes me wait in line."

"Just not fair, is it, wealthy guy like you?"

Casey motioned for him to leave. "Go, see you next week."

Drake routed back through his office to make sure he wasn't forgetting anything and then took the stairs down to the underground parking. The thought of a couple of hours on the freeway listening to some good old rock and roll and a weekend on his farm put a smile on his face. He was leaving Seattle early enough that he should miss the heaviest of the Friday afternoon traffic when he reached Portland.

From Kirkland he took I-405 south for eighteen miles until he merged onto I-5 for the next two hours of driving down the freeway to Oregon. When he got to Tacoma, his mind had already drifted from thoughts about Guzman and terror attacks on Seattle's light rail to the pleasure of a good, long run through the wine country that surrounded his farm with his German shepherd, Lancer. Maybe he'd even have breakfast at his friend's nearby Black Walnut Inn after the run.

While he was imagining being home again, his Bluetooth connection to his cell phone signaled an incoming call.

"Are you still in Seattle?" Paul Benning asked.

"Just passing by Tacoma on I-5. What's up?"

"I'm at the Old Town Burger and Breakfast in Battle Ground. Care to join me for a cup of coffee or a late lunch?"

"Why are you in Battle Ground?"

"I followed James Davis here this morning. Thought you might want to visit the gathering he and his men are hosting at a state park. There are some interesting people out there."

"How interesting?"

"Just your average brown-shirt storm troopers and militia men."

"Do we need an invitation or do we just show up and mingle with the crowd?"

"They're meeting at the Battle Ground Lake State Park. It's a couple hundred acres, so we should be able to get close enough to see what's going on. Take the exit off I-5 to 502E and Battle Ground. The Old Town Burger is on Main Street, you can't miss it."

"All right, see you there."

Drake pulled into the left lane and tucked in behind a string of cars going a lot faster than he was. So much for his relaxing Friday evening on the farm.

It was two fifteen with the afternoon sun at his back when he pulled into a parking space in front of the Old Town Burger in Battle Ground. Paul Benning waved to him when he entered the restaurant.

From the street, the place looked like any other burger joint in a small town. The smells inside told Drake this place was different.

Benning pointed to his pastry. "Pistachio baklava. You need to try some. The menu is a blend of Mediterranean and classic American comfort food. Everything I've tried is excellent."

The exotic smells made Drake's mouth water. He scanned the menu and saw there were stuffed grape leaf appetizers, gyros sandwiches along with a healthy list of burgers and hot dogs. He ordered a Greek chicken sandwich and a cup of coffee when the waiter arrived.

Drake waited for his coffee to be poured and asked Benning, "How many men are attending this gathering?"

"They were still arriving when I drove back here. I'd say a couple hundred, maybe more."

"Are they all from around here? That's a lot of men for a militia rally."

"Judging from their license plates, they're from all over the place; Alabama, Pennsylvania, New York. This is something big and it's not all militia men. It looks like a regular political rally with a healthy mix of bikers and the Minutemen who patrolled the southern borders."

"What do the locals say about the gathering at the state park?"

Benning looked around the restaurant before answering. "The owner says the town's happy to have this many visitors so early in the summer. I get the feeling that some of the locals quietly support the effort to keep refugees from settling around here. I listened to a couple of men talking about giving them handouts when the government won't extend unemployment benefits to our own citizens when they run out. I'd say there's a lot of smoldering anger just under the surface."

Drake's sandwich arrived and he took a hungry bite before saying, "I talked with Liz this morning. She'd just been to a Senate Intelligence briefing about a group from Europe. It's recruiting Americans to patrol our streets to keep citizens safe from roving gangs of immigrants like they're having in Europe. That smoldering anger you mentioned seems to be pretty widespread."

Benning waited for Drake to finish his sandwich and

offered to drive him to the state park. "I think my F-150 will blend in a little better than your Porsche. Let's go have a look at the men promising to take our country back."

Chapter Thirty-Five

BATTLE GROUND LAKE STATE Park was nearby, three miles northeast of the city. Benning gave Drake a rundown on the facility as they drove there.

"Battle Ground Lake is an ancient crater lake surrounded by two hundred eighty acres of evergreen forest. There are camping sites, hiking trails and a boat ramp. Davis reserved a covered kitchen shelter for today and tomorrow that will accommodate one hundred and fifty people, the camp ranger said. It looks like there are about one hundred and fifty of Davis's friends there now."

"Any men you've seen in Oregon?"

"No, the pickups here are from the south and most of the Harleys are from states within a day's ride from here."

"Are they all camping here?"

"The park ranger says they're just here for the day."

"These guys come from all over and they're only here for a day? Why here?"

Benning turned off NE Palmer Road and slowed as they entered the park. He gestured at the forested area ahead.

"I'm guessing that they didn't want anyone taking their pictures from up above. This park gives them a lot of privacy."

He drove through the parking area until he found an open spot. When they got out, he pointed to a trail leaving the area. "This trail will get us close to the kitchen shelter Davis reserved."

Benning led the way. The trail was five or six feet wide and skirted a large open area. The muted sounds of children playing in the distance and a small outboard engine on the lake filtered through the trees.

The fresh scent of fir trees and foliage reminded Drake of camping in the high lakes of the Oregon Cascades as a kid.

They stopped at the edge of the open area beside a vacant picnic table.

"How close do you want to get?" Benning asked.

The kitchen shelter was seventy-five yards away across the open play area. Men were standing shoulder to shoulder, facing a man standing on top of a picnic table at the far end of the covered facility.

"Close enough to hear. Let's walk back to the concession stand near the parking lot. We'll get something to eat so it looks like we're taking a late lunch break. Grab a map from your pickup that we can spread out and look like we're studying it."

Ten minutes later, with two orders of hot dogs and Cokes in hand, they walked back to the closest available picnic table to the covered kitchen shelter. When they sat down on either side of the table, the speaker's voice forty yards away carried to them.

"...the government is busing them here from the border and settling them in our small towns," the man said to a chorus of boos. "We don't know if they're terrorists. We don't know if they have diseases we haven't seen here in fifty years. They can't speak English, how are they going to find work? Yet our business leaders tell us we need them in our workforce. What about our own citizens who can't find work? What about them? What about us?

"We need a homeland here in the northwest where citizens who share our values can work and live safely. We need neighborhoods where kids can play and not be afraid some Syrian jihadist is going to pull them off their bikes and cut their throats because they're not Muslims. We need a place where our women can be out at night and not be afraid of being raped by a gang of refugees like in Europe.

"That's why I'm calling on you to do a couple things right now. First, if you think you would like to live in a part of the country that shares your values, the values of a white working class that values the Judeo-Christian way of life, then move here and join us. We need you here and we need your votes to elect men like me to public office. We can seize power the oldfashioned way, by making sure there are more of us than there are of them."

The speaker raised his hands to quiet the cheers. "The second thing I want you to do is return home and organize neighborhood patrols to keep our communities safe. If the government isn't going to protect us from these immigrants, we'll do it ourselves. When people feel that they're safe and see that it's because of what we're doing, they'll join our movement and we will grow. James has a pamphlet he'll pass out in a moment from our new friends, the Soldiers of Odin, from Finland. It outlines the steps they took to organize. Break into your individual chapters and study the pamphlet. If you have any questions, come see me before we wrap things up."

The clapping and cheers made it hard to hear anything for a long minute.

Drake leaned across the table. "Any idea who that guy is?"

Benning nodded. "I do. The park ranger told me he came with Davis and was introduced as the politician who would be speaking today. His name is Michael Flynn. He's from Spokane and he's running for the state senate."

"That wasn't what I expected," Drake said, shaking his head. "What we heard could have been at a political rally in a lot of places. These white supremacists or Neo-Nazis or whatever we choose to call them aren't just preaching hate, although that's what it boils down to. This is what

the new far-right in Europe is preaching and it's growing in strength in the European Parliament."

"And for the same reason immigration." Benning nodded in the direction of the covered facility. "There's Davis."

Drake turned his head and saw Davis talking with two men ten feet away from the others. Davis raised his hand in protest and started to walk back to the others when the men grabbed his arms and turned him around. One man leaned in close and said something to Davis, who slowly shook his head. Then Davis waved to someone back in the covered kitchen facility that it was okay and walked away between the two men.

"Interesting," Drake said.

"What?"

"I recognized one of the men. He's one of Guzman's crew from his yacht."

Chapter Thirty-Six

THEY DECIDED TO SPLIT UP. Drake would follow Davis and see where he was going; Benning would keep an eye on the gathering until he returned. He wanted to report as much about the men at the gathering as he could to his friend on the gang task force.

Drake followed the men to the parking lot. A black Audi A7 sedan was idling there and Davis was pushed into the back seat. The two men got in beside him and the Audi pulled away.

Before it was too far away, Drake took out his cell phone and took a quick picture of the rear of the departing vehicle. He had a good idea where the Audi was headed. With its license number, he might be able to prove it.

Drake walked back to Benning and sat down at their picnic table. "They left in a big black Audi sedan. I don't think it was something Davis planned on doing. He left sandwiched in the back between the two men who didn't seem all that friendly."

"What do you want to do now?"

"We can't sit here watching these guys too much longer before they decide to come check us out. I'm heading back to Seattle. If Guzman is the one who wants me dead, Davis is the one who can connect the dots for me."

No one appeared to pay any attention to them as they left. The men were standing in small groups reading the pamphlets about how to be effective vigilantes in their communities.

Benning drove back to Battle Ground and the Old Town Burger where Drake had left the Cayman. Before they parted ways, he asked Drake what he wanted him to tell his wife. "You've been out of the office for a long week and she'll want to know when you'll be back. What do you want me to tell her?"

Drake smiled and said, "If she's okay with you working for me as a P.I., tell her what we've been doing and that I'm following up on something in Seattle. If she's not, tell her I'm still working on the PSS assessment and I'll be back as soon as possible. Both are true in a way.

I'll leave it to you to choose the answer that keeps her happy."

"You'll be the first to know if she's not."

Drake got out of Benning's F-150 and walked over to the best employment perk he'd ever had. The gray Porsche Cayman had been Casey's way of rewarding him for agreeing to serve as special counsel for Puget Sound Security and he enjoyed every mile he drove it.

Pulling onto to Hwy. 502E to backtrack his route from Seattle, he thought about where Guzman's goons could be taking Davis. The only place he knew about was Guzman's yacht.

He used the car's mobile phone Bluetooth connection

and called PSS headquarters. The receptionist forwarded his call to Marco Morales. "How's the surveillance of our young Saudi going?"

"It's underway but nothing much so far."

"Are you busy?"

"What do you need and how long will it take me?"

"I'm driving north on I-5 from Battle Ground. Someone I'm interested in was just shoved into the backseat of an Audi A7 here by a couple of men. I recognized one of them, a crewman on Guzman's yacht. If I'm right, the Audi's headed your way. Can you get over to Lake Union and watch for a black Audi A7? I want to know if they're taking Davis to the yacht. If they do, can you watch and see if they keep him there? It will take them at least an hour to get there and I won't be far behind. I'll spell you when I get there."

"Can do, you need pictures?"

"Yes. What are you driving?"

"The boss likes you better than me. I'm driving a white GMC van we use for surveillance."

"Thanks Marco, I appreciate your help with this."

"No problem, I'll keep an eye out for you."

Drake thought for a moment about any other possible places they might take Davis. Guzman was a banker associated in some fashion with a Hong Kong financial conglomerate. He wondered if it owned any banks in Seattle.

It was a quarter to four in the afternoon and Liz might still be in her office. Just in case she wasn't, he called her on her cell phone.

"It's me. Are you still in your office?"

"Hi you. Yes, I'm waiting for a friend to come by and then go to dinner. Have you finished your work in Seattle?"

"I thought I had and now I'm driving back there. It's a

long story. You remember telling me about the banks that Interpol was monitoring that the far-right groups were using?"

"Yes."

"Do you remember if any of those banks were owned by a Hong Kong financial conglomerate and, if so, did the conglomerate have any banks in Seattle?" "I don't off hand. Let me check the stuff Interpol sent me."

Drake drove for ten minutes before she came back with the answer.

"Hong Kong Trust and Financial Services has a bank on Second and Pike Street. It is a member of the banking conglomerate Interpol is watching."

"Second and Pike is downtown and has to be in one of the high-rise office buildings. I don't think they would take him there. Thanks Liz. I'll call you tomorrow. Have a good time with your *friend*."

"Hold on a minute. Take *who* where? And did I hear a little jealousy in your voice?"

"The answer to your second question is no. Should I be jealous? And the answer to the first question is the 'who' is a guy PSS is looking for, so there's nothing you should worry about."

"Remember your promise and I'll promise to have as little fun tonight with my *friend* as possible."

"I'll call you tomorrow and ask if you kept that promise."

"Good night, Adam."

He didn't like telling her there was nothing to worry about, but why tell her there was when he didn't know himself? He might never see Davis again. Even if he did, he wasn't sure what he would do about it.

Unless Walter Guzman was Ryan Walker and Davis was his pawn doing his bidding. Then he'd probably want to kill them both and that was something she should worry about.

Chapter Thirty-Seven

THE WHITE VAN was parked as close to the second dock at the Nautical Landing marina as it could get while still having a clear view of the mega yacht Astrid III. Drake knocked lightly on the passenger-side door and got in.

"Two men got out of an Audi A7 and escorted a man on board twenty minutes ago.

They're still on board." Morales handed Drake a digital camera. "Here's what they looked like."

The three men were the same men he'd seen at the Battle Ground Lake State Park. Davis looked even more uncomfortable than he did when he was led to the waiting Audi.

"Did Davis look like a happy camper to you?" Drake asked.

"They had to pull him out of the car. He looked like he was being led to the gallows.

Who is he?"

"He's supposed to be the leader of Volksfront, a gang that got started in Oregon State Prison. He's sent some of his gang members after me on two occasions. The last time, they tried to take me at my office."

Morales turned to Drake with a puzzled look on his face. "Then why isn't he in jail?"

"Three of his men are, but there's nothing to prove that Davis ordered it. One of his men said that someone else was the one who wanted me dead. My guess is it's the man Davis is here to see, the owner of Astrid III."

"So how does the Saudi we're following play into all of this?"

"I wish I knew. Guzman, the yacht's owner, is involved with them, but I don't know why or how."

Morales looked to his left and pointed. A white Audi A7 drove past them and stopped at the end of the second dock and the stern of the mega yacht. Morales grabbed his camera and started taking pictures of the one man who got out. The camera was set on the fast/continuous shooting mode and continued clicking rapidly until the man boarded the yacht and went inside.

"By the way he checked out his surroundings before getting too far away from the Audi, I'd say the man has seen some action," Drake observed.

"Any idea who he is?"

"No, but you might see if you can identify him when you return to headquarters. I'll stay here for a little longer to see if Davis goes somewhere. Thanks for dropping what you were doing to help me on this."

Drake opened his door and started to get out. "I forgot to ask how you're getting along with a certain vice president at Trans World Marine."

The suppressed smile on Morales' face contradicted his answer as he started the van's engine. "Don't know what you're talking about, *jefe*. Girl like that wouldn't have anything to do with me."

Drake just nodded with his best poker face on and said, "Well, if you ever run into her, tell Stephanie hello for me."

He knew Morales had been seeing the daughter of the owner and CEO of Trans World Marine since the PSS team returned from Nicaragua. The beautiful Stanford MBA had fallen hard for the swagger of the former long distance reconnaissance soldier and called him frequently at work. Teasing him about it was too much fun to pass up.

The view of the yacht from behind the wheel of the low-slung Porsche Cayman was partially blocked and, as Drake started to back out to move to the spot the PSS van had occupied, another car beat him to it. He looked for a space with a better view, but there wasn't one.

He didn't want to attract attention by getting out of his car and strolling around, but he wanted to know if Davis stayed on the yacht or left the same way he arrived. As he looked for a way to keep an eye on the yacht, he spotted a security camera on a pole at the edge of the parking lot that gave him an idea.

He drove to the service road that ran along the row of docks. The marina had placed security cameras all the way down the service road to provide security for the expensive yachts. When he reached the end of the service road, he turned around and drove back to the space he left and called Casey at PSS.

"I'm back in Seattle and have a question."

"What are you doing back in Seattle?"

"I followed the Volksfront guy I told you about to Guzman's yacht. He's on the yacht and I'd like to know if he's staying there or seeing someone else in Seattle. The marina has security cameras all over the place. Could Kevin hack into Nautical Landing's security system and keep an eye on the yacht for me? I'm in the Cayman and I can't find a place where I can see who's coming and going."

"Why do we care if your guy stays on the yacht or not? I thought Guzman was the one we're interested in?"

"Mike, I know I'm asking a lot of you and PSS, but if Guzman is the one who wants me dead, and Guzman's also Ryan Walker, then we need to find out why. And why is he meeting with guys like James Davis and Ali Mohammad on his yacht? That's an odd couple to have over for a sip of champagne."

"All right, I'll get Kevin to see what he can do. Are you going to stay at the marina until he gets it set up?"

"I'll have to."

"Then when he does, you need to come see me. Sound Transit isn't happy about our security assessment. They want to know how they can stop a sarin attack on the light rail system if the Martin Research system won't alert them until it's too late to do anything about it. They're talking about cancelling the installation of the chemical detectors and backing out of the contract."

"Terrific! But they didn't ask us to design a system for them that would prevent a sarin attack. They just wanted to know what we thought about the system they were installing. Is that what they're asking you to do now?"

"Seems like it. We'll talk when you get here."

Drake backed out of the space with the obstructed view and drove to an empty space in front of the marina office where he could see the second dock. The Astrid III towered above the other yachts around it but floated there looking deserted and lonely. He wondered what was taking place on board and what Davis and Guzman were up to.

He also had to think about how a transit operator in

America was going to stop a nerve gas attack. Until the government got serious about terrorism and adopted security practices like the Israelis used so effectively, it would be difficult. And making a recommendation to adopt Israeli practices in a city like Seattle wasn't going to be well received. He knew, though, that it was the bitter pill that would have to be swallowed sooner or later.

Chapter Thirty-Eight

JAMES DAVIS WAS TAKEN below deck where Guzman was just coming out of the sauna with a towel wrapped around his waist.

A spa attendant brought him a glass of water and left, leaving Davis and the two crewmen standing in front of him. Guzman savored the cold lemon water and shook his head when he finished the glass.

"I enjoy a cold glass of lemon water after sweating in the sauna. I would offer you a glass, Mr. Davis, because I see that you're beginning to sweat, but there's no reason to prolong our meeting, is there? You were asked if you had taken care of the one thing I asked you to do. You told my men that you had not. Is that true, Mr. Davis?"

"We don't know where he is. When we find him, my men will finish the job just as you asked us to."

Guzman shook his head, "No, Mr. Davis, not as I asked you to do. Your gathering of the faithful started today. I told you to kill Drake before then. Now you've failed to earn the money I promised you and you owe me for the advance I gave you. Unfortunately for you, I can't think of any way you can repay me in time."

"There has to be a way," Davis pleaded. "With a little more time, we'll find Drake."

"I doubt it," Guzman said with harsh disdain. "Drake is here, in Seattle! He's been on the dock right outside this yacht asking for me! You have greatly disappointed me, Mr. Davis. It's time you understood just how much."

A small, wiry man wearing green surgeon's scrubs entered the spa area and stood beside Guzman. His face was tattooed like Mike Tyson's and his shaved head was covered with scars.

"They call this man the *Confessor*," Guzman explained. "He's going to find out how you led Drake to me. He's also going to find out what you learned about me from the sheriff's deputy in Gold Beach. Then he's going to kill you because that's what he enjoys doing. Goodbye, Mr. Davis."

"You can't do this," Davis shouted as he was led away in the grip of Guzman's crewmen.

"My men will come after you."

Guzman started toward the shower next to the sauna and said, "They're no longer your men, Mr. Flynn is seeing to that. Be a man, Mr. Davis, and quietly accept the fate you've earned."

After a shower and a massage, Guzman waited in his study for the *Confessor* to join him. Davis had been taken in plain sight at the park and brought directly to the marina in the hope that Drake or someone on his behalf would follow Davis.

Then a white SUV had arrived just before Davis did

and parked so that it would have a clear view of Davis when he was brought on board. He felt sure the SUV was connected to Drake and now Josef, his head of IT and communications, reported that he had traced it to the same security firm where Drake served as special counsel.

Guzman knew how the *Confessor* got his name, of course, but he didn't know much about the man's other skills. If he could persuade the *Confessor* to capture Drake himself and then interrogate him, that was the safest possible outcome. He could not afford another failure. He had to leave Seattle knowing Drake was dead or he would face the same fate as Davis had just suffered.

Eric, his bodyguard, knocked lightly on the door of his study. "He's here. Do you want to see him now?"

"Bring him in."

The man came in and sat down across the antique desk in the study. He wore a longsleeve denim shirt with the sleeves rolled up and a pair of black jeans. Guzman couldn't see the shoes he was wearing, but he guessed they would be cowboy boots. "Would you like something to drink?"

"Si, Don Julio."

Guzman snapped his fingers and Eric stepped into the study. "Don Julio and a plate of tapas, Eric."

When his bodyguard left, he raised his eyebrows. "Well, did you learn anything?"

The man's eyes closed for just a moment, as if he was replaying a portion of the interrogation in his mind. "Only that he thought he was more of a man than he turned out to be."

His bodyguard returned with a square bottle of Don Julio Reposado on a tray with two shot glasses and plate of garlic shrimp tapas.

Guzman filled their shot glasses, raised his and said, "*Salud*. Enjoy a tapa and we will discuss business."

After several tapas and another shot of tequila, Guzman continued. "We haven't found your man yet, but we are close. We know where he works and where his company has an account at a luxury hotel for its out-of-town clients and guests. We're checking to see if he's registered there. If he is, how would you like to proceed?"

"Tell me about this man."

"I have a dossier on him that you may have. He was a Delta Force operator when he was in the military. He's intelligent and has been very lucky so far."

"From what I hear, luck has had nothing to do with it. Can your men bring him here?" "I would like to limit our exposure here as much as possible. We'll be leaving soon."

The *Confessor* chuckled derisively. "So, you would rather risk exposing me than your own men? That tells me more about this man than I think you wanted me to know. I am not a *sicario*, a hitman. Have your men bring him to me. I will find out what you want to know. If you don't think you can do that, I will leave now and you can pay me half of the money you were going to pay me."

Guzman rocked back in his chair and considered the *Confessor's* response. The Brotherhood's demand that he kill Drake, coupled with the promise that there would be serious consequences if he failed, gave him little choice in the matter. He needed to know if Drake had learned that he was Ryan Walker, and he needed the *Confessor* to find that out for him.

"All right, I will have my men bring him here. I will leave here by noon Monday. Will you be able to stay that long if it takes a day or two to find Drake?"

"I will stay here on your yacht until then. Send someone to my hotel and get my things and I will enjoy your hospitality a little longer. But you had better hurry and find this man. Two days is not a lot of time if he is as good as I think he is."

Chapter Thirty-Nine

DRAKE'S STAY at the marina lasted another twenty minutes before Kevin McRoberts called.

"Mr. Drake, we have full view of the yacht Astrid III now. You can leave the marina."

"That was fast."

"It was pretty easy, Mr. Drake."

"Thanks Kevin. I'm heading back to PSS now. If James Davis leaves the yacht in the next few minutes, call me. I'll go back and see if I can catch up with him."

"Will do, sir."

Drake took a last look at the mega yacht and left the marina to drive back across the Lake Washington floating bridge to Kirkland. By the time he pulled into his reserved parking space at PSS headquarters, it was a quarter after five and employees were heading out for the weekend.

His first stop was Casey's office.

"Thanks for letting Kevin help out at the marina."

Casey pushed his chair back and smiled. "The kid gets such a kick out of it when he outsmarts someone's system as easily as he does. Tell me about following Davis here to Seattle."

Drake stretched and sat down, pushing his legs straight out in front of him. "I hired Paul Benning to do some PI work for me while he's still on medical leave. He followed James Davis to a meeting at a state park outside Battle Ground and I met him there. It was some sort of get together for white supremacists and Neo-Nazi types from all over the country. One of your political candidates from Spokane got them all revved up about forming vigilante groups to patrol the streets and keep us safe from immigrant refugees. Before the meeting broke up, two goons from Guzman's yacht showed up and led Davis away. I came back to Seattle to find out why."

"How are you going to do that?"

"I thought about that driving back from Lake Union. I want Kevin to hack into the computer system on Guzman's yacht."

"For what purpose? Guzman's not going to keep anything on his computer system if he wants Davis to kill you."

Drake shook his head. "Probably not, but that's not what I had in mind. The yacht has a security system. I saw a security camera inside the ship's loading portal the other day when the crewman wanted to throw us off the dock. The yacht's security system will have cameras all over the place. If we have access to the security system, we might be able to see what Davis and

Guzman are up to."

"You mean if we have 'unauthorized access' to the yacht's computer system, which is against the law."

"Same as it was when you let Kevin gain 'unauthorized access' to the marina's security system. Anyway, under state law, it's only a misdemeanor if you gain 'unauthorized access' and there's no intent to commit some other crime. And since when did you start worrying about misdemeanors and Kevin being caught?"

"There is that," Casey conceded. "Go ahead and tell Kevin he's authorized to make

'unauthorized access' to the yacht's computer system. But before you do, let's talk about Sound

Transit's concerns."

"That's probably my fault. I was very clear about the gap I saw in the security of their light rail system in the event of nerve gas attack with sarin. They probably didn't want it spelled out so clearly, in case something happens down the line, but that's what they're paying us for. And there was nothing in their contract with Martin Research about coming up with a chemical detection system that would detect a sarin gas attack. They knew about the Tokyo attack in '95 and should have made that a requirement if they're the detection system capabilities they wanted."

Casey's assistant buzzed him to let him know he was leaving for the weekend, unless there was something else he needed. Casey told him to go home.

"I suggested that to their lawyer, but since he drafted the contract he wasn't interested in hearing it."

Casey swiveled around in his chair and slid open the center panel of his rosewood credenza.

"The guys gave me this for my birthday," he said, taking out a tall bottle and two whisky glasses engraved with the company's initials. "This is as good a time as any to try it."

"Oh man, I forgot your birthday," Drake moaned.

Casey laughed as he poured two fingers into each of the glasses. "It's okay, I forgot your birthday last year. *Salud!*"

Drake raised his glass and tasted the bourbon. "That's good bourbon."

He reached for the bottle and studied the label. Pappy Winkle Family Reserve. 20-Yrs Old.

"I'm guessing that's expensive bourbon."

"I looked it up. $1,500 a bottle. I'm making it last because it'll be a long time before I spend that much on a bottle of bourbon."

They sat quietly enjoying the buttery flavors of vanilla, honey and a hint of apple.

"What are we going to tell Sound Transit?" Casey asked.

"That the only thing that will keep a terrorist from walking into a train car with a sealed container of liquid sarin is a security guard or guards on each of the station platforms, trained to identify a terrorist. The Israelis know how to do it. It's too PC for our government, but a private company could make it work. A company like yours."

Casey rocked back in his chair and studied the bourbon in his glass. "I like it." Drake tipped his glass toward his friend in agreement.

"No, I mean your idea. Highly trained security guards in plain clothes on each of the light rail stations. Trained to identify and take down the terrorist before he or she ever steps onto the train."

"Do you think you could sell it to Sound Transit?"

"We'd have to move pretty fast to put together a proposal for them, but, yes, I think I can."

"Where do we find and train personnel for the task?"

"We don't find and train, we just find. There's a little country surrounded by hostile neighbors that might have a few men it could loan us for a while."

Chapter Forty

WHILE CASEY GOT to work on the security guard proposal for Sound Transit, Drake took the stairs down to the third floor and the IT division where Kevin McRoberts worked. Not yet twenty-one years old, he was Casey's IT security analyst and white-hat hacker for the company.

Drake found him in his office at the back of the large, open IT area that occupied one third of the entire floor. He was intently studying one of the three computer monitors on his desk with a black, green and gold can of Monster in his hand.

It took four loud knocks on the open door to get the young man's attention.

"Sorry, Mr. Drake, I didn't see you there."

"You were busy. Do you have a minute?"

"Sure, come on in."

There were two chairs in front of the desk and both had a stack of files on them. Drake moved one of the chairs to the side of the desk so he could see around the monitors.

"It looks like you're keeping busy."

Kevin smiled broadly. "One of our clients thinks its IT structure is bullet-proof. I'm showing them it isn't."

"Has there been any activity on the yacht at the marina you've been watching?"

"Not yet. No one has left or gotten on board since I accessed the marina's CCTV system. I'm recording it in case I miss something."

"What do you think of the Astrid III?"

"It's a friggin' 215-foot floating palace, Mr. D! Built in 2014, flying the flag of the Cayman Islands and built in a German shipyard, every billionaire should have one of these to party in. I think WOW!"

Drake had to laugh. He should have known that Kevin would have already studied the Astrid III as soon as it was the target of his surveillance request.

"Do you think you can hack the yacht's computer system?"

The young hacker looked insulted. "Really? Yachts this big will have an autopilot system using signals from GPS satellites. Override the GPS signal and you're in. Are you asking me to hack the Astrid III?"

"That's right, with Casey's blessing. I'm interested in the man who was escorted on board and hasn't been seen leaving yet. He's meeting with the owner of the Astrid for the second time. See if you can find out what they're doing. The owner's going by the name of Walter Guzman, but I don't believe that's his real name. Look for anything that might tell us who he really is."

"I'll have to put together something that will allow me to override the GPS signal, but that won't take me long. Is tomorrow early enough?"

Drake stood up and returned his chair to its place in

front of the desk. "It is. I'm staying in Seattle over the weekend. I'll check with you sometime tomorrow."

There was one more person he wanted to see before he left. He took the stairs down another floor to Operations where Marco Morales had a cubicle in the Competitive Intelligence and Corporate Security section. It was after six o'clock, but unless Morales had a date there was a chance he was still in the building.

He wasn't in his cubicle, but Drake heard laughter coming from Operation's lounge and found him playing darts with three other PSS operators.

Morales towed the line and threw his dart. As he turned to high-five his teammate, he saw Drake and waved.

"Good timing, we just gave these guys a costly lesson," Morales said and walked over.

"You play darts?"

"I do occasionally, but not at your level. Bring me up to speed on your surveillance of Ali Mohammad."

"We're watching his penthouse and follow him when he leaves it, but he's keeping a low profile right now. He's not taking any summer classes and he parties every night. There's a gym in his building and he works out every morning, but that's about it."

"What kind of parties?"

"A dozen guys and maybe twenty girls are there most nights. The men are all of Arab descent and the women are young, pretty and usually blonde. The funny thing is they send the girls home alone about an hour before the guys leave."

Drake's furrowed brow prompted Morales to continue.

"I know, weird, unless ... the girls are there to give these guys cover."

"Cover for what?"

"Cover from being outed as gay Muslim men."

"They're going to great expense with parties every night to keep anyone from finding out they're gay."

"Mohammad can afford it if he can afford to live in that penthouse."

"See if you can find out who his pals are then. It might confirm your theory they're all gay, but it won't tell us why he's visiting Guzman on his yacht. That's what I really want to know."

"You got it. Sure you don't want to throw a few darts with us?"

Drake looked at the three men waiting for Morales to return. "I think your opponents are waiting for a chance to win their money back. I need to see if I have some place to sleep tonight. Call me if you turn up anything, I'll be around this weekend."

He left the lounge to the sound of trash talk and bets being made as he walked to the stairs down to the parking garage. It was after happy hour, but if they had a room available for him at the Woodmark, he still had time for a good run on the bike path along the lake before it got too dark.

Then a quick shower and something to eat in the hotel's restaurant and a good night's sleep. If Kevin was successful in hacking into the Astrid III's computer system, he might find out the next day why Davis was on Guzman's yacht and find out who Guzman really was.

Chapter Forty-One

THE WOODMARK HOTEL and Spa at Carillon Point was the only waterfront hotel on Lake Washington. With a private marina, a spa, three restaurants and meeting rooms for every occasion, it defined luxury accommodations just three miles from the high-tech corridor of Redmond, Kirkland and Bellevue. It was also close to the Puget Sound Security offices.

Guzman sent six men to bring Drake back to the Astrid III. Two men were posted in the lobby sitting area and were standing at the windows looking out at the marina. Two men were sitting at a table on the patio of the Beach Café, extending their happy hour sitting by ordering another round of Heineken. The last two men were sitting in a white Audi A7 with darkened windows in the turnaround in front of the hotel at the end of Lakeview Drive.

Their orders were simple: bring Drake back to the yacht for a word with the *Confessor* or be prepared to take his place.

DRAKE CALLED AHEAD and found that the room he had checked out of that morning was reserved for a client of Puget Sound Security who would be checking in later that evening. As special counsel for the company, the manager said he would keep the room for him and make another room available for the client.

Drake made a note to be sure to let management know how much PSS appreciated the efforts of their manager. He parked the Cayman in the parking lot northeast of the hotel and grabbed his leather weekend duffel bag out of the rear luggage space. He used the back entrance of the hotel on his way to pick up a keycard at the front desk and then changed course to make a reservation for dinner at the Bin on the Lake restaurant.

When he headed back to the front desk, he noticed two men standing at the windows in the lobby sitting area looking out at the marina. The restaurant was a popular dinner destination for boaters on Lake Washington and he thought he'd probably see the men again later at dinner with the party they were waiting for.

After a quick stop at the front desk, Drake took the stairs to his room and changed into gray running shorts, a lightning-yellow Oregon T-shirt with a big gray O on the front and gray Nike trainers. It was always a pleasure to run in Seattle and taunt the Washington Husky football fans.

He used the stairs again and retraced his route to the parking lot and on to the bike path that followed the edge of the lake. The day had been warm and two hours before sunset it was still in the mid-seventies. With the slight breeze coming across the lake, it was a great evening for a run.

Drake ran north for fifteen minutes at a comfortable six

minute per mile pace and then turned back toward the hotel. He kicked it up a notch to a five and a half minute per mile pace to work up a good sweat before the end of his run.

When he was two hundred yards from the hotel, he slowed to a jog and then a walk to cool down. Bicycle riders and skaters passed him on his left and boats motored by on the lake to his right. He'd enjoyed the run and took pleasure in the relaxed calmness he was feeling.

Before he turned off the bike path to avoid entering the hotel through the lobby or the patio of the Beach Café, he saw the two men he'd noticed earlier were still standing at the windows in the lobby sitting area. Instead of looking out toward the marina, they were staring down at him.

He stepped off the bike path and started his stretching routine. Out of the corner of his eye, he saw one of the men waving to someone on the patio of the Beach Café. When he turned to look in that direction, he saw two men get up from their table and start toward the bike path.

Something about the abrupt way the two men left their table triggered an alarm in Drake's mind. It was still daylight and there were plenty of people around, but the two men on the patio and the two men standing at the windows for the duration of his run signaled trouble.

He walked forward, swinging his arms wide and then back across his body as if he was limbering up before a fight. The two men on the patio were now on the bike path and walking side by side toward him thirty feet away. They both had on black polo shirts, tan slacks and deck shoes. From the tight sleeves around their bulging biceps and the width of their shoulders, he pegged them as bodybuilders.

When the men were ten feet away, Drake stepped in front of a woman walking with her son in front of them. He pointed to the cell phone in her hand and asked loudly, "Miss, could I impose on you to take a picture of me with my two friends here? They're leaving tomorrow and I left my phone in my room."

"Be happy to," she said with a smile and guided her son off the bike path while she turned back to take the picture.

Drake closed the gap to the two men and said, "Come on, guys, stand beside me."

Caught in the open with people walking around them to keep from being in the picture, the two men didn't have a choice but to comply. Drake stepped in between the two men and put his arms around their shoulders.

As the woman readied her cell phone, he pulled the men hard to him. "Did James Davis send you?"

The man on his right said menacingly, "Why don't you come with us and find out? When she takes the picture, you're going to turn around and walk with us to the turn-around. Go quietly and no one will get hurt."

"Come on guys, smile," Drake said and then under his breath added, "If I don't, does that mean you will shoot me or something?"

The man on his left said, "Something like that, wise-ass."

Drake dropped his hands down from their shoulders to the middle of their backs and pushed each man to the side.

"Run miss, they have guns. Call the police," he shouted and turned around to run to the patio of the Beach Café.

The two men standing at the windows were now on the bike path blocking his way to the patio and rushing to help their two compatriots. Drake charged straight at them and threw his elbows out, hitting both men in the chest and knocking them off their feet. He kept running, like a linebacker breaking through blockers and looking for the quarterback.

As people turned to see what was happening, he continued to shout for someone to call the police and ran to the front entrance of the hotel. As he reached the front doors, he saw a white Audi A7 idling at the curb of the turnaround at the end of Lakeview Drive.

Inside, he walked calmly across the lobby and on to the stairs. He figured he had time for a shower and drink at the bar before his eight o'clock dinner reservation. If he needed to give a statement to the police about the incident on the bike path, at least he'd be dressed and calmed down by then.

Chapter Forty-Two

DRAKE MADE one phone call to PSS before going to the bar for a stiff drink. The on-duty receptionist paged Marco Morales and found him still playing darts in the Operations lounge.

"Marco, I'm at the Woodmark. Have time for a drink at the bar with me?"

"Is this on the clock or off?"

"We'll decide that when you get here."

"See you in five."

The summer evening temperature was still in the seventies and too warm for a jacket, but he didn't have a choice. He needed to conceal the Kimber .45 holstered on his right hip, which meant he was wearing his blue summer blazer over a dove gray T-shirt and khakis to dinner.

He took a seat at the far end of the bar of the Bin on the Lake restaurant so that he was facing the entrance to the bar area. Guzman's thugs might be smart enough to call it quits for the night, but you never knew.

In between glances at the entrance, he noticed a bottle of Wild Turkey Kentucky Spirit bourbon prominently displayed with the other bourbon whiskeys the bar was serving. If ever there was a night for a little Wild Turkey aged 101, this was the night. He remembered more than one night when, after a mission, a bottle of Wild Turkey was passed around to celebrate a success or salute a fallen comrade. Tonight, his thoughts were more along the lines of letting Guzman know he was messing with the wrong boy.

Morales walked in just as the bartender was pouring his glass of Wild Turkey. "Do you drink whiskey?" Drake asked.

"Only when there's no tequila available."

"Try this and you might change your mind."

He signaled for the bartender to pour another glass and waited as Morales tasted the dark amber liquid.

Morales held the whiskey glass up to the light, took another taste and proclaimed, "A little soft for my taste, but not bad."

Drake laughed and said, "It'll grow on you. Have you eaten?"

"Just some peanuts playing darts."

"Let's have dinner and we'll decide whether you're on or off the clock."

Their waiter led them to a window table and asked if they wanted another round. Drake said yes, but Morales ordered tequila. While the waiter was away, Drake recommended the Kobe flat iron steak and Morales agreed.

With their dinners ordered and a fresh round of drinks on the table, Drake told the young PSS Ranger about his meeting with Guzman's men.

"They were waiting for me when I got back from my

run on the bike path. Two outside on the patio, two inside the lobby and the white Audi in the turnaround for pickup. I guess they expected me to go quietly."

Morales smiled and said, "Guess they don't know you."

"What I can't figure out is why they keep coming for me. If they wanted to take me out, they've had plenty of chances."

"Looks like Guzman's involved in this, with the white Audi showing up again. What do you want to do about it?"

Drake turned and looked out at a large day cruiser pulling into the marina. His first thought was to sink the SOB's yacht with Guzman on board.

His second was a little more pensive: *There's something behind all of this that I need to understand.*

"As much as I want to hurt someone right now, I have to find out what's going on. If Guzman is who I think he is, he's here for a reason and it's not just to take me out."

The waiter served their dinners and the steaks provided a brief lull in the conversation.

"What if we could do a little of both?" Morales asked with a fork of miso-glazed potato paused halfway to his mouth.

"How would we do that?"

Morales' smile was twice as big as before. "You know my background as an Army Ranger. Long range surveillance behind enemy lines was my specialty. My current deployment with PSS requires me to keep up on things. I talked the boss into buying a couple of the latest nano UAVs, the PD-100 Black Hornet 2.

"It's a miniature helicopter drone that fits in the palm of your hand and has both regular and thermal cameras. We could fly one of the Black Hornets into Guzman's yacht, have a look around and leave him something he won't forget."

"Like what?"

"I was thinking a severed horse's head, like in *The Godfather*."

Drake choked on the bite of steak he was chewing. "Seriously?"

"Yeah, but a horse's head unfortunately is too heavy for a Black Hornet. We'll have to come up with something else."

"How close do you have to be to use the drone?"

"That won't be a problem. The Black Hornet has a range of two miles and flies at a speed of up to twenty-two miles an hour. Anywhere close to the marina and we're good."

"Do you need authorization to use a drone on my behalf?"

Morales shrugged. "I figure you and Casey are close enough he's not going to say no if you ask him. The worst that could happen is losing the drone and having to replace it."

"How much would that take?"

"$40,000.00."

Drake just shook his head. "I should have figured that much. Anything designed for the military is not going to be cheap. Here's the deal. We get Casey to approve using the drone and he writes it off if you lose it. If he doesn't, he can take it out of your pay and I'll reimburse you for half of it."

"How about I loan you the drone and you pay for all of it if we don't bring it back?"

It was Drake's turn to smile. "You drive a hard bargain, soldier. I'll pay for all of it if Casey won't write it off as a loss. You come up with something as good as a severed horse's head to deliver to Guzman."

Morales nodded his agreement and asked, "Do we go tonight or tomorrow?"

"Let's go now and leave them something to wake up to."

Chapter Forty-Three

THEY DROVE BACK to PSS headquarters and parked their cars in their respective spaces. Drake waited in the Operations lounge while Morales gathered his gear for the night; the PD-100 Black Hornet 2 kit from the equipment room, his personal Sig P226, tactical flashlight and his CRKT M16 Tanto tactical folder.

When he returned to the lounge, Morales handed Drake a pair of night vision binoculars. "You'll need these to follow the drone's flight. Keep an eye on the equipment for me. I need to run up to my office before we go."

Drake picked up the beige Black Hornet base station. It was small enough to fit in his rear pocket and contained two self-contained helicopters. He opened one storage compartment and took out the small UAV. Morales was right, it fit in the palm of his hand. The control panel for the little drone connected to the base station with a short, computer-like cable and looked like the controls for a video game.

Acting as a pair of flying binoculars, he could see how the little helicopter could be used in combat. Send the little bird out and use its three cameras to spot snipers, look over a ridge and spot an entrenched enemy or fly around corners in an urban environment. It might have been expensive, but the Black Hornet was going to save lives.

Morales came back with a small, black storage container and a brown paper bag. With a huge grin on his face, he opened the paper bag and took out a small shrunken head.

"It's a tsantsa, a shrunken head from the Jivaro tribe of Ecuador and Peru. I got it when I was returning from a mission in Columbia. It's lighter than a severed horse head and I think Guzman or whoever he is will get the message."

Drake stared at the shrunken head. "What message?"

"He's from South America, he'll know about a Jivaro tribe shrunken head. It's the trophy a warrior displays to show he has fulfilled his sacred obligation of blood revenge. Guzman will understand that you're coming to extract revenge for trying to kill you."

They loaded the equipment in the white van Morales was using for surveillance work and drove across the floating bridge to Lake Union and the Nautical Landing marina. The parking lot was only half-full and they had their choice of spaces with a view of the Astrid III.

Morales whistled softly. "It's lit up like a Christmas tree."

"You have anything other than the night-vision binoculars I can use?" Drake asked.

"My Leupold Tacticals are still in the console."

Drake found the binoculars in the center console and searched the yacht. "Even with all the lights on, they still have four guards posted. Two on the lower deck by the swimming pool and two on the aft bridge deck."

"Shouldn't be a problem," Morales assured him. "The ambient noise will cover the sound of the Black Hornet.

Even if one of them is lucky enough to see the Hornet fly by, he'll think it's a bat or bird. Delivering the tsantsa will be more of a challenge."

"Why?"

"The Black Hornet isn't rigged to carry things. It's just for surveillance. The hexacopter in the black container I brought can carry a package, but it makes some noise."

"Let's see what Guzman's up to on the yacht. We'll think of a distraction to cover the sound of the other drone."

Morales reached back and retrieved the base station and control panel for the Black Hornet. He opened one of the two storage compartments and took out the small drone. Sitting in the palm of his hand, it looked like a small, gray dove. He handed the drone to Drake and unsnapped the controller from the base panel.

"I'm going to stand beside the van to fly the drone," he said, putting the base station into the Black Hornet's tactical pouch system and slipping the neck strap over his head. "Stand behind me so you can see the display panel."

Drake got out of the van and came around with the drone.

Morales powered up the control panel and reached for the drone. Holding it in his right hand between his thumb and index finger, he gently tossed the drone into the air and sent it flying toward the yacht.

They watched the display on the control panel as the drone hovered fifty feet off the stern of the Astrid III. The two guards on either side of the swimming pool on the lower deck were standing motionless, holding HK MP7A1 sub machine guns with sound suppressors at their sides.

Morales changed the camera's view to the bridge deck where the other two guards were stationed. They also carried HK weapons but patrolled along the sides of the bridge deck forward and aft. No one else appeared on the exterior of the massive yacht.

Drake tapped Morales on the shoulder. "Fly along the starboard side on the main deck. See if we can peek in some of the windows."

The Black Hornet soared higher and moved to the right side of the yacht. When it was forward of the guards at the swimming pool, it climbed up and moved in close to the row of darkened glass windows on the main deck.

Morales turned the drone so that its forward camera was pointing to the bank of windows and started moving down the line sideways. The first was a long, narrow, tinted glass window. Soft floodlights illuminated the interior of a vast space. White leather sofas and armchairs surrounded several large, glass-topped coffee tables decorated with exotic flowers in crystal vases. Crystal and chrome reflected the subdued lighting. Beyond the conversation clusters, a long, formal dining table occupied the rest of the space that ended with a floor-to-ceiling fireplace made of what looked to be white brick.

The next four windows were also dark glass, but the room or rooms inside were not illuminated. The next two dark glass windows, however, were illuminated. Light from a desk lamp revealed Guzman sitting at a small desk with a phone to his ear. His face was red and the exaggerated movements of his lips suggested that he was shouting at someone.

"I think he's pissed because his men failed to bring you in," Morales said out of the side of his mouth.

"Wait until he sees the shrunken head tomorrow."

The drone continued along the starboard side, but no

one else was visible inside on the main deck. The same was true on the upper deck and the bridge.

"There are lights showing in some of the windows on the bottom deck. Do you want me to fly along them and see what we see?"

"No," Drake said. "That's where the crew will be. On the upper deck, just below the bridge, there's a table sitting under the overhang of the bridge deck. The table looks like it's set for breakfast with a captain's chair at the end. That has to be Guzman's chair. Let's leave our gift for him and call it a night."

Morales flew the Black Hornet back and landed it in Drake's waiting hand.

"What an invention! You're going to have a lot of fun with these."

"I already am," Morales said. "Tomorrow I'm taking the drone out to see what I can get on the Saudi you have us watching. The windows in his condo aren't darkened like the windows on the yacht."

They stored the Black Hornet in its base station hangar and got out the larger hexacopter Morales brought along in its black storage container. Carefully securing the shrunken head in the grips of the drone, he powered it up and got ready to deliver the package.

"If you have an idea for a diversion so they don't hear this drone flying in, now would be the time."

Drake smiled and said, "I've always wanted to do this."

He walked down the line of cars in the parking lot and stopped beside a silver Jaguar XF. Looking back to Morales, he signaled thumbs up. When he saw the hexacopter lift off, he banged the driver's door of the Jaguar with his hand and set off the car's theft alarm and moved along to two more cars to do the same.

Jogging back, he stood next to his partner in crime. Morales flew the larger drone to the upper deck and hovered it over the table in front of the captain's chair. He carefully lowered the drone until the shrunken head touched down on the surface of the table and dropped it there.

When they had the hexacopter back and stored away, they jumped in the van and laughed like school boys after pranking the school principal.

Chapter Forty-Four

WALTER GUZMAN WAS FURIOUS. The men he'd sent to bring the attorney to him were not answering their phones. Now Eric, his right-hand man and bodyguard, was reporting that the GPS tracking device in the white Audi they were using was stationary in the long-term parking lot at SeaTac, the closest international airport.

The cowards were running, afraid to report their failure.

"Find out which flight they're on and send men to meet them. I want them dead before I wake up tomorrow morning," Guzman yelled to Eric standing just outside the door. "I'm going to bed. Don't wake me unless you have good news."

He stepped out of his private office and stormed down the short hallway to the owner's stateroom. When the door slammed behind him, he cursed loudly in his native tongue at the forces that were operating against him. First the damn attorney and now his own men.

Lurking in the dark shadows of his mind was the warning from the Muslim Brotherhood, on whose behalf he had coordinated operations of jihadist groups and the cartels all around the world—Don't fail again!

Or what, they were going to kill him? And lose the use of the banking network that allowed them to move money to any continent, any major city in the world whenever they wanted? Were they naïve enough to think that the Alliance, that provided critical financial services to the world's greatest criminal enterprises and violent drug cartels, would not ask its partners to avenge any strike at its leader? The stupid ragheads had been insignificant and ineffective puppets for his grandfather and the Third Reich. He would make sure they would be again as soon as the far right parties he sponsored around the world gained power.

Guzman poured himself a healthy snifter of cognac and sat in the leather wingback chair beside his reading lamp. His heart was pounding so furiously that his hand was shaking as he tried to drink without spilling it. *Damn them all*, he thought as the cognac burned down his throat. The following day his enemies would suffer for getting in his way!

THE SOUND of a seaplane flying over the Astrid III before setting down on Lake Union woke him the next morning. Sunlight coming in through the stateroom window signaled a summer day warm enough to have breakfast outside on the upper deck.

Guzman got out of bed and put on his monogrammed black spa robe before using the ship's intercom to order his breakfast before heading to the upper deck. Black coffee and his usual boiled egg and wurst, with buttered bread rolls and strawberry jam, would give him the energy he needed for the day.

His bodyguard caught up with him on the stairs.

"They were flying to Australia," Eric reported. "We found them at LAX and turned them over to our friends in Tijuana. By now their body parts are rotting in the cartel's latest graveyard."

"Excellent! Come join me for breakfast. Now we need to make a new plan for getting rid of the attorney."

The two men continued in silence up the stairs. When they reached the upper deck, the bodyguard cleared his throat and said, "Sir, it's possible the attorney doesn't know anything that will interfere with your plans here. Perhaps we should leave him alone for now."

Guzman spun around to face his bodyguard. "Perhaps if you had done your job better, we wouldn't need to think about him at all! I brought the *Confessor* here to find out what the attorney knows about me. Now I'm stuck with the sadistic little man on my yacht because you failed me. You let me do the planning and you do the job I pay you to do."

He turned on his heel and marched across the room to the sliding glass door to the upper deck. With an angry pull on the door that slammed it back into its stops, he stepped out. And abruptly stopped, staring at the table in front of him.

A small, grotesque shrunken head occupied the place on the table instead of the breakfast plate he was expecting.

His bodyguard came through the door behind him and stopped at his side.

Guzman was transfixed, staring at the shrunken head. "It's a tsantsa," he said softly. "I have one on my desk at home."

"What's a 'tsantsa'?" Eric asked.

"It's a trophy for a warrior who fulfills an obligation of blood revenge. It's Drake's way of letting me know he's coming for me."

The bodyguard started to say something when Guzman's chef opened the sliding door on the other side of the upper deck and saw the shrunken head.

"Mein Gott!" he said and dropped the tray with Guzman's breakfast.

Guzman regained his composure. "Send someone to clean up this mess and have my breakfast brought to my stateroom. Eric, get the tsantsa out of here and then come see me. We have work to do."

On the way to the study next to his stateroom, a plan began to take shape in his mind. It was unlikely that Drake would risk being taken a second time at his hotel and it would take time to locate him again. Time they didn't have. As long as Drake stayed in Seattle, there was one place they knew he went every day, the headquarters of Puget Sound Security.

The PSS building had an outer wall surrounding it with a guard shack and a reinforced gate that would be difficult to breach. But even the security of heavily guarded embassies could be breached if you knew what you were doing. He knew people who knew what they were doing.

All he needed to know was when Drake would be in the PSS headquarters.

Guzman checked the time on his Rolex Cellini and saw that it was too early to call the two men he needed to carry out his plan. One would still be sleeping off the debauchery of a tequila soaked night and the other would be saying his morning prayers.

There was enough time before he called them to have breakfast. Planning to finish his business with the attorney was reviving his appetite.

Chapter Forty-Five

IT TOOK Drake a few seconds when he opened his eyes to remember that he had decided to sleep in his office at PSS instead of returning to his hotel room the night before. Guzman's goons tried to take him at the Woodmark and there were no guarantees they wouldn't try again.

He rolled off the brown leather sofa Casey insisted he have in his office for the occasions when he needed to work late at PSS and promised himself this was not going to become a habit. He was stiff and sore and needed a cup of coffee and a hot shower.

While he was slipping on his pair of Timberland loafers, Casey opened the door.

"I heard you spent the night here. Come down to my office and have some coffee and a bagel. I want to hear how the Black Hornet performed last night," he said with a smile.

Drake ran his fingers through his hair and followed his friend down the hall to his office. A black thermal carafe and two cups were sitting on the corner of Casey's desk beside an open Seattle Bagel Bakery box.

Casey selected a bagel and small container of cream cheese. "I like the bacon and cheddar bagels, but the orange cranberrys are good too."

Drake picked up an orange cranberry bagel. It was still warm. "Did you get these on your way in?"

"I had them delivered. There are three more boxes in the conference room. The Israeli security guards flew in last night. I'm briefing them on their assignment in ten minutes. Tell me about your evening."

After a quick recounting of the events at the Woodmark, Drake took full responsibility for the use of Casey's expensive drone. "At first, I just wanted to know if Guzman's guys were on his yacht. I wasn't sure what I wanted to do, other than hit back hard, but I had to let Guzman know that he was messing with the wrong guy. Morales suggested using the shrunken head to send the message."

"Is that it? That's all he gets after trying three times to take you out?"

Drake was surprised. Casey was usually the calm voice of reason telling him he wasn't a soldier any longer. "I can't prove Guzman was responsible for the first two times and there's nothing I can take to the police about last night. What can I do that doesn't wind up earning me some jail time?"

"How about proving Guzman is Walker and putting him behind bars? Let the FBI, DHS or Interpol take him down."

"Liz is working on that. Right now, I'm more concerned about what he's doing here in Seattle, coming after me and meeting up with white supremacists and a young Saudi."

Casey stood up and picked out another bagel. "You'll

think of something. In the meantime, I have to go meet with our new light rail security guards and explain what I want them to do for the next month."

Drake stayed in Casey's office until he finished his bagel, thinking about Guzman and Ali Mohammad. The only conclusion he reached was that he needed to know more about both men. PSS had the resources, the hacking talents of young Kevin McRoberts and the surveillance skills of Marco Morales to find out what he needed to know.

The first stop on his intel gathering tour was the IT division on the third floor. Only a quarter of the desks in the open IT workspace were occupied by the weekend crew. Kevin was in his office in the far corner.

A line of empty Monster cans ran around the edge of his desk.

Drake knocked on the open door. "I hope what I asked you to do isn't the reason you worked all night, Kevin."

Without looking up, the young hacker waved him over. "Astrid's a pretty sophisticated yacht, Mr. Drake. It's using a top-notch encrypted GPS navigation and autopilot system. It took me a little longer than I thought it would to break the encryption, but I'm almost there. Pull up a chair and watch."

Drake pulled a chair from in front of the desk around next to him and watched the young man's fingers flying around his keyboard.

"The spoofing device I built allowed me to send a fake GPS satellite signal to the yacht last night from the marina parking lot. The fake signal had a Trojan horse that got me into the yacht's IT system. I haven't had time to look at everything, but I thought the CCTV security cameras would give you a chance to look around. Have a look."

The monitor closest to Drake came alive with a view

from a camera looking at the aft swimming pool. Two security guards were on each side of the pool standing under the overhang from the deck above.

"See if you can find any interior cameras. I'm looking for the man you used the marina cameras to look for. If you haven't seen him leave, he's still on board."

One by one, they switched from one CCTV camera to the next looking for James Davis. Half a dozen crewmen were seen moving about the yacht, but James Davis wasn't with them. There were no cameras in any of the staterooms or entertaining areas. The security system was focused on anyone coming on board and then moving about the yacht, not what they were doing in their staterooms or while they were being entertained.

Before returning to his exploration of the Astrid's IT system, Kevin asked if there was anything else Drake wanted to see.

"See if there's anything in there about the young Saudi we saw arriving by helicopter. Maybe a file or something that will tell us why he was on the yacht."

For the next five minutes, Kevin searched for anything pertaining to Ali Mohammad. One file was labeled AM and he opened it.

Drake leaned closer to study the image on the monitor. It was a view of a large living area with one wall devoted to an entertainment and video display and another to a service counter and wet bar. The far side of the room had a floor-to-ceiling window that spanned its entire length with a view of the city's skyline. The image appeared to be a still shot of a luxury condo.

"There," Drake said, pointing to a moving spot outside the far window. "It's a plane. This is a live feed from someone's high-rise apartment or condo. If AM stands for Ali Mohammad, Guzman has surveillance on the young Saudi. Now we do as well. Good work, Kevin."

Chapter Forty-Six

DRAKE HURRIED down another flight of stairs to the second floor to find Morales. If Guzman was monitoring the activities and parties of Ali Mohammad, they had more than a casual relationship. Something was going on and he wanted to know what it was.

He walked into the Operations lounge and suddenly remembered that Morales told him he was taking the Black Hornet drone out that morning to spy on Ali's condo. He didn't know Morales' cell number, but the on-duty operations officer would know how to get him to call in.

On the way back to his office, he walked by the conference room as the briefing for the Israeli security guards was breaking up. Casey motioned for him to join them.

Ten men stood around the conference table. They were former airport security guard trainers who traveled around teaching airport and rail security personnel things Israel had learned the hard way. Casey had hired them for one month to demonstrate to Sound Transit a way to back up its new chemical detection system that was effective and unobtrusive enough for its urbane customers.

A two-man team in street clothes would be posted at five stations along the Link Light
Rail line; at Husky Stadium, Westlake, Pioneer Square, the International District and at SeaTac Airport. The trainers were older than the security guards seen at most Israeli airports, but they still had the look of vigilant military men and were fully capable of fulfilling their duties.

Casey introduced him to the Israelis. "Drake was my partner in Delta Force and we fought the same enemy you're still fighting today. He's a lawyer and desk jockey now, but it was his idea to see if we could modify your techniques to work in our ACLU-sensitized society."

Drake shook hands with each of the men and said he would be back later to go over his security assessment with them.

In his office down the hall, he asked the operations officer to patch him through to Morales.

"Good morning, boss. How'd that sofa in your office work last night?"

"Slept like a baby. Kept having dreams about a shrunken head on my plate at breakfast."

"I'm going to miss the little guy." Morales sighed and then laughed. "but that sure was fun."

"Yes, it was. Have you flown the hornet yet?"

"Just setting up."

"Hold off for now. I don't want to spook him if he spots it outside his window. I want you to ID anyone going in and out of his condo."

"There's not much traffic until his parties each night. That gives me plenty of time to set something up."

"When you're finished, come back. There's something I want to show you."

Drake grabbed the file with his Link rail security assessment report and returned to the conference room. When he finished briefing the Israeli teams, Kevin McRoberts was waiting for him in the hallway.

"Mr. Drake, there's something you need to see."

They took the stairs down to the floor below and stood behind Kevin's desk. The image frozen on one of the three monitors showed Ali Mohammad standing in front of a dozen young Arab men.

Kevin hit a key to play the video.

"After he finishes talking to them, they pass around pipes and what looks like hashish and they all have a good smoke. It looks like a ritual of some sort. I don't read lips, but if we can find someone who does we can find out what he's telling them."

Drake studied the faces of the men. He didn't have enough information about any of them to do any predictive profiling. But the eyes of the men, as they focused on the words of Ali Mohammad, told him all he needed to know. They would do anything he asked them to do.

"Kevin, I'll find someone who can read lips. In the meantime, isolate the faces of each of these men and put them in a separate file. Morales is also working on identifying everyone going and coming from this condo. When we have a better idea of why they're passing the pipes around, maybe we'll find out what these guys are up to."

He left the IT division and started upstairs to his office and then turned around and headed down to the parking garage. There was enough time to drive to the Woodmark to take a shower and check out before Morales returned.

With the way things were heating up, he didn't know when he would have time to shave and change clothes for a while.

———

WHEN THE SECURITY gate rolled back at the employee entrance to the PSS headquarters and Drake's gray Porsche Cayman rolled out, two men watched from half a block away. "That's his Porsche," one of the men said. "Let the others know he's moving." "Did you get a good enough look at the security gate?" the other man asked.

"It's reinforced just like the one at the main gate. I'm not sure a semi could ram through it."

"Then they'll have to find a way to get past security at the guard shack today or on Monday."

"What if he doesn't come back here?"

"He will. He didn't go back to his hotel last night, he'll do the same tonight. He's smart enough to know that Guzman will try again. That's why he staying here; this place is built like a fortress."

Chapter Forty-Seven

GUZMAN FINISHED EATING breakfast alone in his stateroom and went to his private study. His first call was to an old cartel friend who was now operating out of Vancouver, British Columbia.

"Armando, *como estas*? I hope I did not wake you."

"Years ago I would have sent men to kill you for using my private number so early in the day. But now I am a new man. I exercise and watch what I eat. The women like me almost as much as they like my son."

"How is Roberto?"

"He's in a bit of trouble. A young woman claims he raped her, but I hear she's going to be leaving the country before the trial. Otherwise, he's fine."

"Is there anything I can do?"

"No, but I think you called because you think there's something I can do for you?"

"Do you remember a small jet that went down a year or so ago? A friend of ours put something under the passenger's seat."

"Yes."

"I need to buy some of that something."

"How much of that something?"

"Enough for a big building."

"That will be very expensive but then you own a bank."

"I do. How soon could the something be delivered?"

"I could have someone deliver it to you in an hour or so."

"Do you know where I am?"

"I always know where important men I might need to call are staying, senor."

"Thank you, Armando. Say hello to Roberto for me."

Guzman opened Drake's file on his laptop and added a list of things he would need for the disposal operation:

1. A list of PSS suppliers who might make weekend deliveries
2. A delivery truck
3. SEMTEX
4. Remote detonator
5. Building permit blueprint for PSS building
6. A martyr
7. Martyr's suicide vest
8. Martyr's video blaming PSS employees/former military men for collateral damage that killed the martyr's family
9. Name of martyr's mosque for donation
10. Name of martyr's family for donation

The Americans preferred to call the jihadists who attacked them "lone wolves". That way they didn't have to dig too deep into their relationships and actual motivations, for fear of offending any of their Muslim citizens. But, if they did, he would make sure there was plenty of evidence to explain the actions of the martyr and nothing that would put them on his trail.

His next call would take a little more finesse than the call to Armando Valencia. Ali Mohammad didn't like him, and cooperated to the degree that he did only because he needed the nerve agent devices for his attack on Seattle's light rail system. Asking him to sacrifice one of his fellow jihadists, and perhaps student friend, had to make sense to the arrogant young man.

Either that or the implied threat that refusal would bring him personal shame or even retribution. Guzman found Mohammad's contact information and called him.

"Hello?

"I need to see you."

"When?" "Now.

"Why?"

"There's something I need you to do."

"You know our schedule. I don't have time right now."

"You'll have to make time or your schedule won't matter. There's an obstacle that must be removed before we go forward."

He thought he heard Ali grinding his teeth.

"Send someone to get me. Same place, fifteen minutes."

Guzman called Eric, his bodyguard, to dispatch the helicopter to pick up Mohammad and then return to help coordinate his plan. Five minutes later, Eric stood in front of his desk.

"We have a lot to do in a short amount of time. Valencia will have the SEMTEX here in an hour or so. When it's here, make the arrangements to transfer the payment wherever Valencia wants it to go. Have IT find out which companies make regular deliveries to PSS. When we know, we will need a truck, one that we can make look like a truck from the delivery company, or borrow one from the company that we can use."

"Will we need to beef up the truck to breach the perimeter?" Eric asked.

"If we can identify a company that makes weekend deliveries, probably not but we'll see. Mohammad will supply the *shaheed*, the martyr, on rather short notice to drive it. Let's plan on supplying the suicide vest and a remote trigger ourselves to make sure it detonates when and where we want it to."

"Is there anything else?"

"Check with the men you sent to follow the attorney and bring Mohammad to me when he arrives. That is all, Eric."

Guzman stood and gazed out the window of his study. The yacht next to his on the starboard side partially blocked the view of the Seattle skyline, but he could see the top of the Space Needle and a few of the taller buildings to the south of it. There were a few things he had wanted to see in the city, but the presence of the attorney on the dock outside the other day had made sightseeing too risky. The next time he visited, however, the man would no longer be a problem.

The thought of the man reminded him the *Confessor* was still on the yacht, waiting to interrogate Drake. There was still a chance they would be able to grab the man before attacking the PSS headquarters. And for that reason, he had allowed the sadistic little man to stay on board. But as soon as the attorney was dead, he wanted the *Confessor* out of his sight and off his yacht.

His bodyguard knocked on the door of his study. "Josef is headed our way with Mohammad, ETA in ten minutes. The attorney checked out of his hotel and has returned to PSS."

"Excellent news! He's mine now."

Chapter Forty-Eight

GUZMAN WAS SIPPING a Campari and soda at the sky lounge bar in the main salon while he waited for Ali Mohammad to arrive. He needed the young Saudi's assistance and counted on his devotion to jihad to deliver it. He hoped it was enough.

He heard the Sikorsky approaching and listened as it flew in and then settled down on the helipad. Two minutes later, Mohammad skipped down the outside staircase and walked briskly toward him.

Guzman moved behind the bar and poured his guest a glass of Campari and soda. "Have a seat while we talk and enjoy this refreshing drink."

Mohammad sat on one of the bar stools and left his drink setting on the counter. "Is this obstacle one of yours or one of mine? I can take care of my own obstacles; that's why I was chosen to lead this mission."

Guzman admired the young man's confidence, but it was time to put his role into perspective. "You were chosen because your father was willing to pay the bill for this adventure. That, however, is beside the point. You are here to prove to the Americans that they need to fear your cause here in America, not just when they travel to Paris or Brussels. I am here to make sure you are successful. Your sponsors have given me the authority to close you down if I'm not satisfied that you will be."

"You were paid to deliver the nerve agents and nothing more!" Mohammad spit out as he stood, knocking the bar stool back onto the floor. "Give me the dispersers and leave. I don't need you hanging around and looking over my shoulder."

Guzman held up a hand to stop two of his bodyguards rushing to his aid after hearing the bar stool crash to the floor. "It's okay. Our guest just stood up too fast. Give us another ten minutes and then you can escort him back to the helipad."

"I don't need another ten minutes. I'm ready to go now," Mohammad said over his shoulder as he turned and started toward the outside staircase.

This time Guzman waved his bodyguards forward and said, "Sit down, Mohammad. You may want to hang around to hear what your father has to say about refusing to help me."

The two bodyguards grabbed Mohammad's arms and spun him around to return him to the sky lounge bar. Guzman stayed behind the bar and took his cell phone out to call Mohammad's father.

"I'm sorry this was required," he said to Mohammad, who was trying to pull his arms free from the vice-like grips of the bodyguards. "There's too much at stake for both of us if we can't work together."

Guzman stood patiently behind the bar as his call went through to Mohammad's father in London.

"Faisal, it's me. I need a minute of your time. Of course, I can wait until you close the door of your office."

Mohammad had stopped struggling and sat still in angry anticipation of what his father would say.

Guzman nodded and continued when Faisal returned to the call. "I need your son to help me with something to assist our efforts here, but he apparently misunderstands my authority and my role here. Would you be so kind as to have a word with him?"

Another nod and he handed his phone to a grimacing and subdued son.

"Father, I—" Mohammad stopped talking and listened. "I will, Father. I won't let you down."

Guzman took his phone back and thanked his London associate before continuing his conversation with Mohammad. "The obstacle I mentioned is someone who has caused us a lot of trouble in the last several years. When I learned that he was here in Seattle, your sponsors told me to eliminate him so there would be no possible way for him to interfere with your mission. That's why I need your help."

"What is it you need?" Mohammad said quietly.

Guzman told him as much as he wanted him to know; he needed a martyr prepared to drive a truck loaded with explosives to a target there in Seattle. He did not disclose the identity of the target or its location.

"This needs to happen tonight. Call me when your man is ready and I'll send someone to come and get him."

"Will there be a reward available for his family?"

"There will be money transferred to his family and his mosque."

"He's already made his video. Do you want him to make another with this man mentioned?"

Guzman considered the question and decided the original video would be enough. With the other *shaheeds* attacking the light rail line, the relationship to the attack on PSS headquarters would be questioned initially. But when the backgrounds of the men who worked for PSS were discovered, the media would quickly connect the dots; a righteous act of revenge for the horrid atrocities committed by the PSS men in the war on terror.

"His video will be enough. Make sure it's discovered along with the other videos," Guzman said, looking at his watch to signal that the meeting was over.

When the two bodyguards left with Mohammad, he saw there was a new text on his phone. The SEMTEX from Armando Valencia had arrived. Now all they needed was a reason to make a delivery to PSS on a weekend and a driver to deliver his response to the shrunken head he'd discovered that morning on his breakfast table.

Chapter Forty-Nine

DRAKE RETURNED to PSS headquarters refreshed after a long, hot shower and a shave in his room at the Woodmark before checking out. Wearing his favorite pair of jeans and a dark blue polo, he was ready for whatever surprises the day had in store for him.

Casey had called before he left the Woodmark to confirm that he'd been able to reach the PSS employee who handled the interpreting and translating needs of PSS. Chris Hayek was a first-generation Lebanese-American who had served as a military interpreter in the 223rd Military Intelligence Battalion. Captain Hayek was fluent in Arabic and acquainted with its various dialects. He was waiting back at PSS for Drake to look at the video of Ali Mohammad speaking to the men in his condo.

On the short drive from the Woodmark back to the PSS building, Drake noticed a black Lincoln Navigator that followed him out of the hotel parking lot. It stayed two cars back and continued on slowly when he turned off and stopped at the employee security gate to punch in the code.

It had the same Alamo rental sticker on the back bumper as the one he drove by earlier a half a block away from the PSS building when he left to drive to the hotel.

He had a good idea the men in the luxury black SUV were Guzman's.

Before he locked the Cayman and took the stairs to meet Kevin McRoberts and Chris Hayek in IT, he slipped a second loaded magazine for his Kimber in the left front pocket of his jeans. If they came after him again, the fourteen rounds of CorBon's 160-grain .45 caliber ammo he was carrying was all the confidence he needed for the encounter.

Drake ran up the stairs to the third floor and found Hayek standing with his arms folded across his chest staring at one of the monitors on Kevin's cluttered desk. Slim and fit in appearance, his thirty-something brown eyes were squinting slightly as he focused on Ali's animated lips.

After shaking hands, Drake thanked him for coming in on the weekend and asked him if he knew what Mohammad was saying.

"Only about thirty percent of sounds can be seen on a person's lips, so I can't give you a word-for-word translation of what he's saying. But I know what he's doing; he's getting these men ready to become martyrs."

Kevin almost dropped the can of Monster he was holding. "You mean he's preparing them to blow themselves up?"

"That or some other way to reach Paradise."

"Tell me why you think that," Drake said. "If you're only getting thirty percent of what he's saying, how can you be so certain?"

Hayek stepped back from the monitor and faced Drake. "I speak Arabic fluently. My parents still used it around the house when I was young. But I've also studied the Koran. I get enough of what he's saying to fill in the blanks, so to speak. When he says "killing" and "way of Allah", he's referring to this passage in the Koran:

'Let those who fight in the way of Allah who sell the life of this world for the other. Who so fights in the way of Allah, be he slain or be he victorious, on him We shall bestow a vast reward.'

"Then he uses the words 'act', 'elevates' and 'one hundred times'. He telling them to remember that the Koran says:

'Another act which elevates the position of a man in Paradise to a grade one hundred times higher, Jihad in the way of Allah! Jihad in the way of Allah!'

"These are a couple of the most well-known verses of violence in the Koran. In my opinion, what you're seeing is this man giving these guys a pep talk before they go off on some mission of jihad."

Drake didn't study the Koran but he was familiar with some of the practices of the Islamic fighters who used it to justify their murderous ways.

"Have you watched the rest of this video where they bring out the hash pipes and all have a good smoke?" he asked.

"I saw that and you're probably thinking about the original assassins of Alamut who were said to use hashish to prepare them for their missions. ISIS today uses an amphetamine known as Captagon that's purported to give their fighters a thirst for fighting and killing. If this guy is using hash for the same purpose, he's going old school. But it supports my conclusion about what he's doing in this video."

Drake thought about what Hayek was saying in the context of Guzman bringing the Saudi to his yacht and having a video recording of the activity in the condo. It didn't make any sense, unless Guzman was partnering with him in some terrorist activity. If Guzman was Ryan Walker, the head of the shadowy organization known as the Alliance, however, it would make sense.

Walker had partnered with terrorists on at least three other occasions he knew of; in San Francisco in a plot to bring down the U.S. energy grid; in Washington, D.C. when he was discovered to be the banker funneling illegal foreign campaign contributions for a Muslim Brotherhood operation; and most recently the plot of the Iranians and Russians to smuggle a missile across the Texas border for an EMP strike.

If Guzman was Walker, it was time to prove it and end his behind-the-scenes reign of terror.

Drake told Hayek and McRoberts to keep working through the available videos they had accessed on the yacht's IT system. He needed to go see how Morales was doing with identifying the men in Mohammad's condo. If these guys were jihadists who were preparing for something, he needed to know who they were and where they lived.

And he needed to get with Casey and figure out their plan of action. This had the potential to be something big if Guzman was involved with jihadists.

Chapter Fifty

DRAKE DECIDED to find Casey before he talked with Morales. He found him in his office with the Israeli team leader going over the plan to deploy the security guards at the five busiest Link Light Rail stations.

When he heard what they were talking about, he stepped in and closed the door behind him.

"We have something you should look at before you dispatch your men," he told the team leader. "We may be able to identify some young men who are being prepared for some sort of jihadist mission here in Seattle."

Casey moved his head slightly from side to side to let Drake know he hadn't said anything about Guzman and/or the young Ali Mohammad. "Have we confirmed any of their identities yet?"

"Not yet, I'm waiting to hear from Morales."

The team leader turned in his seat and asked, "Is this intel from your government?"

Drake looked to Casey. There was no need to involve the Israelis in the investigation of Guzman and Moham-

225

mad, but if the men in Mohammad's condo were jihadists in the making, the man needed to know it.

Casey shrugged. "Go ahead and tell him what we have. Kevin filled me in after I called Hayek."

"We've come across a video of a wealthy Saudi talking jihad with a gathering of young men."

"Have you provided this video to your government?"

"Not yet. We don't have anything to support our interpreter's analysis right now."

"But you believe he's on to something, yes?"

"I do."

The team leader turned back to face Casey. "As you know, in Israel the airlines provide their own security at the airport. I am used to working with my government in situations like this. Would you like me to show this video to a friend in Israeli intelligence to see if he knows anything about these men?"

Casey looked to Drake. "It couldn't hurt."

"If we take this to the FBI or DHS, they won't be pleased that we involved Israeli intelligence before coming to them. We might get the same treatment we did before the attack at the chemical weapons depot two years ago."

"Maybe we should have someone else take it to the FBI, someone like the former FBI agent we know," Casey slyly suggested. "We'll see if she has what it takes to be effective in her new role at PSS."

"If we get the goods on these guys, I'll ask her. In the meantime, we need to talk about that other matter I'm working on. When you finish here, let me know."

Drake excused himself and walked down the hall to his own office. Asking Liz to be their liaison with the FBI was a brilliant idea. As his father-in-law's staff representative to the Senate's Select Intelligence Committee in Washington, she had the connections and the reputation that would make the FBI want to listen to her.

The thought of how Machiavellian his old friend had become as the CEO of PSS made him smile. When they worked together as Delta Force operatives, they had often used deception and cunning to carry out their missions. Casey had since learned to operate at a higher level of craftiness in building PSS into the effective and successful international security firm it now was.

As he settled into the leather executive chair behind his desk and pushed back so he could extend his legs and relax, he let his eyes soft focus on a little, white cloud floating high above Lake Washington. It was time to think about Guzman and Mohammad. What the hell were they up to?

If Guzman was who he thought he was, it could be anything. But who was Ali

Mohammad and how did he fit into the picture? Since 9/11 and the investigations that followed, Saudi involvement in terrorist activities had been largely hidden behind Muslim charitable organizations that covertly funded jihadist activities in non-Muslim countries. Maybe the Sunni Muslims of Saudi Arabia were jealous of the attention the world was paying to ISIS and wanted some press for themselves and Mohammad was their front man.

Or maybe Mohammad was just a pampered and wealthy princeling who wanted his friends to think he was a fierce jihadi who talked of dangerous things and shared some good hashish. Whatever his game was, his association with Guzman made him potentially dangerous and someone to keep an eye on.

So what was he going to do about Walter Guzman, a.k.a. Ryan Walker? The FBI wouldn't waste a minute of its precious time investigating the man based on his association with James Davis, a felon and Neo-Nazi white supremacist from southern Oregon. Nor would they care that he had flown Mohammad to and from his mega yacht, unless they saw the video obtained illegally by PSS's young hacker, which Casey could not afford to hand over.

Even the clumsy attempt to abduct him in broad daylight in front of the Woodmark Hotel wouldn't be enough to interest law enforcement or the FBI because he couldn't prove Guzman was behind it.

It was going to take something convincing before anyone would raise a finger to help him find out what Guzman and Mohammad were up to. If the FBI could interview a terrorist several times and not be concerned until it was too late and the person shot up a nightclub or blew himself up in an airport, Drake's unsupported suspicions would certainly be ignored.

Maybe Morales could come up with something that would be helpful. Maybe use the little drone to video Mohammad passing out suicide vests to his men. Maybe catch Guzman smuggling WMDs into a terrorist cell.

Given his past encounters with the FBI, whatever he presented to them had to be so convincing that J. Edgar Hoover would applaud from his grave.

Chapter Fifty-One

GUZMAN WATCHED the handoff of the sarin gas dispersers to Ali's man on the CCTV display in his study.

Ten aerosol deodorant dispensers in their original packaging were in a cardboard box sealed with packing tape. The modified lookalike dispensers were impossible to distinguish from home mist deodorant dispensers found in any food market and store in America. They could spray their deadly mist automatically on a timer or manually by pushing the test button.

Carried inside a backpack or rolling suitcase, they were undiscoverable. They would even pass the sniff test of the best drug dog because the liquid sarin gas was stored in a speciallydesigned glass container. Made in a chemical plant captured in Syria, the devices were expensive and new; the attack on Seattle's light rail system was to be the maiden test of the devices in the West.

The martyr brought to the yacht appeared to be calm and ready to drive to the PSS headquarters. He'd been instructed to drive the truck to the security gate and tell the guard he needed a signature from someone in purchasing before he could complete his delivery. Once inside, he was to get as close to the building as possible before detonating the bomb and beginning his trip to Paradise.

The truck was also rigged for a remote detonation, should the young man lose his nerve.

Guzman glanced at his watch and saw that it was three thirty in the afternoon. They were running out of time. A delivery after five p.m. on a Saturday would be suspicious, even more so with a driver that looked to be Middle Eastern.

Unless he underestimated the PSS men, their military experience in Iraq and Afghanistan would trigger an immediate alarm when an unexpected truck pulled up to the security gate. In case the truck didn't make it past the security gate, he made sure that it was loaded with three times the SEMTEX required to bring down a building the size of the PSS headquarters and kill everyone inside.

Guzman used an encrypted cell phone to call his head bodyguard. "Eric, is the truck here?"

"It's waiting a mile away."

"Come and take the martyr to the truck. I don't want the truck seen anywhere near the

Astrid."

"Understood. Am I still the trigger man?"

"You are. Video the attack. I want to see that he's finally dead."

He stayed in his studio watching the CCTV display on the wall behind his desk until the martyr left the yacht escorted by two of his men. They were taking him to the Staples business delivery truck Eric had stolen the night before rigged with the SEMTEX. Surveillance had seen a Staples truck make a delivery two days before and Staples'

IT system detailed a purchase of six new Epson printers for PSS when it was hacked. A follow-up delivery of replaceable ink packs for the new printers would be expected, given the way printer ink was used up so quickly.

Guzman used the yacht's intercom to call the yacht's captain. "You may leave the marina now. I want to be underway immediately."

AT FOUR FIFTEEN p.m. on Saturday afternoon, a Staples delivery truck pulled up beside the security guard's booth at the PSS building. The driver rolled down his window to speak with the security guard.

"I have a delivery of ink packs for your printers," the driver said and handed out a clipboard with a purchase order on it. "I need to have the purchasing agent sign the order before I can make the delivery."

The security guard took the clipboard and looked at the purchase order. "Is this a scheduled delivery? Your company was just here a couple days ago."

The driver looked around nervously before remembering what he was supposed to say.

"They forgot the replacement ink packs when they brought the new printers."

Pat Conners was a fifty-nine-year-old retired police officer who worked for PSS as a security guard to supplement his retirement income. In his thirty-year career, he'd worked everything from patrol to robbery and vice. He recognized the darting eyes of someone who was not telling the truth and was anxious about something.

"Let me see if I can find someone to sign your purchase order," Conners said and stepped back to close the sliding bullet-proof window. He picked up the phone to call the operations duty officer. "Mac, there's a Staples delivery driver here and says he needs someone from purchasing to sign for some ink packs. He looks hinky."

"I'll run a scan and see if he's been here before," the duty officer said.

PSS used a facial-recognition system as part of its security apparatus that incorporated national criminal and sex offender database information as well as OFAC, OID and terrorist watch list information. They also added information to the security system the company had developed on its own.

The duty officer ran the image of the delivery driver's face through the PSS facial recognition program and saw it pause and flash a warning.

"Pat, tell him the purchasing agent is on his way out and then slip out the back door of the booth," the duty officer said calmly. "This guy is someone Morales has under surveillance and he's flagged him as a potential jihadist."

"Thanks Mac," Conners said and slid the window open again. "Sir, the purchasing agent is on his way out. Please pull your truck over to the side while we wait for him."

When the delivery driver backed up the truck to be able to move it over to the marked waiting space, he saw that the security booth was empty. With an anguished scream and then a quick prayer, he completed his deadly delivery and hoped that Allah was pleased.

DRAKE WAS STILL in the leather chair behind his desk thinking about Guzman and Mohammad when the building rocked from an explosion. The two framed photos of the Oregon coast on the wall to his left fell to the floor and the brass piano desk lamp on the back bar behind him toppled off as well.

He ran out into the hall and turned to sprint to the east side of the building where he believed the explosion had occurred. His office and Casey's were both on the western side facing Lake Washington. The employee and service entrance to the building were on the other side facing the street and the security booth.

Halfway down the hall that bisected the upper floor he saw shards of broken glass and debris on the carpeted floor of the hallway. The explosion had blown out the bullet-proof band of windows that ringed the top floor of the building. When he reached the hall running north and south in front of the offices on that side of the building, he ran to each office to check for casualties. No one appeared to have been in the offices at the time of the explosion.

That was a blessing because the shards of flying glass would have sliced through anyone at their desks that morning.

Drake crunched across the floor of the last office and looked down. A massive crater marked the location of the explosion at the security gate. The security booth and gate were gone and the reinforced eight-foot high concrete wall along the street was blown away for thirty yards in each direction.

Casey ran into the littered room and stood beside him. "Car bomb?"

"Looks like it with that crater. I'll go see if I can find the security guard," Drake said as he ran out of the office.

Chapter Fifty-Two

HE BOLTED out the door at the bottom of the stairs and ran through the underground parking garage. There were only three ways in and out of the building; the main entrance on the east side and the delivery dock and underground parking garage on the south side. Exiting up the ramp from the underground garage was the quickest way to the detonation site.

Drake punched in the code to open the black, steel, reinforced security gate and looked out as it rolled up into the ceiling. The blast had sheared off the trees and shrubs from the visitor parking area on the east side and scattered them all the way across the paved area at the south end of the building. Debris from the main gate and security booth confirmed the power of the blast.

Running toward the main gate, he looked for the security guard. He expected to see human remains everywhere. He didn't see any until he rounded the southeast corner of the building. The body of the security guard was lying face down twenty feet away.

Blood spread from wounds caused by flying shrapnel piercing his back and legs. Drake knelt and checked for a pulse on the carotid artery and felt a faint one. The security guard had somehow survived the blast.

Drake stood and looked at the front of the PSS building, amazed that it was largely undamaged except that all the windows were blown inward from the blast. The ground floor's exterior solid, fortified concrete wall had withstood the blast, but its overlay of stamped black concrete was pockmarked with fractures and cracks. The thick vertical glass windows on either side of the main door were shattered but the massive carved oak door lined with lead was still standing.

First responders raced toward the PSS headquarters with sirens combining in a cacophony of wailing noise. Drake stayed beside the fallen security guard until paramedics ran around the blast crater onto the grounds and saw him waving his arms.

As he backed away to allow them to work, Casey ran over to him. "We were lucky. No one was injured inside from the flying glass. I'm surprised there wasn't more damage to the building."

"You were smart to build it to foreign embassy specs," Drake said. "Even so, with a crater that big there should be more damage. Maybe Guzman got his hands on some bad explosives."

Casey put a hand up. "We don't know it was Guzman."

"I know it was Guzman and so do you."

"Let's keep that to ourselves right now. I'll deal with the police while you go think of a way to prove it was Guzman."

Casey marched off to meet firemen spilling out of their trucks while Drake jogged back around the building to the ramp down to the parking garage and the stairs up to his office. His mind was racing far faster than his feet as he willed his mind to slow down and think strategically.

His immediate impulse was to swing through the PSS armory and grab one of the

Remington ACR combat rifles the VIP protection teams used and head to the marina to storm Guzman's mega yacht. An innocent man was badly injured because Guzman had used an indiscriminate weapon of destruction to take him out. Two could play that game and he didn't give a damn if Guzman and his whole crew had to go down with the ship.

While that idea soothed his pounding bloodlust for an instant, he knew he needed more than his firm conviction of Guzman's involvement before he went to war with the man. He needed a confession from one of Guzman's men or something that would directly tie him to the car bomb.

Getting the confession might be easier than finding direct evidence from anything that was left of the bomber or his bomb.

Drake called Morales. "Where are you?"

"Headed back."

"Don't. Someone just exploded a car bomb here. First responders are all over the place. Meet me at the marina instead."

"Was it Guzman?"

"Who else could it be?"

"What's the plan?"

"I'll think of one on the way."

Drake stopped at the PSS armory on the way down to his car and picked up two of the new Remington ACRs and four loaded Magpul 30 round 5.56 magazines in case they were needed. The line from *The Untouchables* flashed through his mind, "Don't bring a knife to a gunfight," even though the ACRs were the knives compared to the car bomb Guzman had sent their way.

It took twenty minutes in late afternoon Saturday traffic to reach the Nautical Landing marina. The first thing he saw when he drove past the marina office was that Guzman's yacht, Astrid III, was not moored along the second concrete dock.

Morales was leaning against the door of the white surveillance van.

"I checked in the office. It left an hour ago," he said when Drake got out of the Cayman and joined him.

"They say where the yacht was going?"

"The manager said the captain mentioned cruising Alaska's Inside Passage, but there's no way to know if that's where it's really going."

"Finding the yacht won't be a problem, Kevin will know where it is. The problem is proving Guzman was responsible for the car bomb and getting anyone to do something about it before he leaves U.S. territorial waters."

"What can I do to help?"

Drake looked out to the blue waters of Lake Union Guzman had just sailed through and shrugged his shoulders. "We can't do anything about Guzman right now. Keep working on the men in Ali Mohammad's condo. If we can prove they're involved in some terrorist plot and that Guzman is aiding them in some way, the U.S. will chase him to the ends of the earth."

When he got back to PSS headquarters in Kirkland, the Seattle PD, the FBI and DHS had replaced the first responders and cordoned off the area. The officer who checked his ID before letting him enter through the employee security gate informed him that the security guard had died on the way to the hospital.

Chapter Fifty-Three

HE FOUND Casey in the first-floor lobby talking with a uniformed SPD officer. When the officer left, Casey waved him over.

"Go see Kevin. We ID'd the driver at the guard booth."

"How?"

Casey turned his back to the cluster of law enforcement in the center of the lobby before speaking. "Kevin uploaded the facial scans of the men in Ali's condo to our security system. When Pat, our security guard, called the duty officer to say the guy driving the van looked "hinky", the officer told Pat to get out of the booth. Unfortunately, he didn't get far enough away before the driver detonated the bomb."

"Have you shared that information with anyone?"

"Not yet, I thought we better talk about it first. If we do, we'll have to explain how we acquired the driver's image. I'm not sure we want to do that just yet."

"I agree. I'll go see Kevin and then let's talk upstairs when you can get away."

Drake left and headed toward the stairs. He glanced

over his shoulder and saw the representatives of the various agencies surrounding Casey. FBI or DHS, he knew it would be a while before they finished with the CEO of PSS.

With news of the attack all over the media, employees had returned to work to assess the damage and see what they could do. Most of them had been in the military and had seen worse, but the clenched-jaws and angry eyes expressed their silent anger. There was going to be hell to pay and the men Drake passed on the way to the IT section would want to be in on it.

When Drake walked back to the young hacker's office, his first thought was that he was in some sort of a trance. His head was bobbing back and forth, resting on fingers massaging his temples, and he was softly repeating some sort of mantra.

After waiting a long minute for the ritual to end, Drake knocked lightly on the door. "Kevin, you okay?"

"Come on in, Mr. Drake. I was just taking a five-minute nap."

"Have you been up all night?"

"Technically yes, but I'm used to it from playing in video game tournaments. Did Mr. Casey tell you about the driver?"

"He said you put the images of the men in Mohammad's condo into our security system.

Smart move."

"Not smart enough to save the guard's life."

"That's not your fault, Kevin. Is there any way for us to know who he is?"

"I hacked into the university's admission's office computers to see if he was a student, but he's not in their system. I tried to find him in the government's immigration or visa records, but he's not in any government database I know of."

Drake pulled a chair around the desk so he could see beyond the wall of Monster energy drink cans stacked between the three monitors on the desk. "He's probably in the country illegally. Have you tried to ID the other men in Mohammad's condo?"

"Not yet, but I will."

Drake clasped his hands behind his head and stared at the ceiling for a moment. "The others are likely to be here illegally as well. I also need to know where Guzman's yacht is. It left the marina. When you've found it, see what else you can find on its computers. If Guzman's on the run, I don't care if he knows he's being hacked. I need something that will prove he's involved with these terrorists so we can turn this over to the FBI or DHS."

"If he's moving, the yacht will use its GPS system and my spoofing override will be noticed. When it was moored at the marina, they weren't watching it like they will be now." "Can you send them a little off course if we need to, just enough so they won't notice it?" "If they're in open water, I should be able to do it."

"Find the yacht and let's give it a try. I don't want him to reach international waters," Drake said as he stood up. "Do you want me to send someone up with some food?"

Kevin spun his chair around and patted a stack of three cases of the energy drink along the wall. "I'll be fine, Mr. Drake."

Drake shook his head as he walked back through the empty IT section. He'd be twitching all over the place with the amount of caffeine Kevin had in his system.

Back in his office, he called Morales to let him know that they had positively ID'd the jihadist in the van as one of the men in Mohammad's condo. Time to double the effort to identify and locate all the others.

It was now six thirty, nine thirty on the East Coast. Time to call Washington for help in dealing with two of his least favorite federal agencies.

"Hi Liz."

"Hello handsome."

"What would it take to get you to pack a bag and fly to Seattle tomorrow?"

"There are several things that might work, let me think."

"I need your help."

"That wasn't on my shortlist but that will do. What's going on?"

"Someone just detonated a car bomb at the PSS front gate. We need you to meet with the authorities when it's time."

"My two former employers, the FBI and DHS?"

"Bingo."

Chapter Fifty-Four

ALI MOHAMMAD WAS THROWING another of his parties for his friends as Morales maneuvered the Black Hornet drone outside the window of the luxury condo. The men he was looking for were all there.

So were the provocatively dressed, beautiful women, looking more like prostitutes now than when they arrived by limousine dressed like university students. They were standing along the far wall quietly watching the men who were being inspected military style by Mohammad.

Morales kept the drone's camera on video as Mohammad moved along the line of men. He kissed each man on both cheeks and said something before handing him a small item wrapped in gold foil. When he reached the end of the line, he stepped back in front of them all and raised his hand above his head with his index finger pointing skyward. The men all did the same thing and yelled something in unison.

That was all Morales needed to confirm his suspicions about men in Mohammad's condo. The raised index finger was the gesture ISIS used to identify its cause and affirm its allegiance to the ideology that demanded the destruction of the West. These boys *were* jihadists!

He continued to watch through the lens of the Black Hornet drone as the party seemed to be breaking up. It was time to call the drone in and get over to the condo building.

Two PSS men working surveillance with him were nearby, waiting for him to drive over from the lakeside park where he had deployed the drone. When Mohammad's men left the building, they would each follow one of the men to where they were living. With any luck that night they would be able to identify the men and find out more about them.

The drone returned and hovered an arm's length away until Morales reached out and cupped the small drone in his hand and shut the power off on the control panel. He continued to be amazed at the ability of the little bird to do the things he wished he'd been able to do as a long range reconnaissance patrol (LRRP) ranger; see over the next ridge, see around corners, hunt for the enemy unseen and unheard from the air. Totally awesome.

He parked across the street from the high-rise condo building and checked in with the two members of his team using his handheld digital radio. "Are those two twelve-passenger vans idling at the curb waiting for our guys?"

"Just pulled up, we'll know soon enough."

Morales thought for a moment. "If the vans are for our guys, you two follow the first one and I'll take the second one. Forget about the women. First priority is finding where these guys are nesting."

When Mohammad's men walked out of the building and escorted five women into each of the vans, forgetting about the women was no longer necessary. It looked like the party wasn't over.

"Tailing these guys just got a little easier," Morales said. "They'll be distracted, but their drivers might not be. Keep your distance. Let me know when they get to where they're going."

As soon as the men and women were in the first van, it drove off followed by a blue PSS

Ford Explorer parked twenty-five yards behind it on the same side of the street. When the Explorer passed his position, he watched in his rearview mirror as a white PSS Tahoe pulled out and made a U-turn to follow the Explorer and the first van.

The second van waited until the van and the other two cars drove past and then made a Uturn and drove away in the opposite direction. Morales followed it in his white PSS van. It looked like it was "party on" in two locations.

"My van's headed in the opposite direction from you," Morales reported. "Keep an eye on your GPS and tell me where you are. If they're splitting up just to converge to see if they have tails, we'll switch off and trade vans."

"Roger that."

"Roger."

Morales followed the second van to 5th Avenue NE where it continued north.

Five minutes later, it was clear the vans were heading in two different directions.

"Looks like the first van is headed somewhere on Capitol Hill."

Morales confirmed the divergence. "Second van is heading north. Keep me posted."

He kept two vehicles between his van and the twelve-passenger van ahead. When it slowed to turn left on N. 145th Street, he followed and fell further back. Five blocks later the van turned right onto Meridian Avenue N.

It was a residential neighborhood with small homes fifty or sixty years old. Two cars were parked in most of the driveways he drove by or a pickup and an occasional boat or older RV. While Mohammad was living the high life in his condo, these boys were on a different budget entirely.

The van he followed continued up Meridian Avenue N until he saw its brake lights come on and it turned right into a driveway. He slowed but drove on past.

The house was a small, single-story house that had seen better days. Maybe a thousand square feet with an old, red, brick chimney and a red front door. The windows had wooden shutters that were partially opened and the lights inside were on in every room facing the street.

Morales made a U-turn a hundred yards beyond the house and pulled to the curb two houses away. When he shut of the engine and turned off the lights, the men were still helping the women out of the van. From the laughter and giggles he heard and the way the women were clinging to the men, the party was well on its way.

He picked up the radio and reported his position. "I'm parked in front of a small house on Meridian Avenue N in Evergreen. The occupants of the second van are inside. From the fondling I saw, I'd say this party will last a while."

"Roger that. The first van is in the parking lot of an apartment house on Capitol Hill. Everyone piled into Apartment 105 on the first floor. Same party scene here."

"All right, you two decide who gets the first four-hour shift and then trade off. I'll get someone to spell me in a bit. While we're waiting, I'll have IT find out who occupies these two places. These guys are probably dangerous, so stay alert. Let's meet back at headquarters tomorrow morning when we get some relief out here."

Morales unbuckled his seat belt and got comfortable

behind the wheel. The house had shrubs and overgrown plants hiding the lower half of the windows street-side and he assumed the same was true in the back. The drone would have to fly very close to the house to get a good view inside and, besides, he wasn't sure he wanted to see what was taking place in there. Better to be patient and wait to see what these yahoos were doing the next day.

Chapter Fifty-Five

WALTER GUZMAN WATCHED the video of the delivery truck exploding at the main gate of the PSS offices for the fifth time. He still couldn't understand why the driver hadn't been able to get closer to the building, why Drake was still alive.

He took a deep breath and turned away from the CCTV security display panel on the wall of his study. Perhaps his triggerman detonated the five pounds of SEMTEX prematurely.

"Send Eric in," he told the guard standing outside his study.

He watched the eyes of the man he trusted with his life as he entered the study and stood in front of his desk. His blue eyes were steady and relaxed with no signs of nervousness.

Guzman motioned to the chair in front of his desk. "What happened?"

"When the guard stepped back from the window of the booth, the driver panicked. That building must be heavily fortified because that much SEMTEX should have leveled it."

"Did you trigger the detonation or did the driver?"

"He did. I was waiting for him to get closer to the building."

"You say the guard stepped back from the window, is that all he did?"

"I was across the street, using my binoculars. The guard took the purchase order, looked at it and then picked up a phone. He said something then put the phone down and moved away from the window. Then boom."

"There must have been something else that spooked the driver."

"We'll never know now."

"And there was nothing on the driver or in the truck that can be traced back to us?"

"I wiped down the truck and there was nothing on the driver that could be traced to us."

Guzman shook his head and sighed. "This attorney is like a black cat with nine lives. Four times I have tried to kill him and four times I have failed. When this is finished in Seattle, I will have to find a way to end this."

"Do you want me to fly back to Seattle and keep an eye on the Saudi?"

"We have done everything we said we would. I didn't like this operation from the start, but our client insisted we bring him the nerve gas. Mohammad's on his own while I cruise the San Juan Islands on my yacht to look like a man without a care in the world. Monitor the news in Seattle and see if anyone mentions us."

He dismissed his bodyguard and followed him through the main salon to the viewing deck above the swimming pool. The fresh ocean air was invigorating and the view was spectacular; green forests of the islands on each side of the Astrid III, a light blue sky above and calm waters to sail on the way to Lummi Island and his reservation at the Willows Inn for dinner.

To maintain his image as a billionaire with nothing on his schedule but indulging an appetite for all the best things in life, he booked a reservation at the inn. Epicureans of the world praised the Willows Inn and its award-winning chef. People traveled from all over the world to dine at the inn, especially rich mega-yacht owners, and he needed to do the same. If he had to enjoy himself in the process, so be it.

As a pragmatic realist, with the wealth of the *Alliance* he and his predecessors had accumulated to back his plans, he intended to make a difference in the world. Order had to be restored before the open border policies of the globalists created anarchy in Europe and elsewhere in the industrialized and wealthy nations of the world. Fascism was evil incarnate in the post-war modern world, but authoritarian nationalism worked and would be needed again soon. He saw his mission as being a force behind the scenes to ready the world for a new brand of fascism.

With that inspiring thought in mind, he started down the stairs to the spa for a massage before a late dinner alone in his stateroom. The profit from supplying the nerve gas to the Saudi in Seattle was significant for the little effort it required, but he still had to make good on his promise to eliminate the attorney. A quiet meal and a good night's sleep would help his mind germinate a new plan of action to satisfy his clients and end the life of one Adam Drake, Esquire.

IN HIS SMALL room in the crew quarters, the man Guzman called the *Confessor* read the text message on his phone and smiled.

> If he does not keep his word to kill the attorney, you will be handsomely rewarded if you kill him for us. Our brothers as well as our enemy must know we keep our promises, Insha'Allah.

He detested the arrogant attitude of the man he knew led the shadowy South American organization that called itself *the Alliance*, and now he was being given a chance to make the great man beg for mercy. But he had a choice to make. He knew and trusted the men he served, who lived by the unwritten laws of the cartels. He was their enforcer and their highly-paid interrogator. But he never trusted men who were stupid enough to kill themselves for the promise of an orgy in paradise.

While he relished the thought of the pain he could cause the man who called himself Guzman, he had to choose; the money he would be paid or the real possibility that the cartels would come after him for ending a banking and money laundering arrangement that served them so well.

They thought of him only as a sadistic psychotic killer who enjoyed killing people. He was that, of course, but he was also intelligent enough to survive in a dangerous world that most men in his line of work did not. He would have to be very careful as he considered this offer of the Brotherhood.

Chapter Fifty-Six

DRAKE SAT across the desk from his friend at PSS headquarters eating Chinese takeout and drinking a green bottle of Tsingtao lager. He was treating Casey to the meal for dealing with the SPD, FBI and DHS for the last five hours and missing dinner with his family.

"Never learned how to use the chopsticks," Casey said as he speared a spicy Szechuan shrimp with his fork. "Thanks for the treat."

"I thought you might need a snack before you head home. How's Megan dealing with the news?"

"More angry than upset, once she knew I was okay. She knows Pat Conners's wife from our Christmas parties and retreats. She's at their home now with some of the other wives."

"How are you doing?"

Casey took a quick sip of beer and was quiet for a long moment. "We've both lost friends and seen good men die, so you know what it's like. This is different in a couple of ways. Pat was my employee. It was my job to keep him safe while he was at work. I failed to do that. It's different because in the army you know who's doing the killing and why. Today I don't know who or why."

"Mike, if Walter Guzman is who I think he is, what happened today is my fault. Ryan

Walker has a reason to come after me. Hitting here today while I'm in the building is payback."

"But why now? Why wait until you're here in the company of a bunch of former military guys who know how to defend themselves? If he's after you, why not hire some sniper and be done with it?"

Drake raised his bottle in mock salute and said, "A sniper like you would say that and make it sound so easy."

"You know what I mean. This doesn't make any sense."

"I know it doesn't right now, but I think it will soon. We're sitting on these jihadis of Mohammad's. Guzman's involved in whatever they're up to. When we find out what it is, I think the rest of the puzzle will fall into place."

Casey ate another shrimp and finished his beer. "I've got to get home and relieve the babysitter. You're expensive, but I'm still trying to get used to paying a fifteen-year-old twenty dollars an hour to watch my kids. Call me if anything breaks tonight."

Casey was a good man and his best friend. But it was Drake's job to settle the score with Walter Guzman, a.k.a. Ryan Walker.

Drake finished off the Chinese takeout and deposited the empty containers in the executive breakroom's garbage can. If he was going to spend another night sleeping in his office, it wasn't going to be with the lingering smell of food.

The building was alive with the sounds of workers Casey had called in to repair as much of the damage as possible overnight. Broken glass and debris from the explosion had to be cleaned up, windows replaced and perimeter security restored at the missing front gate.

Kevin was still at work in his office when he got there. A paper plate and a ham and cheese sandwich wrapper from the vending machine in the cafeteria were on the corner of his desk.

The smirking smile on Kevin's face when he turned away from the closest monitor was a good sign.

"You found something?"

"Yesssssiree, Mr. Drake. The Astrid III is in the San Juans headed for Lummi Island. It should get there tonight or early tomorrow morning."

"He must think no one is going to connect the dots from the driver of the truck to Ali Mohammad and then to him. He's just another rich guy cruising the San Juan Islands."

"Oh, he's much more than that. I'm still working my way through the CCTV tapes, but he has some pretty mean looking dudes working security on his yacht and they're armed to the teeth."

"A lot of the *uber* rich have small armies guarding them, so that's no smoking gun. Did you find anything that links him to the driver of the truck or Ali Mohammad?"

"I haven't watched all of the CCTV tapes yet, but I'll keep looking."

Drake patted the young hacker on the back and said, "All right, Kevin. I'm sleeping in my office, wake me if you find something."

On the way to his office, he stopped by the duty officer's desk and was surprised to see Mac manning the desk.

Michael Mackintosh was a retired Marine gunnery sergeant. With his experience as a fire and operations chief for a company of Marines, he was perfectly qualified, if not overqualified, to manage the day-to-day operations of

Puget Sound Security. "Mac, I didn't expect to see you here."

"Couldn't sit at home with everything that's been going on. Besides, the other two who sit at this desk have families at home. My wife got used to being alone when I had to work a long time ago." He turned around and nodded toward the insulated coffee carafe on the counter behind him. "Help yourself to some coffee if you want. Cups are under the counter."

Drake opened the door under the counter and grabbed a coffee cup. "Thanks. How are Morales and the men doing?"

"Bored and anxious to get back here to see the damage. The jihadis have bedded down for the night, and I mean that literally. None of the women have left. It's quiet at the two houses they're watching."

The coffee was strong and bitter, just like he remembered coffee tasting from his time in the service.

"How soon will Morales get back?"

"New team will replace them at midnight. You sleeping in your office again?"

"Yeah, so go ahead and send Morales my way when he gets in." Drake raised his cup and turned to leave. "Thanks again for the coffee."

Despite the loud noise he could hear from the work to repair the damage on the other side of the building, it was a strange feeling to walk down the hall to his office and pass the other empty executive offices. The men who worked in those offices made decisions every day to protect the lives of PSS clients and their businesses.

Today they had failed to protect the life of one of their own, as well as sustaining damage to their own offices. There would be a lot of soul-searching going on that night.

Drake lowered the lights in his office and sat at his desk to finish his coffee. Like the coffee's strong and bitter taste, the thought of America becoming a war zone like Iraq and Afghanistan and Syria and Libya and Europe was hard to swallow.

He set his cup down and leaned back into the soft leather of his chair. He might not be able to stop others from copying the suicide bomber who drove the truck today, but he could stop the man he thought was responsible for it.

His eyes closed as he started thinking of the way he wanted to do it.

Chapter Fifty-Seven

AFTER A SHOWER, a shave and a change of clothes, Drake was behind the wheel of his Porsche driving on I-5 to SeaTac Airport to pick up Liz.

Morales had found him asleep at his desk a little after midnight and let him sleep until six. Now he was late but recharged. He was anxious to see the smiling eyes again of the woman moving across the country just to be closer to him.

Her Alaskan Airline flight had left Ronald Reagan Washington National Airport for its seven-and-a-half hour flight to Seattle and he knew she would be tired and maybe hungry. He'd have to grab a latte and croissant or something at Starbucks on his way through the airport. Or would she prefer getting flowers? He should have thought of buying flowers before he got on I5. Maybe he could find a flower stand somewhere in the airport.

The last two days had been hectic, but the jumble of his emotions this morning was confusing. He prided himself on his ability to stay calm in the midst of chaos, something he'd done in firefights all across the Middle East. So why was he feeling like he was feeling?

He changed lanes and accelerated past a woman putting on makeup while driving her Prius. Maybe that was it; the thought of having a woman in his life again doing the things women did. He was comfortable living alone on his farm with his dog. Liz might suddenly change and he wasn't sure he was ready for that just yet.

Drake took Exit 154B to State Route 518 and headed west for a short distance to the first exit to the airport. He followed the signs to the parking garage, paid the four-dollar day fee for Terminal Direct parking and drove up to the fourth floor. From there it was a short jog over the skybridge to the main terminal to hunt for a Starbucks and a flower stand.

Gate D9 was at the far end of Concourse D. When the passengers from the Alaska

Airlines flight 1097 streamed out, Drake stood with a Starbucks latte in one hand and small bag with one butter croissant and blueberry muffin in the other. He didn't know if she would like either of the pastries but then there were a lot of things he didn't know about her yet.

He waved when he saw her emerge from the tunnel behind two men and look around for him. Her smile and wave when she saw him put an even bigger smile on his face. She was wearing sandals, black skinny jeans and a cocoa brown leather bomber jacket over a white teeshirt. He saw heads turning to follow her as she walked toward him.

She stopped a foot in front of him and looked up. "Miss me, handsome?"

Drake pulled her close and wrapped his arms around here. "More than you know. How was your flight?"

"Seven and half hours of pure delight," she said as she laid her head on his chest. "I knew you would be here to meet me."

He gave her a little squeeze and showed her his presents as they separated. "A latte to help keep your eyes open and pastries if you're hungry."

Liz opened the sack of pastries and picked out the croissant. "Perfect!" she said. "Let's go get my bag and hit the road. I'm anxious to hear about everything."

They made their way down to the baggage claim level, found her black and white print hardside suitcase on carousel fourteen and walked across Arrivals Drive to the parking garage. Five minutes later, with the suitcase stored in the rear luggage compartment, they were driving down the ramp and out of the parking garage.

Liz nibbled on the croissant as Drake told her what he knew about the bombing of the PSS building and Mohammad's men they were watching.

"And you're sure the driver of the truck was one of the men in his condo?"

"Kevin loaded the images of all the men into the PSS security database. The duty officer matched the image from the security CCTV camera from the security booth to the database before the driver detonated the bomb. There's no question it's one of the men in Mohammad's condo."

"How did you get the images of the men in the condo?"

"That's the problem and the reason we haven't taken what we have to the FBI. Kevin hacked into the computers on Walter Guzman's yacht and found that he had a video feed running from Mohammad's condo. If we show the FBI anything, we'll have to tell them how we got the facial images of the men in the first place."

"Now I understand why you asked me to fly to Seattle.

The way the FBI loves you, they'd find a way to throw you in jail if you gave them what you have." "Exactly, so what do we do?"

Liz sipped on her latte and stared straight ahead for several minutes. Drake could see from the silent movements of her lips that she was talking herself through the permutations of the problem.

"Will the FBI be able to identify the driver without your help?" she finally asked.

"There wasn't anything left of him and the truck was stolen from what we're being told, so I doubt it."

"Even if they could, the only thing they could do is question Mohammad and Guzman about how they know the guy. Are they still around?"

"You mean in Seattle or in the country? Guzman's on his yacht in the San Juans within spitting distance from the border with Canada. I don't think we know where Mohammad is right now."

Liz reached over and patted his leg. "Then you're damned if you do and damned if you don't. Keep doing what you're doing and find something on Guzman that will help. I'll meet with the FBI as a soon-to-be vice president of Puget Sound Security and see what I can learn. I'll do that tomorrow. Today I just want to be with you until you wine and dine me this evening."

Drake turned in time to see the mischievous look in her eyes and say with a big grin, "Yes ma'am!"

Chapter Fifty-Eight

THEY DROVE straight to the PSS headquarters in Kirkland so Liz could see the damage and check in with Casey. He was waiting for them in his office when she finished touring the building.

"Thanks for coming, Liz. Did he brief you on what we know and what we're doing?"

"Yes, he did. I'm so sorry about the loss of your security guard."

"Connors was a good man. He almost got far enough away from his guard booth before the bomb was detonated," Casey said and motioned for her to take a seat.

Drake remained standing near the door. "Liz thinks we should keep doing what we're doing until we get something incriminating on Mohammad or Guzman. She wants to wait until tomorrow to go see the FBI."

"They'll be busy over there, but I don't want to meet with the weekend staff. I know some of the senior staff and they may not be there today."

Casey nodded in agreement. "We might have something

by then. Kevin is still going through the CCTV video from Guzman's yacht. Mohammad's men should wake up anytime now and might lead us somewhere. In the meantime, is there anything you need from here that will help prepare you to meet with the FBI?"

"I can't think of anything, other than a nice dinner and a good night's sleep," she said, looking up at Drake.

Casey stifled a grin and kept from looking at his friend. "Thanks again for coming on short notice, Liz. Go get checked in at the Woodmark and make him show you the town. I'll let you two know if anything develops here."

Drake waited for Liz to stand and walk past him at the door before he turned to Casey and said softly, "If something does develop, I want to know about it right away. He's after me, Mike, and I want to be there when we bring him down."

"I know, I know. Go get reacquainted with our new vice president. I promise you'll hear from me as soon as we know anything new here."

Liz was standing in his office down the hall when he caught up with her. "Have you been sleeping in your office?"

"Who told you that?"

"The clothes draped over the end of the couch."

"Just for a night or so. I was headed home Friday night and had checked out of the Woodmark when I changed my mind. There weren't any vacancies there and it was easier to bunk here for the night. No big deal."

He hadn't said anything about Guzman's men waiting for him at the end of his run along the lake and didn't want to admit it now.

She faced him with a puzzled look on her face. "Couldn't they find a room for you last night?"

Drake hooked his arm through hers and led her out of his office. "I'll take you to the Woodmark and you'll see why there are no vacancies most nights. You got lucky and have the same room I had last week."

He'd asked for an early check-in time, but the very polite young man at the reservations desk apologized and said it would be another hour before the room would be ready. Would they like a complimentary beverage to go with a lunch or dinner there, he asked.

They decided to have lunch on the patio of the Beach Café looking over Lake Washington.

When they were seated, Liz put her hand over his and asked about the security assessment he did for the Link Light Rail system. He told her about it and how Casey had hired the Israeli security guard trainers for a temporary demonstration of how Israeli methods could work unobtrusively in America.

When he finished, he asked her about how she was wrapping up her work in his father-inlaw's senate office. She told him about interviewing candidates for her replacement and how she was going to miss her role liaising with the Senate Select Committee on Intelligence and being on the inside on intelligence matters.

They finally looked at their menus and ordered lunch; a bottle of King Estates' Pinot Gris to go with their steak salads. Drake decided to take a risk and bring up a subject he'd been thinking a lot about. "Have you thought about where you want to live when you move here?"

"I need to sell my condo in Washington before I buy anything and I don't know Seattle. Where do you think I should look?"

The waiter arrived with their wine and Drake nodded his approval without tasting a sample. It was time to casually mention his idea. "There's no rush, Liz. In fact—" His cell phone vibrated in his pocket and he saw that it was Casey calling.

"Morales called to say Mohammad's guys just left both houses and drove to a mosque. He thinks it's strange that the prostitutes haven't left yet. He wants to know if he should take a look inside while they're gone. Pose as someone taking a survey or something."

"Is he sure all of the jihadis have left the houses? We don't know if anyone was there when the party vans arrived. If someone's still inside with a woman and he panics, it will blow everything."

"It could also save the lives of ten women."

"Or they could have been paid for the whole weekend. It's your call."

"Let's wait a little longer. I'll call Morales and tell him."

Drake took a drink of his wine and saw that Liz was watching a sailboat on the lake. Her eyes were smiling and he realized how happy he felt when they were together. Maybe after dinner, he would tell her she was welcome to stay at the farm while she looked for a place in Seattle. There was plenty of room.

Chapter Fifty-Nine

WHEN THEY FINISHED lunch and Liz checked in, she decided she wanted to freshen up in her room and change her clothes. Drake returned to the Beach Café and ordered a cup of coffee. While he waited for it, he called Casey.

"Anything new?"

"The jihadis are back from the mosque. They arrived as most of the Muslims were leaving after their noon prayers and stayed for almost an hour. That's a long time to be praying. Morales thinks they were meeting with someone."

"Did they return to the two houses?"

"That's where there are now."

"Liz checked in. She's changing her clothes and then we can head back if there's anything we can be doing."

"Where are you right now?"

"What do you mean? I'm at the Woodmark."

"Where in the Woodmark?"

Drake refused to take the bait. "Sitting on the patio having a cup of coffee."

"Uh huh. There's nothing you can do here. Why don't

you show Liz around town? I'll let you know if anything develops."

"I can do that. You might check with Kevin and see how he's doing. I don't think he's left the building in two days."

"Good idea. He likes a barbeque shack I frequent. I'll see if he wants to get something to eat."

"Stay in touch. Something's going on, I can feel it."

The waiter brought his coffee and he thought about the attractions in the city Liz might like to see. He liked the waterfront and riding the last ferry to Bainbridge Island and back, returning to the terminal with the bright lights of the city reflecting off the water.

She might like Pike Place Market and the shops of the "Down Under", but he wasn't much of a shopper. Wandering from one small shop to the next with no intention of buying anything made him feel claustrophobic.

Then he remembered walking the paths of the Seattle Art Museum's Olympic Sculpture Park. The outdoor sculpture garden graced a seaside bluff north of downtown with views of the harbor, the city and the mountains in the background. The artwork was spectacular, with Calder's "Eagle" abstract soaring bird made of six tons of red-painted steel a main attraction.

Liz liked museums and art, so the sculpture park was a good place to start a tour of the city.

Drake finished his coffee and left money on the table that included a generous tip and went inside to wait for Liz in the lobby. It was two fifteen on a warm Sunday afternoon and he looked forward to the outing he had planned.

When she walked out of the elevator, it was all he could do to keep from whistling. She was wearing a blue, white and green fitted floral dress that displayed well-tanned arms and legs, sandals and a white, floppy, straw hat. Her left hand clutched several brochures.

"These were in the room. I thought the Olympic Sculpture Park would be a wonderful place to visit if we have time," she said.

Drake offered her his arm for the walk to his car. "Great idea, I know the place."

They were on their way to the sculpture park in Drake's gray Porsche listening to Antonio de Lucena on his playlist of acoustic guitar classics when Casey called.

"Mohammad just visited the house in Evergreen. He carried two large cardboard boxes in and stayed for maybe ten minutes. No one walked him out to his car. He left and I'll bet he's headed to the other house where his other guys are staying." "Any idea what was in the boxes?"

"Morales said they didn't look like they were heavy, maybe three feet by two feet and two feet deep. The second box looked like it was lighter than the first."

"That doesn't tell us much. He could be bringing food for all we know. What does Morales suggest?"

"Morales can't stand it that he doesn't know what's going on in these houses. He wants a thermal pocket scope so he can determine how many people are in the house."

"I don't see a problem with that if he doesn't get caught."

"You worked with him in Nicaragua. Not much of a chance that will happen."

"Do we have eyes on Mohammad?"

"No, Morales is trying to identify the guys in his condo. We know where Mohammad lives. Have fun with Liz and we'll see what Morales comes up with tonight."

Drake felt a cool hand on his arm when he reached

down to end the Bluetooth connection and return to his playlist on the car's audio system.

"I know you trust your intuition about things like this, but what if these guys are just foreign university students he's entertaining in his condo?"

Drake's mind drifted back to a hillside above a village in Afghanistan where he and Casey were watching a tribal leader instructing a line of men. They were three hundred yards away and yet the leader's angry face he saw through the spotting scope appeared to be standing right in front of him. The men the leader was amping up had left the village soon after on a suicide mission to attack an American forward operating base. They had warned the base of the attack and the men from the village were cut down before they could breach the outer perimeter.

Drake would never forget the leader's crazed eyes and animated face as he sent his men off to fight. It was the same look he'd seen in Mohammad's eyes on the CCTV footage Kevin pirated from Guzman's yacht.

"Then they're hanging out with the wrong guy. I know Mohammad. He's their leader and he's getting ready to send them straight to hell."

Chapter Sixty

AFTER AN HOUR WALKING the paths of the sculpture garden, Liz wanted to see the city from the top of the Space Needle.

"It was built in 1962 for the World's Fair," she read aloud from another of her travel brochures. "It's 605 feet tall and can withstand 200 hundred mile an hour winds. Twenty thousand people a day ride the elevators that travel at ten miles an hour."

"You sure you want to stand in line with all those people?" he asked, smiling at her enthusiasm.

"The trip up only takes forty-one seconds. How long can the lines be?"

Drake knew because he'd stood in line with Kay for more than an hour. That was before he owned a cell phone. "Download a couple of timed-entry tickets and we won't have to find out."

Even standing in line for an hour would have been tolerable given the pure joy Liz exhibited as she marveled at the sight of Mount Rainier and ferries crossing the waters of Puget Sound.

After the Space Needle, they continued her tour of the city with a stroll along the waterfront, a stop at Pike's Place Fish Market and then to Pier 56 for an early dinner at Elliot's Oyster House.

While they waited for a bottle of Sauvignon Blanc he ordered to be brought to their table, Liz was amazed at how many different types of oysters were on the menu.

"Forty-three! I never knew there were that many kinds of oysters."

"That's why people come here. Do you like oysters?"

She smiled coyly and said softly, "Not really, but I really like crab cakes."

He felt his face redden a little as he remembered the night in her condo when she treated him to crab cakes before their first intimate evening. "I prefer oysters, but I'm a big fan of your crab cakes as well."

"I remember how you enjoyed them."

Drake was about to ask her if she wanted to go back to the Woodmark when the waiter arrived with their bottle of chilled wine.

"Are you hungry?" he asked instead.

"A little, are you?"

"I think so, maybe something light. If you'd like, we can catch the ferry over to

Bainbridge Island before we call it a night."

"I would like that."

With the hint of things to come, Liz ordered a bowl of spicy crab and corn chowder and a butter lettuce salad. Drake couldn't resist the pan-fried oysters.

"Welcome to Seattle, Liz," he said and raised his glass of wine to her. "I'm glad you're here."

She raised her glass and touched it lightly to his. "I never thought I would leave

Washington, especially not for the reason I have. But I'm glad I did."

"I think you'll like working for Casey. He has some big plans for growing the company and he needs you to help make them happen."

"What about you? Will you be getting more involved in those plans and spending more time in Seattle?"

He wasn't sure how to answer her. She was really asking two things; was he going to be doing more work in Seattle and was she going to be seeing him more often. He hadn't told her that he was a shareholder in the company by agreeing to receive shares in lieu of a portion of his fee, so he would certainly be more involved. Whether she saw him more often depended on a number of things.

His law practice in Portland and his farm and the old vineyard he was restoring needed more of his time than he was giving them. And that included his recent decision to have Paul Benning work out of his office as a private investigator. There were things that required a commitment he couldn't ignore.

But he'd be a fool to ignore the commitment Liz was making to their relationship. She was a hot commodity in Washington and could have any job she wanted in any number of agencies or law firms in the capital. Her years of service for the FBI and then DHS and her recent position as the intelligence expert in his father-in-law's U.S. Senate office were worth their weight, literally, in gold in that city.

She had been clear about the reason she accepted Casey's offer to work for PSS; she wanted to see more of him and was willing to move across the country to be closer.

Was he ready to match her commitment with his own?

Drake reached across the table and took her hand. "I will be in Seattle working more and I'll see you as often as you want. But I hope you'll come to Portland as well. There's a lot of work on the farm that needs to be done. I could use your help."

He saw that it was the right answer. Her eyes crinkled up along with her smile and she put her other hand on top of his.

"Would next week when you finish things here be too soon?"

Their dinners arrived and they ate and shared childhood stories until Drake signaled the waiter for their check. "One last thing on your tour of Seattle, a ferry ride over to Bainbridge Island and back at night. You're going to love it."

And she did. The lights of the Seattle skyline reflecting off the water on the return trip covered the spectrum of colors and presented a mesmerizing upside-down image of the city.

"It's beautiful, Adam. Thank you for sharing this with me," she said as she leaned her head back on his chest. They were standing alone on the upper deck of the ferry at the bow railing and Drake had his arms wrapped around her. The night was warm but the breeze off the water was refreshingly cool.

"Would you like to stop somewhere for a nightcap before I take you back to the Woodmark?"

Liz wiggled closer and shook her head. "We could stop at the bar and take something to my room if you want."

Drake answered with a kiss on the top of her head and pulled her a little closer. "I'd like that."

Chapter Sixty-One

IT WAS one o'clock by the time Drake made it back to his office for another night on the couch in his office.

At two o'clock, his cell phone woke him from a deep and blissful sleep.

"We have a problem," Morales said as Drake sat up and looked at the time displayed on his iPhone.

"Where are you?"

"I'm in the house in Evergreen. I used the thermal scope and saw that no one was inside, so I let myself in. They slipped out through the backyard, pulled some boards down off the fence and exited through the neighbor's yard."

"What time did—"

"There's more. They killed the five prostitutes and hid their bodies under blankets in the garage. There's body hair in the tub and sink and an empty bottle of Old Spice in the bathroom. You know what that means."

Drake did. Shaving off body hair and beards and wearing cologne on a martyr's last night was a way of purifying the body so it was clean and acceptable when it entered Paradise.

"What about the other house?"

"The other team is checking it now but I expect they'll find the same thing."

Drake got up and turned the light on. "Have you told Casey?"

"Just before I called you. He's on his way in."

"Is there anything there that tells us where they're headed?"

"The place is a mess, looks like the morning after a frat party. The boxes I saw them carry in are here, some brochures on the counter and prayer rugs rolled up. I'm using my flashlight intermittently, give me a minute to check the cabinets and drawers and those boxes."

Finding the dead prostitutes meant they were going to bring in the police and FBI. He'd leave that for Liz to handle the next day after they had decided how they were going to explain how they became suspicious of the ten men. Right now, they had to find out what the jihadists were planning and what their target was. By the time they got anyone else up to speed, it might be too late.

Morales returned and said, "The brochures were just schedules for the light rail system, but I think you should look at these empty boxes. I'll send you a couple of looks to your cell phone and tell me what you think."

Drake ended the call and waited for the ping telling him the pictures had arrived.

When his phone pinged, he scrolled down and then back up through four pictures. One frame looked down into a large cardboard box. The next three were closer shots of five smaller containers. Expanding the images, he saw that they were shipping containers for automatic air freshener dispensers, the kind that hang on walls and automatically spray fresh fragrances into a room.

He looked again at each picture, wondering why they would need air fresheners in a house that looked like it had just hosted a frat party. Were they trying to make sure the prostitutes weren't offended by something that smelled bad in the house? Or had they ordered the air fresheners to cover up the smell of the bodies of the women they knew they were going to kill? If they had, they were smarter than he thought they were.

Drake called Morales back. "Did you find any of these air freshener things in the house or in the garage?"

"They must have taken them with them when they left."

The image of five martyrs on a suicide mission taking automatic air freshener dispensers with them as they left through the backyard in the dead of night seemed absurd, unless...

"Look at a box those air fresheners came in and see if the actual fragrance refill cartridges came with the automatic spray dispensers."

"Okay. Nope, it says a refillable fragrance cartridge is not included. Why?"

Because in a flash of imagination he saw what the bastards were planning; an ordinary automatic air freshener dispenser with a fragrance cartridge filled with a deadly nerve agent left in a backpack on a light rail car. No one would suspect the device was a small WMD that would operate automatically even if the backpack was searched.

"Because they don't need a refill cartridge, they're going to supply their own and it won't be filled with some sweet fragrance. They're going to attack the Link Light Rail just like the terrorists did in Tokyo in 1995."

"What do we do?"

"Make sure there's no one in the other house and then see if they have the same kind of air freshener containers there too. Then come back to headquarters and we'll think of something to head these ding dongs off."

Drake got dressed and took the stairs down a floor to the IT section to see if Kevin was still there. The Israeli security guards Casey had hired to protect the light rail stations needed to have the facial recognition images Kevin had entered into the PSS security database.

Kevin was asleep at his desk, but bolted awake when Drake touched his shoulder and he promised to get the men's facial images to the Israeli team immediately.

When he got upstairs, he found Casey back in his office on the phone with Morales. Casey put the phone on speaker and they heard Morales say the second house was empty, except for more dead prostitutes and the same empty boxes.

"Get you and your men back to headquarters," Casey directed. "We'll figure something out."

"Did Morales tell you what I think they're planning?"

"He did and I pray to God you're wrong."

"I hope I'm wrong too, but our intelligence agencies have warned that ground transportation is the new favorite target of terrorists. The Link Light Rail system is popular and heavily used, especially downtown and around the university."

"We're lucky, I guess, that we brought the Israelis in for the month. It will take too long to involve the FBI or DHS. We'll have to work with the locals and stop them ourselves."

"If we can figure out where they're going to strike."

Chapter Sixty-Two

MOHAMMAD'S DISTRESS call reached Guzman at a little after one o'clock Monday morning.

"I'm taking you up on your offer. Come get me."

"What's happened?"

"The two houses my men were staying in were under surveillance. They were able to slip out undetected, but someone is on to us."

After the gourmet dinner at the Willow's Inn the night before and several snifters of cognac later, Guzman was groggy but alert enough to sense the panic in the young Saudi's voice. He slid out of bed in his silk pajamas and pressed the call button on the ship's intercom to summon his bodyguard.

"Do your men know who was watching them?"

"Does it make a difference?"

Guzman heard three taps on the door of his stateroom, hit the light switch and opened the door for his bodyguard. "If it was the police, there are a number of reasons they might be watching your men that has nothing to do with what you are planning."

If it's who I think it is, we have a major problem that you caused when your martyr failed to kill the attorney.

"Are you going forward?"

"Yes, they won't know where or what we have planned for them. My men do not believe they can fail and even if they do, it's a righteous sacrifice they will be rewarded for."

"All right, be where I told you to be in two hours."

"Why can't you come sooner?"

"Two hours. If you're not there, your ride will leave. You will be on your own."

Guzman swore loudly and then quickly regained his composure. "Eric, tell Josef to get ready to fly the Sikorsky to Seattle. Mohammad panicked and wants us to rescue him. He'll be waiting on the helipad of his building."

"Yes sir."

The Astrid III was anchored a hundred yards offshore from Lummi Island and the

Willow's Inn. Two hours should be plenty of time for his Sikorsky S-434 to make the flight to Seattle and for him to figure out how he was going to deal with the situation. He wasn't prepared to call it a crisis, unless the attorney had found out what he and Mohammad were planning, and then it was a disaster.

The Brotherhood had warned him that another failure would have consequences. It was clear to him what that meant. On top of that, he promised them he would get rid of the damnable attorney and he'd already failed to do that. Unless he found a way to convincingly explain his failures, he'd be looking over his shoulders for the rest of his life.

Even his beloved *Alliance*, with its financial resources, couldn't provide the protection he'd need to fight off the

Muslim hordes if they came for him. How ironic, he thought, that the same Muslims who fought so unsuccessfully for his ancestors in WWII would spawn another generation of Islamists who were equally inept.

His bodyguard returned to report that the Sikorsky was on its way to Seattle. "Is there anything I can do for you, sir?"

"Perhaps some coffee in a minute. Can you think of any way they could connect the truck bomb at PSS to us? You said the truck itself was wiped down."

"The truck was stolen and we'd never seen the driver until that day. I can't think of anything that would connect to us."

Guzman studied the face of his trusted bodyguard and saw no evidence of deception or nervousness. If someone had slipped up, he was sure it wasn't something Eric was responsible for.

"Could it have been something that Mohammad did when he brought the driver to the yacht?"

"Before we brought the driver on board, I made sure there was no one watching us at the moorage. I guess someone could have been watching Mohammad."

"That's what worries me. I know his sponsors think highly of him, but those parties of his could have attracted attention. There's probably no way of knowing. That's all for now, Eric."

It was becoming clear to him that if anyone was to blame for the surveillance of Mohammad's men, it was Mohammad. If he had proof of that, he might be able to convince Mohammed's sponsors they had chosen the wrong man to carry out their plan.

The only way to get the proof he would need would be to turn the *Confessor* loose on Mohammad. Afterwards, there would be no turning back and no way he would be able to return the young Saudi to his father. Mohammad would sadly never be able to leave the Astrid III again when he returned from Seattle, except as fish food somewhere at sea.

If Mohammad hadn't let anyone know about the backup plan and the distress signal to rescue him from Seattle, Guzman could say he hadn't heard from him. He delivered the sarin devices to him and had no information about his whereabouts thereafter. If the plot failed, it wouldn't have anything to do with him.

Yes, that would work. He would have to be careful with what he told the *Confessor* before the interrogation, of course. The sadist wasn't to be trusted, but his loyalty could be purchased. This day might end well after all.

Chapter Sixty-Three

CASEY GATHERED his team in the conference room next to his office.

Mac Mackintosh, his duty officer, and Drake were already in the building.

Morales and the Israeli team leader, Daniel Asher, came in from the field.

Liz arrived by cab from the Woodmark Hotel, wearing jeans and a sweatshirt.

Thermal carafes of coffee, day-old donuts and mugs from the Operations lounge were on a side table to help them through the early hours before dawn.

Casey introduced Asher to Liz and then nodded to Drake to explain what they were up against.

Drake scooted his chair forward and rested his hands on the table. "It looks like a cell of jihadis is getting ready to hit the Link Light Rail system. The two houses where ten of the them were staying, five in each house, are deserted. The women we think were prostitutes are dead, their bodies left behind in the garage of each house. We think the men prepared themselves for martyrdom before they left, with the body hair Marco found in the tubs and sinks. And they might be using ordinary air freshener dispensers for some sort of chemical attack. Maybe something like the sarin attacks on the Tokyo subways."

Mac raised his hand. "Why do we think it's a chemical attack on the Link?"

"Just an educated guess, Mac. The intelligence agencies have been worried about terror attacks on ground transportation here because it's become a favorite target in Europe. The empty boxes for new automatic air freshener dispensers we found could be modified to spray a nerve gas. All they would need to do is replace the air freshener canister in the dispenser with a canister of sarin. Leave it under a seat when you get off the train and you kill a lot of people when it goes off."

The Israeli team leader drummed his fingers on the table before asking, "Won't this new chemical detection system detect a nerve gas?"

"It will once the nerve gas is in the air. Sarin, for example, isn't detectable as a liquid. In the Tokyo attacks, the sarin was carried in plastic bags inside packages made to look like lunch boxes or bottled drinks. The terrorists punctured the bags with the tips of their umbrellas and got off the trains. The sarin liquid then evaporated into the air and the vapor got on passengers' skin or in their lungs when it was inhaled."

"So how do we stop these guys?" Morales asked.

Drake looked to the Israeli team leader. "You take them down before they get on the trains. We know what they look like from the video from Mohammad's condo. If they wear disguises, you make use of the profiling techniques you developed in Israel and take them on the station platforms."

No one said anything as they considered Drake's answer.

Casey got up to refill his coffee cup and asked on the way, "Which stations will they hit and how do we 'take them down'? There are what, fifteen stations on the line from University Station out to the airport. And Asher's men aren't authorized to make arrests."

Drake pushed his chair back and spread his hands out. "That's what we're here to figure out."

Liz looked around the table before saying, "I'm new to Seattle, but doesn't Sound Transit have a security force protecting these stations? If Mr. Asher has been showing them how they do things in Israel, I'll bet he knows someone with the authority to arrest these men when they show up."

Asher nodded and said, "Sound Transit Police has sworn sheriff's deputies as well as unarmed security guards. I know the chief, but we have been training the unarmed security guards for the most part. They act as extra eyes for the police and call for backup when they feel they need it. I also know the rail operations chief who monitors the surveillance cameras and has access to two hundred views from different cameras all up and down the line."

Drake slapped the table and pointed to Asher. "And that's how we find them. Asher can monitor the stations using the operation chief's surveillance cameras. When he recognizes Mohammad's men or men acting like terrorists, he alerts his team to have the unarmed security guards to call for backup."

"What if the backup doesn't get there in time?" Morales asked.

The Israeli team leader smiled sheepishly. "We are not allowed to be armed while we work with the Sound Transit

Police, but I was able to persuade the chief to let us borrow some of their Tasers. On a crowded station platform, I think my men can close in and neutralize the terrorists until backup arrives."

After a short discussion of logistics led by the Israeli team leader, they agreed that it was likely the terrorists would arrive together at University Station on the northern end of the line and board the individual train cars from there.

As Morales and the Israeli team leader were about to leave to brief the Israeli trainers on their new mission, Kevin McRoberts rushed into the conference room.

He opened the laptop he was carrying and set it down at the end of the conference table, spinning it around so they all could see the screen.

"It's him, that's the driver of the truck that bombed the security booth out front and that's Mohammad." He pointed excitedly. "This is CCTV footage from Guzman's yacht. They're all in it together!"

Drake and Casey were closest to the laptop and leaned in for a better look. Mohammad and a young man were standing just inside the open bow storage hatch of the Astrid III where Drake had taught the unfriendly security guard to mind his manners.

Walter Guzman, the man Drake believed to be Ryan Walker, was clearly involved with terrorists and had to be stopped.

"Kevin, where is Guzman's yacht right now?"

The young hacker bent down and opened another window on his laptop. "He's in open water west of Lummi Island. It looks like he's headed to Vancouver Island and out of U.S. territorial waters."

"We can't let that happen. How long until he reaches Canadian waters?"

"Not sure, Mr. Drake. I know the maximum speed of his yacht is 16.5 knots, or 19 miles an hour, from the research I did on the Astrid III. I don't know the distances up there off the top of my head, but I'd say it's probably forty nautical miles from Bellingham to Sydney on Vancouver Island. Two thirds of that is in U.S. territory. That makes it about two hours before he reaches Canadian waters."

"You still have your Bell Relentless?" Drake asked Casey.

"That and a Bell 429 light twin for shorter flights. They're in a hangar at Renton Municipal Airport, twelve miles south of here. It might be close, but we can catch him in either one."

"Mr. Drake, remember what I told you about hacking the yacht's GPS satellite signal? I might be able to slow Guzman down a bit."

"Do it," Drake said, looking at his watch and turning to Liz. "Get whatever you need from Kevin and get the FBI or DHS to back us up on this. This early in the morning, you might not find anyone who can make a decision, but try. Let them know we think Guzman is Ryan Walker. Maybe they'll jump at the chance to arrest someone with an international arrest warrant outstanding."

Chapter Sixty-Four

GUZMAN STOOD beside the empty captain's chair in the pilot house of the Astrid III waiting for his Sikorsky S-434 to return. A digital display on the bank of navigational monitors to his right charted the yacht's narrow passage ahead between Orcas Island and Blakely Island. The distance to Canadian waters was shorter through the San Juan Islands than heading north to Vancouver, British Columbia, and he wanted to be out of the jurisdiction of the Americans as soon as possible.

The yacht was on autopilot and he'd sent the captain below because he wanted as few people as possible to know that Ali Mohammad had ever been on board the Astrid, and that included the yacht's captain. As soon as the Saudi landed on the yacht's helipad, his bodyguard would take him directly to the owner's stateroom for a private conversation. The conversation would determine if there was any reason to keep the pampered young jihadist alive any longer.

Guzman heard an approaching helicopter and turned to

look out a port-side window in the pilot house. He was relieved to see that it was his Sikorsky flying low over the water and headed straight at the Astrid.

He stood with his arms folded across his chest and watched as the helicopter flared and then settled gently down on the helipad. The rotors continued to spin for the return flight to Seattle as his bodyguard sprinted to the passenger door and waited for it to open.

Ali Mohammad started down the stairs and angrily brushed past the bodyguard and crossed the helipad.

"Take me to Guzman," he shouted over his shoulder.

Guzman stayed in the pilot house for another ten minutes before he made his way down to the owner's stateroom. He was intrigued by the mood of his guest who he had just saved from an embarrassing arrest in Seattle.

Mohammad was pacing back and forth in front of the door of his study when Guzman entered the stateroom. His bodyguard stood in front of the door with his right hand resting on the pistol holstered on his hip.

"This is your fault," Mohammad said, jabbing his finger at Guzman's face. "If you hadn't gone after the attorney, they wouldn't be watching my men! Get your man out of my way. I need a phone to call my father."

"And tell him what?" Guzman demanded coldly. "That your doped-up jihadists couldn't wait until they got to Paradise to have sex? Did you ever consider that bringing a van of prostitutes into a quiet neighborhood and partying all night might attract attention? No, of course you didn't."

"If my men fail, the Brotherhood will demand an explanation. They will never believe you when they learn the truth."

Guzman had heard enough. He nodded to his bodyguard who drew his pistol and pointed it at Mohammad's head.

"I think they will believe me because they will never learn the truth. You see, you were never here. I never saw you after you ran out on your men in Seattle. My truth will be the only truth they will ever hear. Goodbye Mohammad, you arrogant little sand flea. Say hello to Allah when you see him."

Mohammad lunged toward Guzman, but the bodyguard grabbed his arm and hit him behind his right ear with the butt of his pistol as he spun around. Mohammad dropped to the floor and didn't move.

"Take him to the *Confessor*," Guzman ordered as he walked to his stateroom door and knocked twice. "There are a couple of things I still need to know."

Two bodyguards entered and picked up Mohammad under his arms and dragged him out.

―――

ALI MOHAMMAD REGAINED consciousness slumped forward in a chair. A black bag over his head prevented him from seeing and duct tape pinned his arms and legs to the arms and legs of the chair.

As he raised his head, he heard a voice whisper in his ear. "Drop your head back down and listen carefully if you want to live. Groan softly if you understand."

"Ahhhh…"

The *Confessor* walked around the chair and leaned down as if he was listening to Mohammad breathe.

"*Bueno*," he whispered in Mohammad's ear. "Your sponsors want me to kill Guzman. When I do, I will get you out of here. Pretend you are unconscious until I return. If he comes down to watch me interrogate you before I have a chance to kill him, I will have to hurt you a little to make him think I am doing my job. Groan again if you understand."

"Ahhhh…"

The *Confessor* straightened up and walked closer to the door where he looked up at the security camera mounted above it.

"He's still unconscious. Your man must have hit him too hard. I'll give him a little more time. If he doesn't wake up soon, I have something that will bring him around. While we wait, we need to talk. I need to get back home as soon as possible."

The *Confessor* pretended to check on Mohammad again and left the room. He had a Hissatsu tactical folder in his duffel bag on his bunk in the crew quarters, along with his Double Tap Defense derringer.

The knife had a blade shaped in the classical Samurai design that gave it exceptional slashing capability and it opened in a flash with its spring-assisted opening mechanism. The derringer was the smallest and lightest concealed carry pocket pistol on the market and was the perfect backup to his blade for close-quarter work. Each of the gun's two barrels were loaded with a hollow point .45 cartridge and two more .45 cartridges were stored in the butt of the gun for a quick reload.

He knew Guzman didn't trust him and would have a bodyguard present. But it was his speed and ability to dispatch multiple targets that had earned him respect and reputation when he began his career. He was even faster now.

Chapter Sixty-Five

WALTER GUZMAN WAS GETTING his prescribed fifteen minutes of vitamin D on the sundeck when his bodyguard approached. The *Confessor* wanted a minute of his time.

"Did he say why?"

"It's about Mohammad. He thinks he has a concussion."

Guzman sighed and took off his sunglasses. "Send him up and have Josef go down and check on the Saudi. I don't see what difference it makes if he has a concussion as long as he's able to answer a few questions."

"Yes sir."

It wasn't like the swarthy cartel interrogator to worry about the condition his victims were in when he began to ask them questions. There was only one condition they would be in when he finished, and having a concussion wouldn't matter much.

The bodyguard brought the *Confessor* across the sundeck to the side of Guzman's teak chaise lounge and stepped back.

Guzman sat up and swung his feet around to the deck to face him. The man was wearing a white guayabera shirt with long sleeves, black linen pants and a white, Cuban-style fedora. The only thing missing, Guzman thought, was a heavy, gold chain around his neck.

"Well, what have you learned?"

"Your man hit him too hard. He's unconscious. It may be a while before I can question him."

The man was blocking the sun so that he couldn't see his face clearly. He put his sunglasses back on. There was something in the man's voice that he hadn't detected before; a note of disdain.

"You have until we reach Vancouver Island. I need to know if he told anyone he was coming to my yacht. Will you be able to do that?"

"Why does that matter? His sponsors have already decided how they want to handle this matter."

"What?" Guzman exclaimed and started to get up. "How can you know that?"

The *Confessor* withdrew his right hand from his pants pocket and flicked open his knife. He slashed Guzman's neck in a blur of motion, severing the carotid artery, then spun and stabbed the bodyguard up under the diaphragm and into his heart.

"Because they told me so," he said as he twisted the blade deeply in the bodyguard's chest and lowered him to the deck.

HE WAS ALONE on the sundeck but didn't expect that to last long. He wiped the blade of his knife on Guzman's white terry robe and walked quickly to the stairs. By his count, there were three more bodyguards on the yacht, five crewmen and the captain. He knew the bodyguards were armed, but he wasn't sure about the others.

If he could get to the captain and persuade him to change course to Vancouver, British Columbia, where he had cartel resources, he was home free. With the money Mohammad's sponsors had at their disposal, he was sure the captain would get them safely to Vancouver. If money failed to be persuasive, there were other ways.

The captain was alone in the pilothouse sitting in his chair. He appeared to be studying a possible course between two nearby San Juan Islands on one of the yacht's navigational monitors. The two islands looked to be so close together that they were almost touching each other.

The *Confessor* quietly walked up behind him and said, "Don't get up, Captain. I have a small but very powerful gun pointed at your head. Put your hands on top of your head for the moment. Mr. Guzman and his bodyguard are dead. I want to know if you think you could be persuaded to change course to Vancouver, B.C., for a sizeable contribution to your retirement fund?"

"Did you kill them?"

"I did."

"Are you the man Guzman calls—called—the *Confessor*?"

"I am."

"Then you know the *Alliance* will never rest until you are dead," the captain said and started to lower his hands.

"Ah, ah, Captain. Keep your hands where I can see them. I am not concerned about the *Alliance*, but you haven't answered my question."

"Even if I wanted to, the others on this yacht will never let you leave this yacht alive."

"We'll see about that. Will you take me to Vancouver?"

"Do I have a choice?"

The *Confessor* chuckled. "You are a smart man and possibly a rich one soon, if you do as I ask. You may lower your hands to change our course to Vancouver if you need to."

He watched as the captain lowered his hands and reached forward to the controls on his navigation workstation. The yacht began to slow but didn't alter course.

"Why are you still steering toward those islands?" the *Confessor* demanded to know.

The captain jabbed repeatedly at an icon on the touch screen of the workstation.

"Something's wrong. This says we're on the course I set but we're still heading straight at that little island."

The *Confessor* angled away so he had a view of the pilothouse door behind him as well as the captain. "If this is a trick, you're a dead man, Captain."

Dead ahead were three islands. On the navigation panel, he saw the larger island on the right was Orcas Island. On the left and to the south, the other large island was Blakely Island. In between the two was a small island appropriately named Obstruction Island. The passage on the south side of Obstruction Island was adequate for the large mega yacht, but the passage on the north side required a right turn of ninety degrees. On their present course, they were going to run aground on Obstruction Island.

The captain kept jabbing at different controls. "I can't steer away! I can't get her slowed in time! We're going aground on that damn little island!"

Chapter Sixty-Six

THEY WERE FLYING five hundred feet above the blue waters of the Rosario Strait in Casey's Bell 429 light twin helicopter. Thirty minutes into the flight, the PSS duty officer called using the helicopter's Honeywell satellite communication system.

"Fly to Obstruction Island. The yacht has stopped there on the east end of the island for some reason," he advised.

"Is Obstruction Island that little island sitting between Orcas Island and Blakely Island?" Casey asked.

"That's the one. It's privately owned and isn't open to the public. We don't know why they've stopped there."

"Was Liz able to meet with the FBI?" Drake asked over the copilot's headset.

"She met with an assistant special agent in charge she knew from Washington. The FBI is cooperating and sending help from the Navy to assist you from its naval station on Whidbey Island."

"Are we authorized to stop Guzman?" Drake wanted to know.

"You have permission to locate and detain him until help arrives."

"That sounds like the FBI. Any word from Morales?"

"He should be calling in any minute. He's with the rail operations chief watching for the jihadis to show up. He thinks they'll wait for the heaviest travel times to kill as many people as possible."

"Call me, Mac, as soon as you know anything," Casey said, ending the call and veering left a couple of degrees toward Obstruction Island.

"How did you know about Obstruction Island?" Drake asked.

"I kayaked up there several years ago with some of the guys. It's not someplace you'd expect a yacht like the Astrid III to stop."

"Can we land on the island?"

"I'm not sure. It's not very big and has a lot of trees. If we can't find a spot to set down, we'll land on the yacht if the helipad is empty."

"Guzman won't like that. We might have to go in hot."

"That's why those Remington ACR combat rifles are back there." Casey pointed over his shoulder with his thumb. "You didn't get to use them when you went after him at the marina. Maybe you'll get a chance today."

Drake nodded and looked ahead at the cluster of islands in the distance. They were flat and covered with dark green forests, floating between the dark blue water and light blue sky. To his right was the mainland and to his left the larger mass of Vancouver Island.

He'd taken a ferry to Victoria with Kay before they were married and watched the fireworks at Butchart

Gardens on a Saturday night. She insisted on taking tea in the stately old Empress Hotel and then pulled him eagerly from one display to another in the natural history museum. It had been one of his favorite memories in this part of the world. Now he was going to add another memory that he would never forget.

Walter Guzman, a.k.a. Ryan Walker, had tried to kill him three times in one month and he didn't know why. Today he was going to find out.

Casey tapped him on the shoulder and pointed straight ahead. "That's Blakely Island.

Orcas Island is just beyond it. Mac said the yacht's on the east end. We'll swing west and use Blakely for cover on our approach."

The Bell 429 dropped down to one hundred feet above the water and hugged the western shore of Blakely Island. As they neared the northern end of the island, Casey dropped even lower until they rounded the tip of Blakely Island and then flew across the narrow channel.

Obstruction Island's shape resembled the continent of South America occupying the middle of the channel, one hundred and fifty yards north of Blakely Island. Two small docks jutted out from shore on the western end and the entire surface of the small island was heavily forested.

"Why would Guzman stop here?" Drake asked.

The answer was apparent when they reached the eastern end of the island and turned north. The Astrid III had run aground on Obstruction Island.

A panel as large as a two-car garage door in the port side of the yacht extended out. Two cables were attached to a rigid hull inflatable tender that was suspended out over the water. Six men were in the boat, staring at the helicopter that hovered at eye level fifty yards away.

Drake jumped out of his co-pilot seat wearing his headset and stepped back into the passenger compartment. "Turn broadside to the yacht, I'll keep them from leaving."

He picked up one of the Remington ACRs and pulled back the charging handle to initiate the firing cycle before he opened the door on the left side of the Bell 429. He motioned for the men to raise their hands and they complied.

"They're giving up too easily if Guzman's in that boat."

"Could be a trap," Casey warned.

Drake studied the men standing motionless with their hands raised. Except for one welltanned man who looked to be forty or so, the rest looked to be in their twenties. "Guzman's supposed to be at least sixty. Either he's incredibly fit or he's still on the yacht."

"Hold on," Casey yelled and veered right, throwing Drake back inside. "Two men shooting at us from up top."

Drake got up and grabbed onto the handrail on the side of the open door.

"Swing back around so I have a shot."

Casey turned back and circled around the stern of the yacht. The two gunmen ran to the other side of the sundeck, shielding their eyes from the sun directly behind the helicopter.

"Hurry up before they start firing blindly. I can't hover here much longer."

Drake fired a burst of 5.56x45mm-NATO rounds at the first gunman as he started to raise a Heckler-Koch HK G36 German army assault rifle to his shoulder. He moved his aim right and fired another burst at the second gunman. Both men dropped to the deck next to each other.

Casey dropped the nose of the helicopter down and flew

back around the stern of the yacht in time to see the tender speeding west along the southern shore of the island.

"The Navy's coastal patrol boat is headed our way. Let them run down the tender," Drake said as he slipped back into the co-pilot seat beside Casey. "I recognized the weapons the two I shot were carrying—German army HK assault rifles. If they're that well equipped to guard Guzman, he's not going to run from a fight. He's still on the yacht and I want him."

Casey circled the yacht looking for any other men with automatic assault rifles he could see. "I can set down on the helipad but we'll be a sitting duck if they're waiting for us. We could keep an eye on the yacht and wait for the Navy Seahawk to get here."

"I can't let this guy get away, Mike. Get me down close enough and I'll jump out. You can lift off and watch for rats fleeing the ship."

"Sorry pal, if you go, I go. Someone has to watch your sorry six."

Chapter Sixty-Seven

WHEN THE ASTRID'S captain convinced him the yacht was too damaged to continue on to Vancouver Island, the *Confessor* rushed down to the interrogation room to free Mohammad. He found Guzman's bodyguard standing over the Saudi whose chair had tipped over onto the deck when the yacht ran aground.

"Is he still unconscious?" the *Confessor* asked as he thumbed open his knife and held it low against his leg.

"See for yourself. He's not responding."

The *Confessor* moved closer behind the man to get a better look. When his left shoulder nudged against the bodyguard's back, he threw his left hand around the man's head and pulled it back to expose his throat. At the same time, his right hand looped around and drew the razorsharp blade of his knife deeply across the bodyguard's neck and shoved him aside. "Are you alright?" he asked Mohammad.

"What happened? Why have we stopped?"

The *Confessor* reached down and lifted Mohammad and his chair upright. "Stay still while I cut you loose. The yacht hit some little island. We need to get off and find a way to an airport."

Mohammad stood when he was freed and rubbed his wrists. "How do we get by Guzman and his men?"

"Guzman's dead and you're rich. Don't worry about the guards."

As they started to leave the interrogation room, they heard gunfire on the upper decks.

"We must have company. Stay behind me," the *Confessor* ordered and led the way to the stairs to the upper decks.

The gunfire stopped and they were able to hear the sound of a helicopter somewhere above them. They waited to see if it was landing or moving away from the yacht. The yacht shuddered slightly as the helicopter touched down on the helipad.

"That's our ride out of here," the *Confessor* said. "You stay out of sight on the main deck.

I'll have a word with this pilot, whoever he is."

"What if it's the police? I can't be arrested."

As a feared enforcer for the drug cartels, the *Confessor* was embarrassed by the fear he saw in the eyes of the young jihadi. "Then you will have a decision to make, *amigo*."

He sprinted up the stairs to the upper deck and the helipad. When he reached the salon deck, two of Guzman's bodyguards crouched at the bottom of opposite flight stairs up to the sundeck and the helipad.

"Where's Guzman?" he yelled.

The closest man pointed up with the barrel of his assault rifle. "He was on the sundeck."

"Go up on your side and I'll go up on mine. We'll catch them in a crossfire. Don't hit the helicopter. It's our way out of here."

He waited until the first bodyguard reached the top of

the stairs on the other side of the salon before he started up. The sound of the helicopter masked the men's run up the stairs but not well enough. He was halfway up when he heard two short bursts from an assault rifle and saw the second man fall back down the stairs.

Before he started back down the stairs, he heard someone call out.

"Stay down and push your weapon away if you want to live. Mike, leave the Bell running, but go see if the guy in the spa robe is dead. I'll take care of this one."

The *Confessor* remembered the layout of the sundeck. The chaise lounge where Guzman's body lay was ten feet away from the top of the stairs he was standing on. The man who was coming to check on Guzman had to be the pilot.

He waited for a moment and then quietly climbed to the top of the stairs and popped his head up for a quick look. A tall man wearing a baseball hat and aviator sunglasses stood with his back to the stairs, staring down at the blood-soaked corpse of Walter Guzman.

Now was his chance. If the other bodyguard was out of the fight, it might be his only chance. He took three quick steps to the back of the man he hoped was the pilot.

"Don't move, *señor*, I have a nasty little gun pressed against your back. Tell your friend to lay down his rifle and stay where he is."

"Adam, some guy's behind me with a gun poking in my back. He says to lay down your rifle and stay where you are."

"Is it Guzman?"

Without turning, the tall man asked, "Are you Guzman?"

"Guzman's the man in the robe. It's not important who I am."

"He says Guzman is the guy in the robe with his throat cut."

"Then ask him if he knows if Guzman is also Ryan Walker, the man we're after."

The *Confessor* moved a little to the right to get a look at the man across the sundeck asking questions. Baseball hat and sunglasses, but shorter than the man in front of him. He held a short assault rifle loosely in his left hand. "Lay your rifle down and perhaps I'll tell you."

He saw the other man smile. "Sorry, I can't do that."

"Then your friend dies."

Again the smile. "Go ahead, pilots are a dime a dozen. But don't you need him to get you off this yacht before the Navy gets here?"

The *Confessor* had to laugh. "Let me guess. You are Drake, the man Guzman wanted me to interrogate and kill. He was right, you are a nuisance cat with nine lives. But I don't think the

Navy is coming."

"Suit yourself. Why did Guzman want you to interrogate me?"

"He wanted to know how much you had learned about his organization."

"You mean *the Alliance*?"

"*Si, the Alliance*. That is what he called it."

"Guys, I'm sure this conversation is important, but I have a gun in my back and I left my helicopter running," the tall man said. "Why don't you let me shut it down so we'll have the fuel to fly out of here?"

"Why don't you let me do that for you?" the other man said. "What do I have to do?"

"Just turn the red knob to the left. It's as simple as one, two, three."

The tall man spun to his left, pivoting around the elbow he threw back into his chest.

Before he could react and get off a shot, his head blew back and a bright light pierced his eyes.

Chapter Sixty-Eight

CASEY BENT DOWN TO pick up the small derringer the man had poked in his back.

"Double Tap .45 pocket pistol," he said as he broke it open to see what it was loaded with. "Remington Golden Sabre hollow points. Glad you decided to listen to me to get that little beast out of my back. When I saw you were holding your Kimber by your leg in your right hand, I knew we were on the same page."

Drake walked over and looked down at the man he'd just killed. "Wonder who this guy was?"

"He said he was here to interrogate you and he's Hispanic. Maybe cartel?"

"Possible. Let's search the yacht and see what we can find before everyone shows up. There might be a couple more of these guys still on board."

After searching the pilothouse, they took the stairs down to the deck below.

"Now this is living high on the hog," Casey said quietly as they moved through the main salon. "Crystal chandeliers, gold fixtures that are probably real gold, this boat is gaudy to the max."

"It takes a lot to impress people who own these things. Let's see what's in here," Drake said and moved to one side of an intricately-carved mahogany door at the end of the grand salon. Casey went to the other side.

"One, two, three," Casey whispered.

Drake entered first with his Kimber .45 drawn. "Well, well, look who we have here."

Mohammad Ali was sitting in a canary yellow wingback chair next to a massive king bed. He held a brandy snifter in his hand.

"Are you here to fly me to the airport?" he asked.

Drake looked to Casey and they both laughed.

"You could say that," Casey said. "Unless the Navy's taking you to Gitmo on a ship. I'm sure there's an airport somewhere in your future. Set the snifter down and get on your knees, Mohammad."

"You're making a mistake," Mohammad sneered. "I've done nothing wrong. I'm a guest on Mr. Guzman's yacht."

Drake exchanged a look with his friend that said, "Allow me," and walked forward and stood in front of Mohammad. "You're not paying attention, Ali. Mr. Casey told you to set the snifter down. You should have done what he said. One of your jihadis tried to blow up his building and he's upset about that. In fact, he'd like to rip your heart out and feed it to the pigs because you killed one of his employees. I won't say it again. Get on your knees or he'll come over and make you."

Drake stepped back and pointed his gun at the thick, white carpet in front of the wingback chair.

Mohammad set the snifter on the chrome and glass end

table and slid to his knees, never taking his eyes off the muzzle of Drake's Kimber.

"Did you work for Guzman or did he work for you?" Drake asked.

Mohammad lifted his eyes briefly to Drake's and then stared at a spot on the carpet in front of his knees.

"That's okay, it doesn't make a difference. You were in it together." Mohammad continued to stare at the floor.

Drake walked back and stood next to Casey. "What do you want to do until the Navy gets here?"

"There's not much we can do, except secure the place and wait. I'll look for something to tie him up with. Then we can look around."

While Casey was gone, Drake kept his gun trained on Mohammad and looked in the walk-in closet. Nothing but expensive-looking clothes.

He crossed to the other side of the stateroom to a half-open door of a small study. A thin, silver Lenovo laptop and a satellite phone docking station occupied the top of an exquisite leather top, oval writing desk. He ducked his head in and saw a wall-mounted CCTV screen behind the desk. On the wall in front was a framed photo of an imperial-looking German officer.

He was wearing a World War II SS dress uniform with the red swastika armband on his left arm.

Casey returned just then with a roll of duct tape in his hand and a broad smile on his face. "This should do the trick. Keep him covered while I truss this turkey up."

Drake stepped away from the study and watched as Mohammad was ordered to lie flat on his stomach with his hands behind his back. When both wrists were wrapped round and round with the tape and then his ankles as well,

Casey raised his hands in the air as if to stop the clock on a calf he'd just roped at some rodeo.

"While you were keeping an eye on our little doggie over there, I called Mac to hear how things went on the light rail stations. The jihadis showed up at University Station in staggered groups every couple of minutes with their backpacks. Morales was with the rail operations chief and identified them. As soon as he did, the Israelis moved in with their Tasers and took them down.

"Every backpack had an automatic air freshener dispenser in it, just as we thought. The Sound Transit police are having the dispensers tested, but they're confident they're loaded with sarin. The jihadis almost wet their pants when the dispensers were taken out of the backpacks for inspection. They backed away and looked like they were afraid the things would go off. Marco's convinced they planned on surviving the attack."

Drake nodded toward Mohammad on the floor. "Like their brave leader. First chance he had he was getting out of town with Guzman. Speaking of Guzman, step into the study over here and tell me what you think."

He waited while Casey looked around in the small study. The uniform the German officer was wearing in the framed photo didn't have a name tag on it, but he was willing to bet it was Ryan Walker's father or grandfather.

Casey stepped back into the stateroom shaking his head. "Looks like that hunch of yours about Walter Guzman being Ryan Walker was right on. It still doesn't explain why he wanted to kill you."

Drake looked down at Mohammad hog-tied on the floor and thought about the times he'd crossed paths with Walker.

"Who knows? Maybe he just got tired of losing."

Chapter Sixty-Nine

AFTER FIVE HOURS of questioning by naval officers from the Protector class patrol boat who took custody of the Astrid III, followed by agents from the FBI and DHS, Drake and Casey were allowed to return to Seattle.

They met a second wave of unhappy government officials at PSS headquarters. They were relieved, of course, that a major terrorist attack was foiled, but angry they weren't called on to handle the threat. At the end of the day, Drake suggested that the government agencies take full credit for preventing an attack on the light rail trains and apprehending Ryan Walker, a NeoNazi wanted internationally by Interpol.

In exchange for any concerns said agencies had about the way PSS obtained information about Walker or their activities on his yacht, PSS was willing to become an FBI

Counterintelligence Strategic Partner. In that way, any information PSS had about Walker and his involvement in three known plots to attack America, that the government had failed to uncover or prevent, could remain classified in any future investigation. Liz Strobel, the new PSS vice president for governmental relations, said she would be willing to work with Senator Hazelton, her former boss and Drake's father-in-law, to make sure that happened.

It was six o'clock in the evening when Drake and Liz joined Casey in his office for a celebratory drink before they went their separate ways.

Casey set three whisky glasses on his desk and poured them each a generous two fingers of amber gold. He handed two glasses across his desk and raised his in toast.

"To a memorable day."

"*Salud*!" Drake and Liz echoed.

Liz sampled her drink and then reached for the bottle of Pappy Winkle Family Reserve 20-year-old bourbon. "Wow! I'm not a big bourbon drinker, but this is good."

"Best in the world," Casey said with a smile. "Birthday present from my employees, but I won't expect you to buy me another bottle for my next birthday."

Drake laughed. "You are shameless, my friend, hinting that another fifteen-hundred-dollar bottle of Pappy's isn't expected but wouldn't be rejected for your next birthday. You better double her salary if you want to be treated like that."

"Don't give her any ideas, counselor. Where did you come up with the idea for a strategic partnership with the FBI?"

"Something Liz mentioned once. The FBI's Counterintelligence Strategic Partnership Program involves a partnership with businesses, academia and defense contractors. The partnerships directly support FBI operations and enable partners to share information about emerging threats to national security. I didn't know if they'd bite, but I thought it might help to smooth things over."

Liz set back in her chair and held her glass with both hands to her lips. "Might also help heal some of the FBI toes you've stepped on in the past."

"That too," Drake said with a grin. "What do you think they'll do with Mohammad?"

"That will be interesting. The administration won't want to upset Saudi Arabia, but they can't let Mohammad return home without some consequences. If the president closes Gitmo, I don't know what they will do with him. If they brief the Senate Intelligence Committee before I leave, maybe I'll find out."

"Speaking of leaving Washington and moving here, how soon will that be?" Casey asked.

Liz shrugged her shoulders. "My condo is on the market, but I still have a lot to do for Senator Hazelton before Congress returns from its summer break. Is the first of September too late?"

"September first it is. I want to have the company's restructuring completed by the end of the year. That should give us enough time. If I can get my special counsel to drag himself away from his vineyard and spend a little more time up here, that is."

Drake exchanged a look with Liz before responding. "I told Liz she was welcome to stay at my place until her condo sells and she finds something here. I'm trying to get her to come sooner than September first."

"Sure, that would give you two more time to, ah, discuss my plans to take PSS to the next level." Casey looked at his watch. "I'd better head for home. Will I see you both tomorrow?"

Drake set his glass down and got up. "I talked Liz into flying out of Portland when she heads back to D.C., so we'll head home tomorrow morning. I need to get back and get some work done this week before my secretary leaves me. I'll be back next week on my usual day, unless something comes up and you need me sooner."

"Okay then," Casey said. "If you're hungry and want to have dinner at the Woodmark, charge it to the company account. My treat for the day we've had."

Drake stopped by his office to get his things and then drove Liz to the Woodmark. When they stopped in front of the hotel at the parking valet stand, Liz saw that he was leaving his travel duffel in the car when they got out.

"It's been a long day. Would you like to shower in my room before we head down for dinner?"

He caught the valet trying to suppress a grin in his peripheral vision as he hit the trunk release on his key fob to get his duffel. He tossed the keys to the valet and waited until his Porsche was pulling away to say, "I thought you'd never ask. We could even call room service for dinner if you'd like."

Chapter Seventy

AFTER A LIGHT BREAKFAST in the Beach Café the next morning, they were on the road and headed south by mid-morning. The temperature was already seventy-two and the day promised to be a warm and breezy Northwest summer day.

The mid-week traffic on the freeways through Seattle was congested, as usual, and not any lighter when they merged onto I-5 South. Drake saw that Liz was smiling as she looked out at her new home passing by.

"Penny for your thoughts."

"It will cost you a lot more than that for these thoughts."

"Name your price."

"Are you sure you want to know?"

"I am. What's your price?"

"What did you think of me when we first met?"

Drake drummed his fingers on the steering wheel as he thought back to the time they met. It was a little after 3:00 a.m. in the morning on his farm. He'd just killed three armed terrorists and called his father-in-law, Senator Hazelton, and was told help was on the way. A woman and Secret Service agents arrived a half an hour later in two white SUVs. The woman had taken charge and told him she was doing his father-in-law a favor by taking the bodies away. She also said that frankly she didn't care if he spent the rest of his life in jail for using deadly force that night, even if he was defending himself. His impression? He'd just met the reigning queen of mean, the original Ice Lady.

"I thought you were good-looking, confident and tough. You took control of the situation. I was thankful for your help getting me out of a tight spot."

Liz laughed, a throaty guffaw. "I remember the look in your eyes! The only thing you were thankful for was that I was leaving your farm before the sun came up."

"That might be true, but I still thought you were good-looking. Your turn. What were you smiling about?"

Liz remembered leaving Drake's old vineyard before dawn. Three young Muslim men were dead and in the back of her SUV, two of them literally killed at the hands of the man she had just met. She had been around men who had killed in the line of duty before and none of them had reacted as calmly as he had. There was a look of smoldering cold anger in his eyes that night, but no remorse, just a hint of sadness. The way he had handled the violence had both frightened and attracted her. She'd driven away thinking that cleaning up the mess he'd made was just part of her job but getting to know him better might be a perk.

Her eyes softened as she turned toward him. "When we first met, I thought you might be a dangerous psychopath and that your father-in-law was getting me involved in something that night on your farm that was going to end my career. I was smiling at how meeting you ended the career I thought was so important and how happy I am that it has.

I'm moving across the country to be closer to the man I never wanted to see again. Now I'm hoping I'll get to see him every day."

Her words triggered an emotion that surprised him. Their relationship had grown from one of undisguised animosity to a reluctant professional admiration and then slowly from a strong physical attraction to affectionate companionship. But what he was feeling now was love and he knew it.

"I'm not sure that would be a good thing. I have some habits you might find pretty disgusting."

"Such as?"

Before Drake could tell her, his cell phone buzzed. He saw it was his secretary, Margo.

"Good morning, Margo. I have you on speaker and Liz is here with me. We've just passed Olympia on I-5 and should be in Portland by noon."

"Hello Liz. Will I get to see you before you return to D.C.?"

"I hope so. How's your husband doing?"

"He's feeling better than when you saw him in Nicaragua. Have you found a place in Seattle?"

"Not yet. Do you need to talk to Adam?"

"No, sweety, I'll save it until he finally decides to come in and gets back to work. Paul's the one who needs to talk with him."

"Good to talk with you too, Margo. Is Paul there?" Drake asked.

"I am," Paul Benning said. "Two things I thought you'd like to know. I found the chef's son. He was staying with a friend of his father's. He's identified the men who killed his dad. They've been arrested, but we haven't been able to locate Davis. No one seems to know where he is."

"Good work, Paul. You closed your first case as a P.I."

"About that. If the offer's still good, Margo's decided she likes having me around in the office if I really want to start a new career as a private investigator. So I have a new client lined up, if you approve."

"The offer's still good. Who's the new client?"

"The Archdiocese of Portland. There have been some threats made and the police aren't taking them too seriously. My priest gave my name to the archbishop. With what's happened in France and the threats ISIS is making toward the church, the archbishop wants to know how seriously he should take the threats made here locally."

"Go for it and congratulations. Nice way to start your new career."

"Just a second. Margo's saying, since you have Liz with you and you won't get much work done until she leaves, take the rest of the day off and come in tomorrow."

"Tell the boss thanks. I'll do just that."

Drake reached over and squeezed Liz's hand. "Since I have the rest of the day off, would you like to stay with me and I'll cook you dinner tonight?"

"I thought you'd never ask."

Next in The Adam Drake Series

vinci-books.com/sacredtarget

Convert to Islam or die is the stark choice people are facing... not in the Middle East, but in Oregon.

Adam Drake, lawyer and former Tier 1 operator, has three days to determine if the threat is real. With the FBI dismissing it as a hoax, he must go it alone before innocent lives are lost.

Turn the page for a free preview…

Sacred Target: Chapter One

THE MAN SITTING in the parked green Prius watched the dark form stealthily run down the sidewalk on the other side of the street. It was two o'clock on a drizzly Sunday morning in Portland, Oregon's Nob Hill district. Printed notices were being stuffed in the doors of random residences and businesses in the area.

He knew the area was chosen because it was just west of St. Patrick's Catholic Church. He also knew what each notice said. He'd drafted the warning.

In the name of Allah, the merciful, full of grace. You who are not believers will be beheaded in three days in your house.

You must choose one of the following to stay alive:
1. Convert to Islam.
2. Pay the jizya (religious tax) for protection.

If you choose to ignore this warning and do not make one of the two choices you're being offered, you will be beheaded.

Do not expect the police to prevent your murder or save you from death.

Several of the catholic churches in the city had received an earlier notice to convert or die nailed to their front doors. Now the next phase of the plan was being implemented to create fear and panic among the Catholic parishioners of St. Patrick's, as well as in the minds of the owners of a few of the trendy Nob Hill boutiques and restaurants in the area.

It had taken him just a year to develop his plan and find the person who would carry it out. From there, it took another year to recruit the other members of the group and test them to ensure their professed pledge of loyalty was sincere. He found that young Americans were easily attracted to the idea of violent jihad. Few had the ability, however, to fully embrace the sacrifice and commit their lives totally to the cause. Fortunately, the leader he had chosen had the fire and the ability to do both.

She also had the natural gift of leadership. The acolytes she chose obeyed her without question. When she'd required them to go far beyond the societal norms they were accustomed to, they hadn't hesitated. Her final test for each of them was to behead a sheep in the dark of night in some farmer's pasture and bring the sheep's head back to her.

He was shocked when she told him about her final test, but he was not surprised. He had recognized her psychopathic personality soon after she enrolled in his entry-level computer science class at Portland State University.

He'd been fascinated by how she charmed and manipulated the others in class. But he was fully convinced of her psychopathic personality by what she offered to do when he was being reviewed for termination by the administration. One of his students was a loud-mouthed football player who voiced anti-Muslim sentiments one time too many in his class. He'd made the mistake of responding out loud to the bigoted lout in class. When the student's well-known and wealthy alumni father persuaded his Catholic church to protest the anti-Christian and discriminatory outburst toward his son, he'd been called on the carpet by the administration and terminated.

That's when his chosen had offered to take care of the loud-mouthed student for him, if he wanted. She had flirted with the football player and embarrassed him by calling him out as gay when he rejected her advances. When he tried to get back at her for embarrassing him, she offered to go to the police and claim she'd been raped. If he didn't like that idea, the football player thought he was such a stud, she said she was willing to castrate him and let the world know about it.

The young student delivering the notices this morning was a new member and hadn't been fully tested. That's why he was interested in how she delivered the last items on her list. In her backpack remained three items; a stencil for gang-style graffiti in bubble letters for the word "ISIS", a black can of spray paint and a gallon Ziploc bag with a small wooden cross soaking in sheep's blood.

He watched approvingly as she ran up to the front door of the turn-of-the-century Victorian home toward the end of the block. She took her backpack off and set it at her feet. From inside, she took out the stencil and the can of spray paint. Holding it up against the heavy solid oak front door, she sprayed the word "ISIS" in gang-style bubble letters onto the door. She replaced the stencil and spray can in her backpack and took out the Ziploc bag. Carefully opening it, she lifted out the wooden cross dripping in sheep's blood and laid it on the front door welcome mat.

With a quick survey of her work, she replaced the Ziploc bag, slipped on the backpack and jogged down the sidewalk and turned left up the street. Her ride was waiting one block away.

When she turned the corner at the end of the block, her watcher started the Prius and followed her up the street. He was now satisfied that he had a cell of warriors with the capability to carry out his plan.

Sacred Target: Chapter Two

ADAM DRAKE MADE a note in the margin of a copy of the complaint he was reviewing that had been filed against Puget Sound Security, where he served as its special counsel and attorney. A former PSS client had sued them for negligently failing to prevent a theft of its intellectual property.

The former client suspected one of its employees of selling proprietary information to a competitor. It felt that PSS should have discovered the possibility of the theft if they had conducted a thorough background check on the individual. The client apparently had forgotten that the individual was the nephew of the company's CFO and that his recent financial difficulties had been reported but overlooked, due to his relationship to the CFO. Drake smiled at the thought of deposing the CFO and asking about her role in the hiring of her nephew.

It was Monday morning and he'd driven in from his farm and vineyard to get a start on the stack of files on his desk. The one day a week he was spending in Seattle working for his friend, Mike Casey, the CEO and major shareholder of Puget Sound Security, was taking more of his time than he'd anticipated.

Drake finished his review of the complaint filed against PSS and walked down the stairs from the loft in his office to get a fresh cup of coffee. Paul Benning was coming down the back stairs from the condo he rented from Drake above the law office.

"Morning, Paul."

"You're here early."

"Your wife made an indelible impression on my ego last week, telling me I wasn't the attorney I used to be. I thought I'd prove her wrong."

"She does have a way of getting us to do things her way, doesn't she?"

Drake walked to the break room to refill his coffee cup. Benning followed him.

"How's your new PI case for the archdiocese going?"

Benning waited until Drake stepped back from the new Moccamaster coffee maker. "If you have a minute, I'd like to talk with you about that."

"Sure, grab a cup and join me."

When they were seated upstairs in the loft, Benning sat back in the black leather side chair in front of Drake's desk and recounted the phone call he'd received that morning.

"The archbishop's executive called me at seven thirty. One of their parishioners found their front door had been spray-painted gang-style with the word 'ISIS' and there was a bloody wooden cross left on the welcome mat. There was also a notice beside the cross warning that if they didn't convert to Islam or pay a religious tax for protection in three days, they'd be beheaded in their home. It was the same notice the owner of a boutique dress shop nearby found stuffed in the door when she opened up this morning. The archdiocese wants to know how they should handle these new threats to its parishioners."

"Does the archdiocese have any idea who's leaving these notices?"

"They've reported them to the police, but there are no leads so far. The Vatican sent out a general notice based on similar threats and notices in Europe two years ago, in Sweden, I think. Nothing came of those threats and police there attributed it to a lone-wolf ISIS wannabe follower. Law enforcement here is responding the same way."

"Is the FBI or DHS involved in this?"

"Not actively, as far as I know. The Portland Police Department says it hasn't received any intel from the FBI that identifies any locals who might be doing this."

Drake sat his coffee cup down and sat back with his hands clasped behind his head. "The archdiocese is asking you if these are serious threats, not just the general threats ISIS has repeatedly made worldwide to nonbelievers."

"That's pretty much what they're asking."

"I don't know what to tell you, Paul. Portland Police and the FBI could try to work with the local mosques and ask for help, but they haven't had a lot of success with that in the past. Radicalized lone wolves are hard to spot until they reveal themselves online or by making threats that someone reports. The big thing will be to keep the parishioners advised of what's going on and give them assurance that everything possible is being done to protect them."

Benning cocked his head. "Even when it's not?"

Drake knew his friend well enough to know he hadn't just stopped by to brief him on his new P.I. case. There was something else. "What are you thinking?"

"This is the first time this kind of terrorist threat has been made in America. The FBI has to know more about

Soft Target

this than they're telling us. I think they might share more if they're sharing intel with someone they like and know."

"You know that person isn't me?" Drake smiled.

"I've come to understand that. When do you go to Seattle this week?"

"I'll drive up tomorrow night, work Wednesday and drive back Thursday morning. But Liz isn't there yet. She's still wrapping things up in D.C."

Benning got up and raised his coffee cup. "Okay, just a thought. Then say hi to Liz for me the next time you talk with her."

Sacred Target: Chapter Three

DRAKE WATCHED his friend leave and thought about the change in his demeanor and attitude since he'd decided to retire from the Multnomah County Sheriff's Office.

Benning had been with the MCSO for twenty-five years and worked as a senior detective for the last eighteen. He was eligible for retirement with full benefits but wasn't planning to retire for another ten years. After being diagnosed with stage-two prostate cancer recently and having had surgery, however, he was reconsidering an early retirement. Seldom leaving the condo and suffering a debilitating bout of depression, he'd lost interest in just about everything.

That ended when he'd agreed to help Drake for a client with business in Nicaragua. A confrontation with a rogue Russian general there and being captured by an Iranian terror cell had revived his fighting spirit. It had also led to his decision to retire from the MSCO and begin a career as a private detective working out of Drake's office.

That decision was serving him well. Working out of Drake's office where Benning's wife, Margo, was the office manager/paralegal/executive assistant and, yes, ran the place, allowed him to see his wife more often and establish a new line of work. Benning was a skilled detective and solving cases was something he was good at.

This case for the Archdiocese of Portland was different than the cases he was used to working. If the threats were genuine, and ISIS was behind it or promoting it, then advising the archdiocese on how to respond to the threats wasn't going to be the end of it. He knew Benning would keep after it until the terrorists were identified, arrested and behind bars for the rest of their lives.

That worried Drake, not only for his friend's sake but for the sake of his friend's marriage. Margo was resigned to *his* "adventures" as she called them but still hadn't forgiven him for involving *her* husband in Nicaragua. It wasn't hard to imagine her reaction if her husband started chasing terrorists who were threatening to behead people in their city.

Drake decided not to wait until he saw Liz in Seattle.

"Hello, good looking. Got a minute?"

It was eleven o'clock in D.C. He knew she normally returned to his father-in-law's senate office following the morning's hearings she attended and then left for lunch. Liz served as the senator's liaison with the intelligence community because he was the chairman and ranking senator on the Senate Select Committee on Intelligence.

"How are preparations for your move out west going?"

"I'm getting there. The condo sale is pending in escrow, I have an offer to sell my car and a mover lined to move my things. It's all the little things, like getting in touch with people I know I won't see for a while."

"When you tell people you're moving, how do they react?"

"Usually they're shocked that I'm giving up what I have here to move across the country. Working in the capital is the penultimate achievement for most of the people I know here."

"Are you having second thoughts?"

"Not one. Is that why you called, to see if I've changed my mind?"

"No, I wanted to hear your voice and get some advice. Paul Benning has a case that I think you know about. He asked me this morning if I would run something by you."

"For the Archdiocese of Portland? His first case that you told me about?"

"That's the one. They're getting more serious threats and the police don't seem to be taking them very seriously. This morning someone spray-painted 'ISIS' on the front door of a residence and left a bloody cross and a warning. The warning said convert to Islam, pay a religious tax or die in three days. The explicit threat was that they would be beheaded in their own home if they made the wrong choice."

"Wow. Is the FBI involved?"

"Paul says they are, but they're not sharing anything. The archdiocese wants to know if these are genuine threats and what precautions they should take, if they are. Do you know someone in the intelligence community who might be able to help Paul evaluate these threats?"

Drake waited while Liz considered his request. She knew a lot of people, but he was hoping she had a close relationship with someone with the intel to take a hard look at the threats.

"There is someone I trust and have lunch with occasionally. But's she very careful about discussing her work, except in general terms, unless there's a good reason for doing so."

"Would a request from Senator Hazelton be a good enough reason? He represents Oregon and his state office is in Portland. The archdiocese is a constituent of his."

"Relax, Counselor, I can fill in the blanks. Her name is Marta Halim. She's a senior analyst with the National Counterterrorism Center at Liberty Crossing. I'll invite her to join me for a late lunch or a drink after work and see if she'll help."

"Thanks Liz. I hope this turns out to be someone's idea of a sick joke, but I want to help Paul in any way that I can. He seems to like working as a P.I."

"Is Margo okay with his new career?"

"Hey, she's your new best friend. Maybe you should ask her, as chummy as you two are now. That's a subject I'm not willing to bring up right now. It's been a little chilly in the office since Paul helped me with that matter last month in Seattle."

"You're still curious about the girl-talk we had in your office, aren't you?"

"What? No, why would I be?"

"Maybe I'll tell you why you should be, if you'll come see me."

"That sounds like blackmail."

"You *are* a smart attorney."

Drake knew he was losing this round. "Why don't you call your analyst and see if you can do something to help your new best friend's husband?"

He knew she was grinning as she said goodbye.

Grab your copy...
vinci-books.com/sacredtarget

About the Author

Scott Matthews got hooked on reading thrillers – especially the James Bond thrillers – as an escape from the required reading in his high school English class; *The Odyssey*, *The Scarlet Letter*, *The Great Gatsby* and all the other "great" literature meant to prepare him for college and life beyond.

But Bond was fun! When Scott studied for the Oregon bar exam, he rewarded himself after a long day of study, reading a dog-eared Fleming paperback for fifteen minutes before turning off the bedside light each night.

His collection of thrillers later expanded to include the novels of John MacDonald, Nelson DeMille, Barry Eisler, Randy Wayne White, Daniel Silva and Steve Berry. And when his favorite authors took too long releasing their next books, he started jotting notes for a thriller he would write someday.

Scott still lives on the Left Coast in Oregon with his beautiful wife, and now writes his own thrillers that carry on the tradition of a brave and patriotic hero battling evil enemies and terrorists to protect his homeland.